ACCLAIM FOR COLLEEN COBLE

"Engaging characters, irresistible intrigue, and a slow-burning romance make *Fragile Designs* a captivating read."
—MARY BURTON, *NEW YORK TIMES* BESTSELLING AUTHOR

"Excitement, evil antagonists, action, and romance are a few of the items that stand out in *Break of Day* by Colleen Coble . . . The world-building is excellent."
—*MYSTERY & SUSPENSE MAGAZINE*

"A law enforcement ranger investigates a cold case and searches for her kidnapped sister in this exciting series launch from Coble (*A Stranger's Game*) . . . Coble expertly balances mounting tension from the murder investigation with the romantic tension between Annie and Jon. This fresh, addictive mystery delivers thrills, compassion, and hope."
—*PUBLISHERS WEEKLY* ON *EDGE OF DUSK*

"This Christian romantic suspense novel packs a lot of plot into its pages, wrapping up only two of its biggest plot lines while leaving plenty of material for a sequel. Some of the plot twists were excellently paced surprises . . . Fans of Colleen Coble's works will welcome this brand new series set in the same world as her previous thrillers. Her love for the UP is palpable, and I really liked learning about the Finnish influences on the area. Ms. Coble is a great ambassador for the UP's natural beauty and cuisine, and speaks knowledgeably and at length on celiac disease, including recommendations at the end of the book that are super helpful for anyone wanting a list of gluten-free brands."
—*CRIMINAL ELEMENT* ON *EDGE OF DUSK*

T0037004

"Coble's clear-cut prose makes it easy for the reader to follow the numerous scenarios and characters. This is just the ticket for readers of romantic suspense."

—PUBLISHERS WEEKLY ON THREE MISSING DAYS

"Colleen Coble is my go-to author for the best romantic suspense today. *Three Missing Days* is now my favorite in the series, and I adored the other two. A stay-up-all-night page-turning story!"

—CARRIE STUART PARKS, BESTSELLING AND AWARD-WINNING AUTHOR OF RELATIVE SILENCE

"You can't go wrong with a Colleen Coble novel. She always brings readers great characters and edgy, intense story lines."

—BESTINSUSPENSE.COM ON TWO REASONS TO RUN

"Colleen Coble's latest has it all: characters to root for, a sinister villain, and a story that just won't stop."

—SIRI MITCHELL, AUTHOR OF STATE OF LIES, ON TWO REASONS TO RUN

"Colleen Coble's superpower is transporting her readers into beautiful settings in vivid detail. *Two Reasons to Run* is no exception. Add to that the suspense that keeps you wanting to know more, and characters that pull at your heart. These are the ingredients of a fun read!"

—TERRI BLACKSTOCK, BESTSELLING AUTHOR OF IF I RUN, IF I'M FOUND, AND IF I LIVE

"This is a romantic suspense novel that will be a surprise when the last page reveals all of the secrets."

—PARKERSBURG NEWS AND SENTINEL ON ONE LITTLE LIE

"There are just enough threads left dangling at the end of this well-crafted romantic suspense to leave fans hungrily awaiting the next installment."

—PUBLISHERS WEEKLY ON ONE LITTLE LIE

"Colleen Coble once again proves she is at the pinnacle of Christian romantic suspense. Filled with characters you'll come to love, faith lost and found, and scenes that will have you holding your breath, Jane Hardy's story deftly follows the complex and tangled web that can be woven by one little lie."

—LISA WINGATE, #1 NEW YORK TIMES BESTSELLING AUTHOR
OF BEFORE WE WERE YOURS, ON ONE LITTLE LIE

"Colleen Coble always raises the notch on romantic suspense, and One Little Lie is my favorite yet! The story took me on a wild and wonderful ride."

—DIANN MILLS, BESTSELLING AUTHOR

"Coble's latest, One Little Lie, is a powerful read . . . one of her absolute best. I stayed up way too late finishing this book because I literally couldn't go to sleep without knowing what happened. This is a must read! Highly recommend!"

—ROBIN CAROLL, BESTSELLING AUTHOR
OF THE DARKWATER INN SERIES

"I always look forward to Colleen Coble's new releases. One Little Lie is One Phenomenal Read. I don't know how she does it, but she just keeps getting better. Be sure to have plenty of time to flip the pages in this one because you won't want to put it down. I devoured it! Thank you, Colleen, for more hours of edge-of-the-seat entertainment. I'm already looking forward to the next one!"

—LYNETTE EASON, AWARD-WINNING AND BESTSELLING
AUTHOR OF THE BLUE JUSTICE SERIES

"In One Little Lie the repercussions of one lie skid through the town of Pelican Harbor, creating ripples of chaos and suspense. Who will survive the questions? One Little Lie is the latest page-turner from Colleen Coble. Set on the Gulf Coast of Alabama, Jane Hardy is the new police chief who is fighting to clear her father. Reid Dixon has secrets of his own as he follows Jane around town for a documentary. Together they must face their secrets and decide when a secret becomes a lie. And when does it become too much to forgive?"

—CARA PUTMAN, BESTSELLING AND AWARD-WINNING AUTHOR

"Coble wows with this suspense-filled inspirational . . . With startling twists and endearing characters, Coble's engrossing story explores the tragedy, betrayal, and redemption of faithful people all searching to reclaim their sense of identity."

—PUBLISHERS WEEKLY ON STRANDS OF TRUTH

"Just when I think Colleen Coble's stories can't get any better, she proves me wrong. In Strands of Truth, I couldn't turn the pages fast enough. The characterization of Ridge and Harper and their relationship pulled me immediately into the story. Fast-paced, with so many unexpected twists and turns, I read this book in one sitting. Coble has pushed the bar higher than I'd imagined. This book is one not to be missed. Highly recommend!"

—ROBIN CAROLL, BESTSELLING AUTHOR
OF THE DARKWATER INN SERIES

"Free-dive into a romantic suspense that will leave you breathless and craving for more."

—DIANN MILLS, BESTSELLING AUTHOR, ON STRANDS OF TRUTH

"Colleen Coble's latest book, Strands of Truth, grips you on page one with a heart-pounding opening and doesn't let go until the last satisfying word. I love her skill in pulling the reader in with believable, likable characters, interesting locations, and a mystery just waiting to be untangled. Highly recommended."

—CARRIE STUART PARKS, BESTSELLING AND AWARD-
WINNING AUTHOR OF RELATIVE SILENCE

"It's in her blood! Colleen Coble once again shows her suspense prowess with a thriller as intricate and beautiful as a strand of DNA.

Strands of Truth dives into an unusual profession involving mollusks and shell beds that weaves a unique, silky thread throughout the story. So fascinating I couldn't stop reading!"

—RONIE KENDIG, BESTSELLING AUTHOR
OF THE TOX FILES SERIES

"Once again, Colleen Coble delivers an intriguing, suspenseful tale in *Strands of Truth*. The mystery and tension mount toward an explosive and satisfying finish. Well done."

—CRESTON MAPES, BESTSELLING AUTHOR

"*Secrets at Cedar Cabin* is filled with twists and turns that will keep readers turning the pages as they plunge into the horrific world of sex trafficking where they come face-to-face with evil. Colleen Coble delivers a fast-paced story with a strong, lovable ensemble cast and a sweet, heaping helping of romance."

—KELLY IRVIN, AUTHOR OF *TELL HER NO LIES*

"Coble . . . weaves a suspense-filled romance set during the Revolutionary War. Coble's fine historical novel introduces a strong heroine—both in faith and character—that will appeal deeply to readers."

—PUBLISHERS WEEKLY ON *FREEDOM'S LIGHT*

"This follow-up to *The View from Rainshadow Bay* features delightful characters and an evocative, atmospheric setting. Ideal for fans of romantic suspense and authors Dani Pettrey, Dee Henderson, and Brandilyn Collins."

—LIBRARY JOURNAL ON *THE HOUSE AT SALTWATER POINT*

"Set on Washington State's Olympic Peninsula, this first volume of Coble's new suspense series is a tensely plotted and harrowing tale of murder, corporate greed, and family secrets. Devotees of Dani Pettrey, Brenda Novak, and Allison Brennan will find a new favorite here."

—LIBRARY JOURNAL ON *THE VIEW FROM RAINSHADOW BAY*

"Coble (*Twilight at Blueberry Barrens*) keeps the tension tight and the action moving in this gripping tale, the first in her Lavender Tides series set in the Pacific Northwest."

—PUBLISHERS WEEKLY ON *THE VIEW FROM RAINSHADOW BAY*

"Filled with the suspense for which Coble is known, the novel is rich in detail with a healthy dose of romance, allowing readers to bask in the beauty of Washington State's lavender fields, lush forests, and jagged coastline."

—BOOKPAGE ON *THE VIEW FROM RAINSHADOW BAY*

"Prepare to stay up all night with Colleen Coble. Coble's beautiful, emotional prose coupled with her keen sense of pacing, escalating danger, and very real characters place her firmly at the top of the suspense genre. I could not put this book down."

—ALLISON BRENNAN, *NEW YORK TIMES* BESTSELLING AUTHOR OF *SHATTERED*, ON *THE VIEW FROM RAINSHADOW BAY*

"Colleen is a master storyteller."

—KAREN KINGSBURY, BESTSELLING AUTHOR

FRAGILE DESIGNS

ALSO BY COLLEEN COBLE

FRAGILE DESIGNS

A NOVEL

COLLEEN COBLE

THOMAS NELSON
Since 1798

Library of Congress Cataloging-in-Publication Data

Names: Coble, Colleen, author.
Title: Fragile designs : a novel / Colleen Coble.
Description: Nashville, Tennessee : Thomas Nelson, 2024. | Summary: "Family secrets can be the most dangerous of all. The journey to find the truth and protect her family will have Carly delving deep into the lost treasures of Eastern Europe--if she can survive that long"--Provided by publisher.
Identifiers: LCCN 2023022845 (print) | LCCN 2023022846 (ebook) | ISBN 9780785253822 (paperback) | ISBN 9780785253853 (library binding) | ISBN 9780785253839 (epub) | ISBN 9780785253846
Subjects: LCSH: Family secrets--Fiction. | LCGFT: Thrillers (Fiction) | Novels.
Classification: LCC PS3553.O2285 F73 2024 (print) | LCC PS3553.O2285(ebook) | DDC 813/.54--dc23/eng/20230605
LC record available at https://lccn.loc.gov/2023022845
LC ebook record available at https://lccn.loc.gov/2023022846

For my buddy Denise Hunter.
Twenty-five years of critiquing and encouraging!
I couldn't write or do life without you!

PROLOGUE

Pawleys Island

Another wave of nausea hit Carly Harris the minute she opened her car door and got out in the garage. It was the stench of gasoline and oil mixing with the humid South Carolina heat swirling around the space that upset her stomach. The tourist trade in Pawleys Island was in full swing, and it had taken her longer to get home than she'd planned.

Eric's truck was in its bay with the engine running, and she gritted her teeth. He knew better than to leave it running with the garage door down. For a police officer, her husband was surprisingly unconcerned with safety issues.

Her hand drifted to her belly, and she sighed. How would he take the news she needed to share tonight? They'd been fighting nearly every day, and she'd threatened to leave if he didn't start to stick up for her with his mother. Ever since Carly and Eric had been married three years before, Opal's criticism of Carly had gone unchallenged. And this past year had been unbearable.

Everything Carly did was wrong—she didn't organize the kitchen right, she didn't call often enough, she didn't send Eric off with the perfect lunch every day. And the greatest sin of all was that Carly didn't want to give up traveling to flea markets and selling the collectibles she'd happily curated from garage sales, online websites, and estate sales.

When she'd first broached the idea of attending a writers' conference this weekend, he hit the roof, and she knew it was because he didn't want to tell his mother she was gone. Opal was constantly whispering in Eric's ear that he couldn't trust his wife to be faithful if she was out of town without him.

Carly was afraid Eric was beginning to believe it. Even worse, now that she was pregnant, she was beginning to doubt her career choice herself. What she'd wanted to do since she was a teenager was to write historical novels. Selling collectible items had seemed a good option instead of putting a toe in the craziness of the publishing world, but the itch to create her own novel had blossomed lately. Maybe she was finally ready to try. Eric wouldn't be on board with a pie-in-the-sky move like that, which was why she hadn't brought it up yet.

With the grocery bags dangling from her arms and hands, she opened the door from the garage and stepped into the kitchen. "Hello?"

She set the groceries on the kitchen counter and headed for the hall. "Eric?"

The house had that empty feeling, and she glanced out the sliding glass door into the backyard. The door to her shop stood open, and she smiled. Eric must have followed through on his promise to start organizing the items belonging to her great-grandmother. He'd been poking around them for several weeks but hadn't done the heavy lifting she'd asked. Carly planned to take them to the flea market next weekend.

After putting away the groceries, she opened the sliding door and went across the deck and down the steps to the yard. The scent of freshly mown grass mingled with the roses blooming in the garden bed along the back of the deck. He'd been on a roll today. Mowing the grass was his least favorite chore, and she usually had to prod him to get it done.

The dark interior of her shop gave her pause. "Eric, are you in here?"

When he didn't answer, she reached around the edge of the opening and found the switch. Light overhead flooded the interior, and she found things moved around. Her great-grandmother's antique desk and chairs had been transferred to the other side of the building, and some of the boxes sat with their tops open. Eric had at least made a start on the work, but he hadn't gotten as far as she'd hoped.

Her sisters had been pushing her to sell the items so their inheritance could be split. Even though she'd told them the items were unlikely to bring much money, they were impatient. So was Eric. He'd had his eye on a new truck and had thought their share might be enough for a down payment. Some of the sentimental items had been left to Carly alone, but the valuable, sellable antiques were for all of them.

Her hand drifted to her belly again. A new truck would have to wait with the news she had to give him. The money would need to be used for a crib and other baby paraphernalia.

"Eric, where are you?"

The place felt empty, so she went back outside and checked the cement pad behind the garage. Nothing was out of place. They had no close neighbors, so there was no one to ask if they'd spotted him. Could a buddy have picked him up?

3

She pulled out her phone and called him. After a few seconds, she heard the distant sound of Eric's ringtone from inside her shop. He had to be in there.

She went back across the grass and stepped into the building. The sound of his phone came from a back corner where the majority of the boxes had been stacked. As she neared the area, she caught a whiff of an unpleasant coppery scent, and nausea rose in her throat again.

She increased her pace and was nearly running by the time she rounded the end of the boxes and looked down at the open floor space.

Eric lay on his stomach on the floor. A wound in his back had saturated the green tee he wore with a hideous red stain. "Eric—honey?" She knelt beside him and touched his arm. His skin was already cooling.

She rocked back on her heels and didn't realize she was screaming until she felt the pain in her throat. His phone quit ringing, and she lowered her gaze.

She'd dropped her cell phone in the pool of blood beside Eric's body.

She snatched it up and wiped the blood from it on her jeans so she could call for help.

But it was too late for her husband.

ONE

Nine Months Later
Beaufort, South Carolina

The scent of South Carolina salt water and marsh blew in from the water, and the breeze caressed Carly Harris's face. There was nothing like a low-country spring morning, and she wanted to enjoy every minute of it before the day got busy. Two-month-old Noah had nursed and fallen asleep to the drone of boats out on Beaufort Bay, and she shuffled her son to her other arm. Her black cat, Pepper, gave her a disdainful stare when she jostled him with the movement. She kept the swing moving with one foot so the baby didn't awaken.

Her attention lingered on her son's sweet face, and a fresh wave of grief closed her throat. He looked so much like his daddy. If only Eric could see him, hold him. Instead he'd died without ever realizing he was going to be a father.

The door to her left opened, and her grandmother stepped out onto the wraparound porch. People took Mary Tucker for fifty instead of seventy. Her boho attire added to her youthful air. Today's outfit was enough to make Carly want to reach for sunglasses. The bright yellow top contrasted with the red-and-blue patchwork skirt that swirled around her grandmother's slim figure in voluminous folds. Crystal clips kept her white hair in an updo that accented her cheekbones. The soft blue reflection of the porch ceiling enhanced her grandmother's creamy skin and deepened the color of her eyes.

She carried a Bolesławiec tray with two mugs. Carly eyed the traditional Polish peacock design of the mugs and straightened.

Gram set the tray down on a table beside the Adirondack chair near the swing and leaned over to drop a cube of sugar into each mug of tea. She stirred the tea with a prized Sheffield spoon before handing one of the mugs to Carly. "Here you go, sweetheart. Herbal, of course, so Noah doesn't get any caffeine."

Carly accepted the mug and saucer with her right hand and balanced it on the swing. "What's wrong, Gram?"

"Why would you think anything is wrong?" She settled on the chair and lifted her mug to her lips.

"You only bring out your favorite peacock mugs when you want to stay calm. What are you trying to talk me into now?" Carly smiled to take the sting out of her question.

"Busted." An impish light danced in Gram's blue eyes. "Have you thought about what to do next, sugar?" Her soft southern drawl was one Carly could listen to for hours. "I mean, you've been here for seven months now. The flea market season is in full swing, and you haven't made a move to look at my mama's estate pieces to get them ready for sale. I know little Noah has consumed every waking minute since he was born, but it seems unusual you haven't made any noises about resuming your previous life. I've heard you typing a bit on your computer at night, and I suspect you're finally writing a novel like you've talked about for years."

Carly nodded. "I'm trying, but I still haven't landed on the right story." Her smile faded as she examined her grandmother's face. "Noah's been keeping you up, hasn't he? I can change rooms and stay at the other end of the house." The huge Georgian home was over five thousand square feet. Surely there was a place where Noah's colicky cries wouldn't disturb her grandmother.

Carly had moved in right after Eric's death and had spent seven months of her pregnancy here before the baby came. It had been a lot to ask of her grandmother.

Gram put her tea down and reached over to place her hand on Carly's knee. "No, that's not what I meant at all. He never awakens me. It's been so wonderful—like having my babies all over again. I'm going about this all wrong. I don't ever want you to leave."

"I'm confused, Gram. If you don't want me to leave, what are you trying to say?"

Gram gestured at the expansive porch and view. "I want to restore this place and turn it into a bed-and-breakfast. And I want you to run it. You won't have to leave Noah, and you can putter around with your writing if you want."

Carly's gasp made Noah stir, his rosebud mouth puckering as if he was about to cry. She gave another push of the swing with her foot, and he settled. "But what about Amelia and Emily? They'll think I'm trying to cut them out."

Gram's lips pursed. "You've babied those girls way too much, Carly Ann." When Carly opened her mouth to protest,

Gram waved her hand. "I know—I know. They needed you after your mama died. Lord knows I love my son, but Kyle has never grown up. You shouldn't have had to shoulder the burden of raising your sisters. The problem is they expect you to rush in and fix things for them. If they want a part of this house, they need to help restore it. Emily can design the interior to her heart's content, and Amelia will give it the finest paint job in all of Beaufort."

Carly found her voice. "Gram, I don't know anything at all about running an inn."

"Lordy, I never met anyone with more of a gift for gab than you, Carly Ann. You could talk the paint off a fence post. And it's not fake—it's always clear to people that you care about them and are genuinely interested. We'll buy baked goods from friends for breakfast, and we'll have the best coffee anywhere in town."

Carly looked across Bay Street to the water. The house boasted one of the best views in town, and the two "angel" trees on the front lawn had drawn amateur photographers for years. If a live oak tree branched down and rooted itself in the ground before stretching up to the sky again, it was a highly prized specimen of southern beauty. The biggest one in Gram's yard had done its magic trick the year Carly's mother died of a stroke at the much-too-young age of forty-five. Carly had always taken it as a sign Mama was looking down on them and smiling.

The massive home had been built in the early 1800s, and Carly had loved it for as long as she could remember. Huge verandas wrapped around both floors, and its red metal roof made a cheerful statement of invitation to passersby. She'd itched to bring it back to its former glory since she was in her teens, but Gram had always insisted it was perfect just the way it was with its worn rugs, uneven plaster, and wide plank floors.

"Gram, do you realize how much work it will take to reconfigure it for guests? For one thing, we'll need more bathrooms. And we'd have to put in air-conditioning. Visitors won't put up with sweltering all summer long like we do. You can talk until you're blue in the face about opening the south-facing windows and letting the sea breeze lift the heat up through the top floor vents, but guests expect all the comforts of home."

A frown settled on Gram's face. "People are too soft these days. All that artificial air is bad for the lungs."

"We'll still have to fix it. And the cost. Gram, it will take a *lot* of money."

"Mama left me enough to do it. I've already consulted Ryan about taking on the job."

Carly caught her breath at the mention of the next-door neighbor who had broken her heart all those summers ago. So far, she'd managed to avoid him, and she hoped to continue that good luck. "I see," she muttered.

"I'm going to do this, Carly. It's not up for discussion. Are you game to be an innkeeper, or do you long to go back to the hectic life of selling collectibles at flea markets?"

Carly stared down into the sleeping face of her infant son. A stable life for him would be right here in this home she'd loved all her life. "I'm in." And she just might find more time to write.

———

Today was one of those days when Lucas Bennett wondered why he hadn't chosen construction as a career instead of law enforcement. The spring breeze held the scent of salt and confederate jasmine, and puffy clouds blocked the worst of the sun's scorching rays. He didn't even mind the insects buzzing around his head as he and his brother, Ryan, nailed the last of the shingles on the garage in their backyard.

While their house had once been the most dilapidated on Bay Street, he and Ryan had worked diligently over the years since they'd inherited it from their parents to turn it into the beautiful lady it had been in 1850.

His gaze fell on the decaying porch of the house next door. Now Mary Tucker's house held the distinction of being the most dilapidated. She'd had a metal roof put on last year, but it was the most current item on the grand old lady. Lucas had often thought about the things he'd do if he owned the mansion. But it had been in the Tucker family for generations, and he didn't see it ever going on the market.

Not that a homicide detective could afford the prices the Bay Street houses brought these days. If this house hadn't been left to them, he and Ryan never could have bought it, though Ryan's net worth was increasing quickly as the reputation of his construction business blossomed.

Ryan paused to wipe a red bandanna across his forehead. He took a swig from his thermos. "Yeah, I know Mary's porch is about to fall off, but she's asked me to renovate the place. Things will look a lot different by this time next year."

Lucas turned to stare at his brother, and it was like seeing a version of himself—same hazel eyes and dark hair. Ryan was slightly shorter and more tanned from his construction work. "Sounds like too big of a job with the new apartments you're working on."

"I can handle it."

Lucas didn't like the smile on Ryan's face. "I don't know, Ryan. We both like Mary, but don't bite off more than you can chew."

Ryan's mouth twisted, and he shrugged. "You just don't want me around Carly."

"She broke your heart once. Don't mistake pity for something deeper."

"It's been six years since we broke up, and I've moved on."

"Oh really? Carly's been living with her grandmother for seven months, and in that time, you haven't repeated a date with anyone that I know of. You sure you aren't just waiting for her to get over Eric's death?"

Ryan tossed down the last bundle of old shingles. "I just haven't found the right one. And aren't you the pot calling the kettle black? When was the last time you went on a date?"

The faint wail of a small infant filtered through the rustle of live oak leaves and the whisper of Spanish moss. Babies made Lucas uncomfortable, and he tried to tune out the sound. How did someone even figure out what made a tiny human like that cry? Give him a file full of evidence any day over figuring out emotions.

When he was twenty-five, his fiancée had told him she couldn't bear the constant worry his job had brought to her life. He realized then that law enforcement and a romantic relationship made for uneasy friends. Now that he was thirty-two and the department's top homicide detective, he was convinced it was better to stay single. He was called out in the night way too often to deal with a wife and family.

A soulful look in his dog's eyes was enough to send Lucas on a guilt trip, and he didn't need a crying kid to add to his stress. "Ryan, she chose her sisters over you. She's got a kid now too. Everyone and everything will take precedence over you."

They both knew how devastating that felt growing up. Dad had pushed them all aside to tend to Mom's constant ups and downs. Lucas wanted more for his brother.

Ryan hooked his hammer into the loop on his tool belt. "You've never given her a chance. She was the only mother her sisters had. Of course she was going to take care of them."

"And she probably still does." Lucas eyed his brother. "Have you talked to her since she moved in?"

Ryan's gaze didn't meet Lucas's. "Well, no. She's been busy and so have I. That should tell you I'm not interested."

Lucas swung a boot over the edge of the ladder and began to climb down. "Then why do I have the feeling you'd like something to develop?"

"Because you're paranoid and can't stand her. You need to get over it."

Lucas pressed his lips together and stepped off the ladder. He hefted the discarded shingles onto his shoulder and stepped around his red golden retriever, Major, to move toward the garage door. Maybe a shower would wash off the uneasy feeling that had coated his skin at all the talk about Carly.

It wouldn't do any good to argue about it with Ryan. He'd never seen through Carly. Lucas had always considered her a spoiled brat. Mary had lived next door his entire life, and her granddaughters had lived with her after their mother died. Mary never made them grow up. It was understandable she'd had sympathy for the loss of their mother, but at some point, she needed to make them stand on their own two feet and become adults.

And Lucas had heard enough from Eric over the years to know that his brother had dodged a bullet. Carly ruled the roost at home and hadn't been the supportive wife Eric had hoped for. But his brother had always been blind when it came to Carly Tucker. Like Ryan said, he was a grown man. His life was his own to ruin if he wanted to.

TWO

Carly thought she should have about two hours before Noah woke from his nap. Taking the baby monitor and Pepper with her, she hurried up the creaky stairs to the third-floor attic, where most of her great-grandmother's possessions had been stored after Eric's death. While Carly told herself the items wouldn't prep themselves for sale, the real reason for her decision to go through them today was to try to wrap her head around her grandmother's offer.

A text from her sister Emily had contributed to the final push. According to Emily, her sisters had been patient long enough. It was time to get this job done so Carly could distribute the income from the antiques. And if Gram was serious about her plan to turn the place into a B and B, the attic needed to be cleared out anyway.

Dust motes danced in the rays of sunshine streaming through the windows, and Pepper batted at them before he went hunting for spiders and mice. Carly sneezed and flipped on brighter lighting. Boxes along with antique furniture of every variety, from sofas to tables and bookcases, filled nearly all the floor space. The movers had brought it all here after Eric's death, and it was a mountain of old belongings. If the job didn't need to be done now, she would have retreated. Two hours wouldn't begin to touch organizing this.

An area to her right held enough space to squeeze between the items, so she started there and immediately saw a genuine Tiffany lamp. Her great-grandmother had liked nice things. The French Provincial cabinet would bring a pretty penny too. Carly moved things as she examined them and marked them in a notebook.

By the time she reached an old chest at the end of the row, she realized most of these things needed to go to auction. She'd never get their full value at a flea market. Much as Carly hated to admit it, Emily had been right. As an interior designer, Emily must have paid attention the few times she'd gone to visit Gramma Helen.

Noah could awaken any minute, but the old chest of memorabilia Gramma Helen had left to Carly caught her eye. One quick peek wouldn't derail her too much. She knelt and opened the lid of the chest. A folded note with her name on it lay nestled atop yellowing christening clothing. Was that *Eric's* handwriting? When had he looked inside this old chest—and why?

Her hands shook as she picked up the paper and opened it.

Carls, I'll put out some feelers about the names on the certificate. Pretty exciting stuff for your grandma. Do you think she knew about this? I'll let you know what I find out.

What on earth? She laid aside the note and began to lift out the items inside. Under the christening gown and hat, fragile with age, she found more baby clothes as well as an old brown file with papers inside. The wool garment under it was a rich black mixed with brighter colors, and she recognized it as a highly prized Russian Pavlovo Posad shawl. She caressed its soft folds, then picked it up and shook it to make sure no spiders lurked within. Something hit the floorboards, and she looked at her feet. A small red egg lay beside her left foot. It seemed hardly worth the effort it had taken for someone to wrap it up. She picked it up and laid it aside with the shawl.

She opened the file and pulled out a sheaf of papers. It took a moment for the words on the top page to coalesce in her brain. Adoption papers. The child's name was Mary Balandin, and it had been changed to Mary Padgett, Gram's maiden name.

There was a note in Gramma Helen's spidery handwriting.

Carly, I'm sorry to leave this on you to deal with. Somehow, I never found the courage to tell my sweet Mary she was adopted. I was fearful she would love me less. Do with this as you wish. I know you'll pray about it and do the right thing.

Carly set aside the note to examine the documents under it. The top paper was from a nurse named Adams. A faded picture of two babies in a pram was clipped to the top, and Carly scanned down the text.

Mr. and Mrs. Padgett,
I thought perhaps you would like to have this photo of little Mary and her sister, Elizabeth. It was a shame we had to separate twins, but at least they both have good homes

now. Thank you for your generosity in welcoming Mary into your home. Her mother, Sofia Balandin, is grateful as well and enclosed the shawl and the egg so Mary had something to remember her by.

It was signed by a Nurse Adams at an orphanage in Savannah. Carly flipped the paper over to see if there was more information, but it was blank. Gram had a sister out there. She'd always wished she had a sibling but had grown up an only child. Carly was certain her grandmother had never seen the contents of this chest.

Carly had to find out if Gram's sister was still alive. Wouldn't that be the most amazing birthday present? Gram's seventieth was in two months, and Carly had to try. Why hadn't Eric mentioned this to her? She thought back to the week prior to his death. They'd been fighting a lot and barely talking.

But Eric had always detailed everything. She'd gotten his laptop back after the murder investigation had gone nowhere, and it was in her closet. Maybe he'd made notes about this and what he'd found out.

She scrambled to her feet, picked up an indignant Pepper, and rushed down the steps. Noah was beginning to squawk as she reached the second floor, so she set her squirming cat on the floor, then quickly washed the dirt from her hands before she picked up Noah. Carrying him in one arm, she grabbed the laptop from her closet and plugged it in beside her bed. While Noah nursed, she scanned through Eric's files.

Bingo. A file titled *Mary Tucker* had been created a week before he was killed. The first notation mentioned that Eric had called the home of Natalie Adams and spoken to her grandson. He confirmed that his grandmother had worked at the orphanage for many years. The man, Roger Adams, had asked odd questions about old belongings. A day later, Eric noticed he'd picked up a tail. His final note mentioned he was going to install extra security at the house.

Carly closed the computer and gulped. Was Eric's death connected to this somehow? Eric's old partner would want to hear about this and see if it opened any doors.

——

Carly had Eric's partner's personal number, so she carried Noah out to the porch swing and called Kelly Cicero directly instead of trying her at the station. The baby's eyelids drifted closed at the gentle movement of the swing and the sound of the water across Bay Street.

The phone rang twice. When the call was picked up on the other end, the first thing Carly heard was the sound of an infant crying.

"Carly? Is everything okay?" Kelly asked with a hitch of concern in her voice.

The sound of Kelly's tired voice brought Eric back somehow. The last time they'd spoken was three months after Eric's murder. At that time the police hadn't made any real headway. "I'm not sure, Kelly. I-I found something I can't explain."

She launched into what she'd found in the chest and on Eric's laptop. "Did you make a copy of his personal laptop information?"

"Sure, but no one mentioned that file. You say he picked up a tail after that call? It's probably a coincidence, but the tail could be related to his murder. Is there any information about who was following him?"

"No, nothing." Saying it all out loud made it seem unlikely, but Carly clung to the hope it might lead to finding Eric's murderer. "It all seems very odd, though."

"I think it's likely unimportant. Anything interesting in the old furniture that might explain it?"

"Not really. The usual things like collectibles. Even an old toy egg." She paused at another infant wail. "I hear a baby in the background."

"That's Caroline. She's four months old."

No wonder Kelly sounded tired. "Congratulations! I didn't know you were pregnant."

And as far as she knew, Kelly wasn't married. Carly hadn't even heard she was dating anyone seriously. "I'd love to see a picture. I'll send you one of Noah. My mother-in-law sent me baby pictures of Eric, and they're identical."

"I wish Eric could have seen him."

"Me too. Are you missing your job?"

"I don't really want to go back, but I have to work."

Carly knew how Kelly felt. Every time she held Noah, she was thankful she got to care for him. "Should I call the chief or should you?"

"I'll do it. Maybe I can learn more information. I'll let you know what I find out."

"Thanks." After hanging up, Carly jotted down a note to pick up a gift for the baby.

She stared at her phone. Her sisters still hadn't been notified of Gram's decision about the house, and Carly needed to quit putting off the calls. It would need to be all-hands-on-deck if they had a chance of getting this project done. Maybe she should have her grandmother make the calls, though. The last time she'd spoken with Amelia and Emily, both of them had been cool. While they had good reason to be upset, it hadn't been Carly's doing, and their treatment stung.

She put her phone down on the swing beside her when the front door creaked open behind her and Gram came out.

She fanned her pink face and settled into the Adirondack chair. "Land's sake, it's hot today. The idea of getting air-conditioning in the old place isn't a bad idea."

Carly propped Noah on her chest so her grandmother could see his sweet face. "Except for the cost."

"I don't even want to know how much that will cost."

"Gram, we haven't talked about the price tag of all this. Are you sure Gramma Helen left you enough? The bill will be enormous."

Her grandmother leaned over and cooed at Noah until he smiled, then leaned back again. "You let me worry about that, sugar."

Carly zoned out as her mind listed all the things that needed to be redone. She realized her grandmother had spoken and was waiting for an answer. "I'm sorry?"

"I asked if you called your sisters."

"I hoped you would."

Gram reached for her phone. "Let's do it together. Use my phone."

Gram must have realized Carly was fearful that her sisters wouldn't answer a call from her. She rang Emily first so she wouldn't have to deal with Dillard yet.

Emily answered on the first ring. "Hi, Gram."

"Um, it's Carly, Em."

"Is Gram okay?"

"She's right here and wants to talk to you. I'm putting you on speakerphone."

Gram leaned closer to the phone in Carly's hand. "Emily, dear, I have some wonderful news, and I need your help to execute it."

Carly breathed in the sweet scent of her baby's head and listened to Gram explain her plans. Emily's enthusiasm wasn't a surprise. She was a home designer, and landing a project like this could open some new doors here in Beaufort and across South Carolina. Emily mentioned several color ideas, but Carly couldn't picture what her sister had planned. Carly's view of design was to paint everything white and put in the furniture. She didn't have an artistic bone in her body, but Emily thrived on that kind of thing.

"I'm in," Emily said. "When do you want me?"

"As soon as you can come, my dear. There's a lot of work to tackle before we get to the design phase, and your sister will need help."

"I can be there next week. What about Amelia?"

"I'm about to call her next."

"You know Dillard will be on this like a duck on a June bug."

"I certainly hope so, my dear."

And within ten minutes it was all arranged. Amelia was just as enthusiastic. Carly's sisters would be descending on the house in a week. And Carly would have to decide if she should tell them about the papers she'd found in the chest. She still had no idea what to do.

THREE

After a shower and a bottle of kombucha, Lucas felt almost human. The sun still tingled on his tanned arms, but in a good way. The roof looked great, and he could spend the rest of the day doing something mindless like reading a good thriller or pulling weeds. A Saturday off was a rarity, and it wasn't uncommon to get called in to investigate a crime on a Friday night, but last night had been unusually calm.

After glancing out the window, he decided the weeds won the toss-up. He went out to the big porch and down the steps to his grandmother's prized rose and camellia garden. Though she'd passed twenty years ago, the family had worked hard to preserve her legacy. He and Ryan had such crazy schedules, they sometimes had to hire out the gardening, but he could knock this out in an hour.

The physical effort felt good as he worked on his task. He quickly had a pile of weeds beside him, and he straightened to move to a different section. Someone moved in the shadows, and he looked up into the face of a drooling infant. The baby's mouth lifted in a toothless grin, and he found himself smiling back. He glanced at the mother's face.

Carly Harris wore a frightened expression, and she shifted her baby boy to her other arm. "Um, do you have a minute?"

She sure was a looker, even with a newborn in tow. He'd always understood her appeal on a purely physical basis. A guy could lose himself in her large brown eyes, and her long dark hair invited a man to plunge his fingers into it. She wore shorts that highlighted her showstopper legs and a pink top with the word *tattarrattat* across it. But he disliked women who knew they were beautiful and used it. She'd reeled in Ryan first and then his friend Eric.

He wiped his muddy hands on the grass. "Sure. Let's get out of the sun, though."

"Thank you."

She followed him up the wide staircase to the big porch and settled in a rocker. When the baby started to squawk, she rocked him gently until he settled. He waited for her to speak, but she rocked without a word for several minutes.

Awkward. She was the one who had initiated the contact, and he couldn't figure out what she'd want to talk about. It wasn't like they were friends. Their last conversation had been fiery, with her bursting into tears at its conclusion.

He took a surreptitious glance at his phone. The afternoon would slip away quickly at this rate. "Sorry about Eric." He'd gone to the funeral but hadn't spoken to her. And though she'd lived next door for months, he'd managed to avoid her.

She looked down and licked her lips. "Thanks." Her long hair swung against her cheek, obscuring her expression. "Eric's death is why I'm here. I discovered something that might have played into his murder."

He shifted on the Adirondack chair. "Shouldn't you be talking to the detective in charge of the case?"

He didn't want to step on the lead detective's toes. Though the murder had occurred on Pawleys Island, it wasn't good police etiquette to go poking his nose in another officer's case.

"I tried, but with his reaction, he might as well have patted me on the head and said, 'There, there, little lady.'"

Lucas's lips twitched. He'd dealt with some boneheaded men himself. No one looking at Carly's intelligent eyes could think she would be bringing baseless concerns. "What did you find?"

"My sisters and I inherited our great-grandmother's belongings. I hadn't had a chance to go through them and get them ready for sale. They'd been in my shop, and Eric had a day off. He promised to organize them for me and start taking pictures so I could list them. He'd been poking around them for a few weeks. That's where he was killed. After his death, I didn't have the heart or energy to get that big job done, but I started it today. I discovered some papers in an old chest. It appears Gram was adopted and didn't know about it."

He listened to her story of a missing twin and the accompanying notes Eric had left. His interest tingled when she mentioned Eric had picked up a tail after the call to the nurse's grandson. "Did you try talking to Eric's partner? She might be more invested in getting to the bottom of his murder."

"I did. Kelly is on maternity leave, and I don't know when she's going back to work. She sounded vaguely interested and told me she would try to get the information to the chief. She has a new baby, and I think she was overwhelmed."

At least Carly had hit all the right places first. He and Eric went way back. They'd met at a basketball camp, and they'd gone to police academy at the same time. The bond they'd shared from their teens had deepened over time, and he'd been grieved at Eric's death. Didn't Lucas owe it to their longtime friendship to do what he could to bring Eric's killer to justice?

His gaze landed on the infant. A baby with Eric's nose and chin. Justice was what had always driven Lucas, and while Carly wasn't his favorite person, Eric had loved her. And he'd lost out on the chance to raise his son.

"Did anyone search his work computer for something about the things in the shop?"

"I don't know. My questions were dismissed immediately."

"I'll run up to Pawleys Island to take a look at the evidence, see what I can find out."

"Thank you. I know I'm asking a lot, but you and Eric were tight. I didn't know who else would have the contacts to help."

True enough. He fidgeted in his chair waiting for her to leave. Did she expect him to say something else—maybe promise results? She should know it didn't work that way. Any police department had cases that landed in the cold files. Usually the murder of an officer took high priority, and he had no doubt this one did too. Maybe they had a suspect and were gathering evidence. He could call, but an in-person visit might tell him more.

"I'll go Monday after I get off. I don't work tomorrow, but I'd like to talk to the chief and get the green light to look at Eric's work computer."

She finally stirred and rose. The baby had fallen asleep in her arms, and she moved carefully so she didn't awaken him.

Ryan would have a field day when he found out she'd talked him into this.

———

Carly shooed a fly away from Noah in his bouncy seat on the porch. He loved sitting in it and facing the honeysuckle, but the insects loved him as much as the hummingbirds loved the blossoms.

Her phone rang, and she saw it was Eric's partner. Carly hadn't expected to hear back, though Kelly had said she'd call.

"Kelly, good morning."

"I hope this is a good time to call. I talked to Chief Robinson."

"It's fine. We're just out on the porch enjoying the sunshine. What did Robinson say?"

"The chief brushed me off. He doesn't think it's connected. I mean, your grandmother's birth parents are probably dead by now. He didn't see how something like that could lead to murder."

Robinson had a point. "But what about the tail?"

"Eric told Robinson about a white Ford pickup following him, and while it could have been the killer, it's unlikely to be connected to your grandmother. I saw it the day before he was killed, but it was one like a million others. There wasn't anything distinctive about it, so I always thought it was coincidence that he spotted it a few times. It might not have been the same one."

"Did Eric say why he thought it was the same pickup every time?"

"Something about the wheel covers, but they didn't look distinctive to me."

But Eric had always been a truck and car guy. He'd done some racing when he was a teenager and had dragged her to car shows all the time during their three-year marriage. If he thought it was the same truck, it was. He wouldn't make that kind of mistake, but it was clear Kelly didn't think there was a connection. Maybe because they were close to an arrest. Another thought struck Carly—maybe she didn't want to reveal anything and have Carly meddle in the case.

"Any movement on finding Eric's murderer?" she asked.

"Dead ends from what I've been told. You probably remember Trevor Lloyd? He got out a week before Eric's murder."

The hit-and-run case. "He threatened Eric at the sentencing." If it hadn't been for Eric's persistence in following the leads, Lloyd would have gotten away. The guy had a rap sheet as long as her arm, and tracking him down had led to other charges.

"Right. So we looked at him pretty hard, and at first, his alibi didn't seem to hold water. But we got hold of some street video, and he was telling the truth about being in Charleston at the time of the murder. He'd been our best lead. But strangely enough, he does drive a white Ford pickup."

So the case was stalled. Carly knew they wouldn't give up, though. "I talked to Captain Robinson too. He didn't seem to think Eric's investigation into my grandma's past had any bearing on his murder, but I'm not so sure. Would you mind reviewing his notes to see what you think?"

"Sure, send them over. I'm not going back to work for another month, though, and I'm not sure I'll have time to do much about it."

At least it was something. "I think your email should be on Eric's computer. I'll send the notes from there."

"I'll look for them." She sounded a little impatient and distant like she wanted to get off the phone.

A baby's cry sounded in the background, and Carly hurriedly thanked her and ended the call so Kelly could tend to Caroline. Noah had fallen asleep, so she picked him up in his bouncy seat and carried him inside to her bedroom. She eased him from the sling seat and put him in his crib, then grabbed the baby monitor and the papers she'd found on her way back to the porch. She had only a few days before her sisters descended to help begin the restoration on the house, and she wouldn't have as much time to investigate her grandmother's birth family.

She still hadn't decided if she would tell her sisters about the papers she'd found. They might think she should leave it alone, and she couldn't do that. Why had Gramma Helen been so fearful to tell the truth about Gram's birth? It wouldn't have negated the love they'd shared. Maybe Gram was better off not knowing, but it would take more information for Carly to make that decision one way or another.

She spread the papers out to take another look. Should she call Natalie Adams's grandson herself, or was it too dangerous? If he'd had anything to do with Eric's death, the call might bring deadly attention their way. But he was the only lead they had.

Her attention went to the birth certificate. Sofia Balandin. She could start there.

FOUR

Balandin wasn't a common name. A brief internet search didn't bring up any likely names for Carly to contact, which might have been why Eric had started with the Adams connection. She didn't want to jump into a dangerous call right off the bat, so she decided to spend a little more time digging around in the chest where she'd found the documents.

With the baby monitor in the pocket of her shorts, she went back to the attic. Pepper chased her feet up the steps. Her grandmother volunteered at the Pat Conroy Literary Center, and she'd be gone for another couple of hours. Carly sneezed again when she flipped on the attic light and looked around. Nothing had been disturbed since she'd been here on Friday.

The chest was still closed and partially hidden in the back corner. She dragged it out into the light and opened the lid to inhale the aroma of the cedar lining. She lifted out every clothing item one by one and shook it to make sure there wasn't another paper or document hidden in the folds. The last item was the colorful wool shawl. The rich colors contrasted with the black, and it was in excellent condition. No moths had destroyed the heavy fabric in all these years. She hated to sell it. Maybe she'd keep it.

She gently lifted the red egg from the final fold of the shawl and studied it. Had it been a favorite toy so Sofia tucked it away? It seemed rather small—only between three and four inches. Had this shawl belonged to Gram's birth mother, too, or had it been used as a wrap for the baby? She brought it to her nose and sniffed, but it held only the scent of cedar.

The egg was such a gaudy red that it made Carly wrinkle her nose. Who had thought that color would be good? She supposed a baby might find it fascinating. She turned it over and over in her hands and a tiny fleck of paint fell off. She squinted at the white under it. Using her nail, she scraped away another piece of red to reveal more of the egg's true appearance. It looked like white enamel, which would be much better than flaky paint.

It would take more work to get the egg back to its original appearance—maybe more work than it was worth, but she was like that with old items like this. She had to uncover the beauty and original use. Carrying the documents, the egg, and the shawl, she went down the stairs to the kitchen and laid aside the items before finding some white vinegar in the pantry. She filled the sink with hot water and added the vinegar and some dishwashing soap to the mixture before she put the egg in to soak for a few minutes.

While the vinegar had a chance to penetrate the red paint on the egg, she looked over the documents again but found no new clue to follow. She would have to call that Adams man unless Lucas came up with a better idea. When she went back to the sink, she took a utility brush to the softened paint, and it peeled off easily.

She lifted the egg into the light and caught her breath. The luminous white porcelain glowed in the sunlight streaming through the kitchen window. The trim appeared to be real gold, and Carly's eyes widened as she took in the details.

For years she'd been obsessed with Fabergé eggs. Several museums housed the treasures, and she'd visited several of them—Richmond's Virginia Museum of Fine Arts, the Hillwood Estate in DC, and the Walters Art Museum in Baltimore. She hadn't been able to touch any of them, of course, but if Carly wasn't mistaken, this egg in her hands could have held its own against any of the beauties she'd seen in the museums.

She'd studied the list of missing eggs and had often fantasized about finding one of them at a flea market or garage sale. The appearance of this one with its opaque white enamel seemed to match the description she'd read of the missing Hen with Sapphire Pendant, made for the tsar himself.

If this was truly a Fabergé egg, it should open. She held one hand on the top and one on the bottom and gave the egg a twist. It seemed to move but didn't open. Maybe it had some paint in the crack. She ran her fingernail around the thin line between the two halves and tried again.

This time the egg opened to reveal a beautiful interior of real gold. Nothing was inside, which wasn't unusual. The "surprise" inside the egg could have been taken out sometime in the past. According to the imperial archives, if this was indeed that famous missing egg, it should have contained a gold hen studded with rose-cut diamonds taking a sapphire egg pendant out of a nest. No photographs of the surprise existed, so all that was known about it was the description. Some accounts said there was a golden yolk held inside the hen and pendant, but others didn't list that detail.

While the history was murky, there were between six and ten Fabergé eggs still missing, and the only one with an opaque white porcelain exterior was the mysterious Hen with Sapphire Pendant. The last egg found had been sold for thirty million dollars to a private collector.

Could Roger Adams suspect that Gramma Helen had possessed this priceless egg? That much money could tempt someone to kill for it.

Carly snapped several pictures of the egg with her phone. Who could she trust with this information? Not her sisters, probably not even Gram. Not yet. She would need to authenticate it, and until the egg was safe in a vault or museum somewhere, they could be in danger.

Lucas's intelligent hazel eyes flashed into her mind. He didn't seem the type to talk, and he was a detective. Maybe she could trust him with this information.

———

Traffic was light on 17 into Pawleys Island. It had been a pleasant two-and-a-half-hour drive from Beaufort. Lucas parked in the lot outside Gilbert's Ice Cream. It was a hangout spot for everyone in town, including police officers. Chief Robinson had suggested meeting here, and Lucas hadn't had the homemade treat in a couple of years. The place was quiet at this time of day. May wasn't a usual month for tourists, and the ice cream shop had just opened.

He stepped inside and walked around to the ice cream counter. The front blackboard had flavors listed in colorful chalk, and more chalkboards behind the counter displayed the full menu. He ordered a banana split with coffee, chocolate, and strawberry ice cream.

Chief Jamal Robinson stepped behind Lucas. "I'll have what he's having." The officer wore the usual navy shorts and white short-sleeved uniform of the town. A navy cap covered his tight black curls.

Lucas turned and shook hands with Robinson. "Thanks for coming, Chief."

He'd met the fiftysomething man a couple of years back when he'd been with Eric. Robinson was just as fit and buff now as he'd been back then. Lucas paid for the sundaes, and the two men went out to a secluded table on the porch of the plantation-style building.

Robinson scooped up a spoonful of ice cream. "Did Carly put you up to this interview?"

"Chief, you have to admit what she found is odd. Eric picked up a tail as soon as he started digging into Mary Tucker's heritage. You have to at least consider there's a connection and it's not a coincidence."

"Answer me this then. If there's a connection, why did the murderer stop? The papers Carly just found were still there along with Eric's note. There have been no break-ins or attempts to recover more information."

True enough. Lucas had noticed that too. "The guy could have been picked up for something else. He might have taken whatever it was he was interested in. The contents from Mary's mother's house haven't been cataloged. We don't know what all was in that shop when Eric was killed. Maybe the guy's job took him away. Do you have a suspect?"

"Nothing solid. Eric had a run-in with an ex-con by the

name of Trevor Lloyd a couple of weeks before the murder. He's at the top of the list, but so far, his alibi has held up." He lifted a thick black brow. "You're not going to leave it alone, are you?"

Why was he even sticking his nose in like this? Something about seeing that baby without his daddy had tugged at Lucas's heartstrings. "Eric was a friend, and his wife is my next-door neighbor. She has a little son who will one day want to know what happened to his father."

Eric had been a good judge of character, and he'd thought the world of his captain. Lucas didn't think Jamal would be the type to shut out help. He led a small cohort of officers and could probably use the assistance anyway.

Robinson shrugged. "Have at it then, Bennett. What do you need from me?"

"A look at his work computer might show more of what he learned about Mary's birth family."

"I already went over it after Carly called. There were no personal files on it at all. Eric was a man who liked to keep his professional and personal lives separate. I printed out the call log from his phone for you, though. It's in the truck."

Lucas thanked him, and the men finished their treats and tossed away the trash. Lucas followed him to his SUV, and Robinson reached inside and retrieved a sheaf of papers. "There's another call log I included, but you'll need Carly to help you sort out anything important. I've done all I can."

And that *all* was a lot. "I appreciate it." He stared at a circled number. "Looks like it's a Pawleys Island number."

"It is. Guy by the name of Gage Beaumont. He lives in the True Blue Condos."

Lucas knew the area. The condominiums were surrounded by golf courses, and it was just down 17 from here. He could make a stop and try to catch the guy at home, though in the middle of the day on a Monday, he was most likely at work.

He shook Robinson's hand. "I appreciate it, Chief."

"You'll let me know what you find out?"

"Sure will." Lucas slung his long legs into his truck and waved to the police chief as he pulled out onto 17.

Lucas turned in at the True Blue complex and drove back to the condos. Golf carts cruised slowly along the road, and golfers were out on the greens enjoying the perfect weather. He followed the road to the right into the complex and found the condo number jotted down beside the phone number. He parked and decided to call the number before he went to the door.

The condo was on the first floor, and he got out and watched the door as he placed the call. No one answered, and he debated whether to leave a message. He shrugged and left his name and number.

The trip hadn't been a complete bust—at least he'd gotten ice cream.

FIVE

Carly's mouth was dry as she carried Noah across the yard to the Bennett house in the late-afternoon sunshine. A flash of white caught her eye, and she smiled to see a little blue heron in the grass across the street.

The egg was safely tucked into one of Noah's blankets in the diaper bag. She had to be crazy taking such a huge chance with the priceless egg. She'd done some research last night and was convinced the egg was all she suspected. It would take an expert to make the final determination, and she wasn't sure she wanted to know. Her sisters would demand the egg be sold and the money split between them, and though the contents of the chest had been left only to her, Carly knew she'd do what they wanted. She already mourned its loss when she loved it so much.

Lucas's bright blue Jeep pickup was in the drive, so he was home from work. She went up the steps and pressed the doorbell. The front door stood open, and she could see through the screen door into the entry where a room opened on each side. The oak woodwork appeared newly redone and glowed with a matte shimmer. A long rug ran the length of the entry past the wide stairway. The guys must be working on redoing their house too.

"Coming!" Ryan's voice called.

Carly's heart hitched in her chest. She'd seen him from a distance several times since coming back to town, and her attraction to him still simmered under the surface, though he didn't act like he felt anything for her.

His dark hair glistened with water like he'd just hopped out of the shower. He wore khaki shorts and a red tee that showed off his muscular arms and chest. She knew the taut muscles came from hefting beams and heavy construction materials, not from visiting a gym.

She wetted her lips and forced a smile. "Hi, Ryan."

His smile came easily. "This is a nice surprise." He held open the screen door. "Come on in. I was about to have some sweet tea. Want some?"

"Sure. Um, is Lucas home?"

"Yeah, he just got here and is in the shower. Have a seat in the living room, and I'll let him know you're here. He told me he was looking into Eric's death for you. I think he went to Pawleys Island this morning and poked around."

His feet pounded up the stairs as she went to the living room and dropped into the rocker. Noah was fussing a little, so she put him on her shoulder and patted his back as she looked around the room. It was a man's room with leather furniture, no rug on the gleaming oak floors, and nothing on the end tables but lamps. No pictures or decorations of any kind on the furniture or the plaster walls, which were painted a pleasing taupe. It had to have been done recently because the air still held the faint odor of paint. But it was clean and newly redone.

Neither man would have the inclination or time to fuss

over decorations. It was a utilitarian room and that was enough. She could see a glimpse of the dining room through the large opening opposite where she sat, and it was the same way—no touch of softness. What would the kitchen be like? Maybe a freezer full of pizzas and frozen dinners. Or maybe they mostly ate out. Ryan had never liked cooking when they were dating.

Footsteps came back down the stairs, and she turned toward the entry doorway as Lucas stepped into view. He wore shorts and a tee also, and she was struck by the similarity between the two brothers. Both had dark hair and muscular builds. Both had hazel eyes and aquiline noses, but Lucas was a little taller and carried himself with a confident stride that reminded her of a Marine. He'd never been in the military, but his police training had probably been similar.

Lucas was two years older than his brother. Had he ever been in a serious relationship? He was thirty-two, so it was likely, but she couldn't quite see those serious eyes smiling with love. His expression always said he was evaluating and searching for a reason to be suspicious.

She shifted her son in her arms and gave an uncertain smile. "I hope I'm not bothering you. I had something I needed to talk to you about."

He went to the brown leather sofa and dropped onto it. "I was going to come over to your grandmother's anyway. I spoke to Robinson today, and he gave me permission to poke around. He isn't following up on your grandmother's past, so I'll see what I can find out." He lifted a brow and nodded at her shirt. "*Murdrum*? What's that mean? And yesterday you wore a shirt that read *tattarrattat*. That's a tongue twister, whatever it is."

"*Tattarrattat* is a word coined by James Joyce in *Ulysses*. It means a knock on the door. I've liked palindromes since I was in high school. I love words, especially obscure ones. Palindromes are fun, and they're a great conversation maker. I collect shirts with them on them. *Murdrum* is the act of murdering someone in a secret manner."

"Isn't all murder like that?"

"You might have a point." She laid Noah onto her lap to free her hands so she could reach into the diaper bag. "I found some compelling evidence for murder today."

Her hands shook a little as her fingers touched the smooth porcelain surface of the egg. After glancing around to make sure no one was peeking in a window, she pulled it out and held it up for Lucas to see. "This was covered in red paint and seemed worthless, but I-I think it's priceless."

He frowned and rose to take a closer look. "It's an egg."

"Not just any egg. I believe it's one of the lost Fabergé eggs of the Romanov imperial family. It's worth at least twenty million dollars. Probably more. If the surprise inside could be found, I can't even imagine what it would be worth. If someone suspected it was in our possession, they might kill to get it."

His face remained expressionless except for a slight tightening of one brow. "I've never heard of Fabergé eggs."

"In 1885 Emperor Alexander III commissioned Peter Fabergé to create an Easter egg gift for his wife, Empress Maria Feodorovna. She loved it so much that the tradition continued to 1911, both by Alexander and his son. Only the best gold and jewels were used to make them, and each of the fifty eggs was unique. When the Bolshevik Revolution occurred, the eggs were seized. Some were sold and some went into storage. There are between six and ten still missing today, including the Hen with Sapphire Pendant."

"You're sure this is one of them?"

"As sure as I can be without an expert verification, but I don't see how it can be anything else. All the expected markings are there. It's been hidden in that chest for decades."

"But someone might be searching for it. I'd better take a closer look at Roger Adams and his family."

"Or find the Balandin family. I struck out looking for them. The mother who left it for Gramma Helen was Sofia Balandin." Carly tucked the egg away in the diaper bag.

"How are you going to keep that safe?"

"I have no idea. Maybe a safety-deposit box?"

"That's a good idea."

It would crush her to lose it now, and she glanced at her watch. If she hurried, she could get to the bank before it closed.

What had possessed him to offer to watch the baby? Lucas stared at the infant sleeping beside him on the sofa. Major stood, watching Lucas with his red ears cocked as if to ask him the same question. When Lucas had seen the panicked expression on Carly's face and realized how late it was, the offer popped out of his mouth before he thought about it.

What if the kid's diaper needed to be changed? What if he cried? The possible scenarios swirled in Lucas's head. No way was he changing a diaper.

The floor creaked, and he looked up to see Ryan in the

entry. His brother had a date, but for a moment Lucas considered throwing himself on Ryan's mercy and begging him to stay. Stupid idea, though. Ryan didn't know any more about babies than Lucas did.

Ryan's eyes widened when he entered the living room and saw the baby. "I thought Carly left in your truck."

"She did. She had to make a quick run to the bank, and I offered to keep the baby. It would have been closed if she'd gone home to get her vehicle and car seat."

Ryan released a slow grin. "You falling under her spell, big brother?" The strong scent of Eternity cologne wafted into the room with him.

"What? Of course not!" Lucas wrinkled his nose at the thought. "She's the last woman I'd ever be interested in."

"Why? She's pretty and smart. She's loyal with a lot of heart."

"And she made her husband's life miserable. No thank you."

"You're listening to Eric's mother too much. No one was good enough for her baby boy."

Lucas shook his head. There was no getting through to his brother. Lucas was too jaded from his job to trust much of anyone, least of all a woman with Carly's track record.

He decided to change the subject rather than fight about it. "Who you going out with tonight?"

"Cicely."

"Three times in a row? Must be serious."

"Nah, but she's fun. We're going to a country music concert." The baby stirred, and Ryan's hazel eyes darkened with concern. "You sure you know how to hold that kid and everything? I think he's waking up."

To Lucas's dismay, his brother was right. The baby lifted his head and yawned. His eyes opened, and he put his fist in his mouth. The sucking noises made Major move closer, and Lucas grabbed his golden retriever's collar. "Stay back, boy."

The baby made mewling noises, and his head bounced up and down as if he couldn't quite keep holding it up. Maybe he couldn't. The sounds grew louder and more demanding. Those little lungs were gearing up to burst into a full-blown cry.

"Now what?" Lucas muttered.

"So now you pick him up. I think you have to watch his head and neck, though. They aren't strong yet."

"Since when did you become the baby expert?"

"I dated a girl in high school who had a newborn sister. It was one reason we broke up—she went on and on about the things you had to know about babies, and I wasn't interested at the time."

Lucas bit back a laugh. "I don't doubt it."

Little Noah's lungs were in full bellow now, and Lucas bent down to scoop him up, but he wasn't sure how to start.

"Roll him over on his back," Ryan suggested. "Then you can lift him more easily."

Lucas gently moved the baby onto his back and found himself looking into the little guy's blue eyes. When the baby's gaze fixed on Lucas's face, Noah's rosebud mouth opened in a gummy smile. The warmth that spread through Lucas's chest startled him, and he smiled back without thinking. The baby began to kick and make sounds.

"Aw, he's cooing at you," Ryan said.

Cooing? That was the weird sounds? "Is that good?"

"Sure, it means he feels happy and content. He must like

you. You've got a natural touch with kids." Ryan glanced at his Apple Watch. "I gotta go, bro. Good luck."

Lucas wanted to laugh at the "natural touch" comment, but he felt strangely touched at the thought that the baby liked him. If there was a person with less experience with babies, he didn't know who it might be. "Can't you stay a little while?"

"Not if we want to use our tickets. You're a big, strong cop—you can handle it."

Lucas was sure he *couldn't* handle it by himself, but he had no choice as Ryan turned and vanished through the door onto the porch. Lucas watched his brother walk to his Camaro and drive off before turning his attention back to the baby who was watching him. Noah broke out into another toothless grin when he saw Lucas look at him.

"You're going to be a lady killer, Noah."

Noah kicked his legs in agreement, and his little fists waved in the air. He was doing that cooing thing again, and Lucas kind of liked it. It wasn't like anything he'd ever heard before. Should he let the baby continue to lie on his back or pick him up?

Picking him up might provoke an unhappy response, so Lucas decided it was safest not to disturb him. He stood with his hands on his hips and stared down at the boy. What did one talk about with a baby? Or was it even necessary to talk? He wasn't about to be one of those people who jabbered baby talk at a kid. He'd heard a dad doing it at the hardware store once and thought the guy sounded like an idiot.

He reached down and touched Noah's hand. The little guy grabbed hold of Lucas's index finger. "Um, you doing okay, buddy?"

Noah brought Lucas's finger to his mouth, and Lucas flinched as the small gums went to work on his finger. "You've got quite the bite there, little dude."

Noah chewed on his finger for a few more seconds before turning to his own fist. Lucas wiped his wet finger on his shorts. Maybe this wasn't as bad as he thought it would be. As long as the kid didn't require a diaper change.

SIX

Carly felt naked and bereft without the egg in her posses-sion as she drove away from the bank. She'd never dreamed she'd really find a Fabergé egg in her lifetime, and everything in her wanted to keep it, to treasure it. But that dream was not to be.

Traffic was light as she maneuvered through Beaufort back to Lucas's house in his bright blue Jeep pickup. The vehicle drove like a dream, and after parking in his drive, she was sorry to slide out of the comfortable seat. She listened for Noah's cry as she hurried up the steps to the front door. He wouldn't be hungry for another hour, but he didn't know Lucas and she feared he might have gotten scared and fractious.

The only sounds she heard were of the waves across the street mingling with the bees checking out the rose bed along the front porch. Lucas didn't strike her as the type to be good with babies, but he'd offered, and she needed help to get the egg to the bank on time.

She peered through the screen door past the open entry and spotted his red golden stretched out on the floor at the foot of the stairs. The living room wasn't visible from here, and Lucas had told her to come on in when she got back rather than knock. The screen door squeaked as she eased it open and stepped inside. Major lifted his head to flare his nostrils her direction, then plopped his head back on his paws and closed his eyes.

Could Noah still be sleeping? Carly slipped past the dog into the living room and stopped short at the incongruous sight of her baby boy sleeping peacefully on Lucas's chest. Lucas lay stretched out on the sofa with his eyes closed and one arm thrown protectively around the baby so he didn't slide off. A shaft of late-afternoon sunlight fell on Lucas's face, and she allowed herself the chance to look over his handsome features, from the deep-socketed eyes and dark brows to the straight nose above firm lips. His strong features spoke of his inner strength as well.

Her heart stirred at the sight of that muscular arm around Noah. Even in rest, Lucas's nature tilted toward protection.

Without warning, his hazel eyes opened, and she found herself staring into them. Heat rushed to her cheeks to be found drinking in the sight of him. She cleared her throat. "Um, sorry to wake you. Did Noah give you any trouble?"

He shook his head and eased into a seated position. "We had a nice chat. He's quite talkative."

"He's just started to coo at people he likes."

"He pretty much talked nonstop. I didn't change him or anything. I wouldn't know how."

"Thanks for taking care of him." She hurried to lift the baby from Lucas's chest. Lucas's warmth had transferred to the baby, and she caught a faint aroma of masculine cologne.

"Not a problem. Any trouble getting a safety-deposit box at the last minute?"

She shook her head and went to sit on the chair across from the sofa. "They were very kind, and I got it tucked away safely without anyone seeing." She dug into her purse and pulled out the key she'd just gotten. "Would it be all right if I left the key in your possession? I'd feel safer if you had it."

Surprise lit his eyes. "Sure. I'll put it in our safe. No one knows the combination but Ryan and me."

"That's perfect. There's no safe at Gram's, and I was worrying about where to hide it."

She really should take her baby and go home before he demanded dinner, but she couldn't look away from Lucas's intent expression. Being around him centered her in some way—which was weird because he disliked her. She wasn't fond of him either. And after Eric's death, she'd firmly put away any thought of a man in her life. That part of her life was dead and gone, leaving only the grief behind.

"Anything else I can help you with?"

She scrambled to her feet at his pointed question. "I'm sure you have things to do this evening. I'm so sorry to have taken up so much of your time, but thank you. I'll sleep easier tonight." She shouldered the diaper bag and her purse and went toward the entry.

He trailed her. "You're welcome. I hope to find out something about the Balandin family once I get in my office tomorrow. There has to be some trace of them. You should make sure you don't poke around online. There are all kinds of electronic snooping devices these days. Someone could be watching your online activity to see if you've started to go through your great-grandma's items."

Too late. "It's odd nothing has happened since Eric's death.

Maybe whoever was interested decided there was nothing to find."

"Maybe. Or the guy could have moved away or gotten sent to jail. We just don't know. Better safe than sorry when you've got Noah."

At the mention of his name, the baby stirred. His head bobbed up off Carly's shoulder, and he turned to look at Lucas. When he began to coo, Carly laughed. "I've never heard him be quite so talkative."

"Told you he was a chatterbox."

What magic had Lucas woven around the baby to get him to respond like that? Maybe it was because Noah was used to being around women, and he liked Lucas's deep voice. The baby wasn't the only one affected. Carly had to admit Lucas's voice resonated in her chest, too, and reached inside with some strange power.

———

That hadn't been so bad. Lucas went into the kitchen to fix something to eat. The little guy had been pretty cute with all the smiles and coos. Carly had seemed surprised too. He hadn't spent that much time around Carly over the years, and she'd been—different than he expected. For one thing, she hadn't been flirtatious at all. Maybe she didn't want to run the risk of having him quit helping her.

Or maybe she doesn't find me attractive.

He shoved away the stupid thought. There was no attraction on either side. Sure, that thick dark hair was attractive in a messy bun. And her brown eyes made him think of rich, heavy chocolate, but he'd always dated blondes. There was no denying she was cute, though, which was how she'd roped in Ryan and then later Eric.

Her palindrome tee had been unexpected. He'd never heard those words before, and he prided himself on having a good vocabulary. He had to admit there was more to Carly than first met the eye. Not that he was interested in her that way.

He pulled out sirloin steak and sautéed it with onions and garlic before adding mushrooms and making the thickening. All he had to do was cook the noodles, and dinner would be ready. The rich aroma of beef stroganoff would linger until Ryan got home, and he would be sorry he left Lucas to fend for himself with Carly and the baby.

He heard Noah fussing through the open window. Once the full heat of summer hit, his air-conditioning would be going full blast, and he wouldn't be able to hear what was going on next door. That might be a good thing.

He stared at the generous amount of food he'd prepared. Carly had gotten home late, and Mary was still gone at her volunteer job. He could share the food he'd made. That was a neighborly thing to do. Maybe he should just have them come here rather than him take it all over there. Decision made, he turned down the meat mixture and shut off the boiling water until he could get back and cook the noodles. He called Major, and they went out the back door and across the lush green grass to where Carly sat on the back deck with the baby.

Noah had quit crying, and as Lucas and Major neared, he saw the baby kicking his feet and reaching for a cat on Carly's lap. Major's ears went forward, and he woofed at the scent.

Lucas grabbed Major's collar as the dog jumped forward

to check out the cat. "Stay." The dog fell back and sat on his haunches but looked up at Lucas with reproachful dark eyes. Keeping control of his dog, Lucas crossed the last few steps of the yard.

"You've got a cat."

Carly looked up and smiled. Her dark hair had escaped her bun and hung in thick curls down to her shoulders. She rescued her cross necklace from the baby's fingers. "Noah loves Pepper. I've had him for about three years."

"He's cute. Is your grandma coming home soon? I made too much beef stroganoff, and I thought you two might help me eat it."

"She's going to dinner with her best friend, Maude, so I'm sitting out here trying to decide if I should order pizza or warm up leftovers. Stroganoff sounds much better. I haven't had it in forever. That's very kind of you." She rose quickly as if she was afraid he'd withdraw the offer.

And for an instant he regretted the invitation, but it was done now.

He reached down and snagged the diaper bag for her. "You might want to put Pepper away. Major is way too interested. I think he believes Pepper is a squirrel and fair game for chasing. He's never been around a cat."

"I'll put him inside." She situated Noah in his bouncy seat before carrying the cat to the back door. She returned in less than a minute. "He's happily eating his dinner." She picked up the baby, seat and all, and came down the deck steps.

Lucas turned with Major and walked back to his yard. What should they talk about? Maybe the case. That would eat up some time. "How did you find that egg anyway? It's hard to believe someone would bury something so beautiful in a chest."

"It was painted a gaudy red, and I saw a speck of white porcelain when a fleck of it flaked off. White vinegar and dish soap soaked the old paint right off. I've been obsessed with Fabergé eggs for years. The history is fascinating. My egg was given to Empress Maria in 1886. All the art in the palace was supposed to have been cataloged and stored away when the Bolshevik Revolution occurred, but some pieces went missing. No one knows if they were sold or stolen."

"I've never heard of them." He reached the back deck and went up the steps to hold open the door for her and the baby. "Have you ever found anything else valuable from flea markets and garage sales?"

"I've found a few valuable paintings, but their worth was more in the hundreds, not the millions. And I've scored some Polish pottery for Gram. A few pieces of valuable furniture, too, but nothing close to the value of the egg. It's the find of the century—maybe two centuries."

She entered the kitchen and sighed. "That smells heavenly. What can I do to help?"

"I've got it under control. You could get out the sour cream and some plates. We'll be ready to eat in a few minutes." The already-hot water went back to boiling quickly when he set his induction range on high, and he dropped the noodles into the froth.

She went to the new gray cabinets and found the plates. "Ooh, these are Spode Blue Italian! I love them."

"They were our mom's. She collected Spode for years."

"What happened to your parents?"

His gut tightened and he turned his back to her to stir the noodles. It wasn't something he liked talking about. "My mom started the car in the garage and lowered the door, then sat out there. Dad found her, and I think he didn't want to live without her, so he just climbed into the car and waited for death too. She'd struggled with depression for years. The only reason we know it had to have gone down that way was because of stomach contents and time of death."

He felt her hand on his shoulder, and her sweet breath lifted the hair on the nape of his neck. "I'm so sorry."

"I was supposed to be home by four to go with them to a family reunion, but we had a missing swimmer, and it was all-hands-on-deck for the police force. I was late. I suppose I should feel guilty, but mostly I'm just angry. She didn't think about how the rest of us would feel, and neither did he."

"I know how it feels."

Sympathy radiated off her in waves, and he remembered how her dad had abandoned her and her sisters after their mother died. His dad had done the same thing—just in a slightly different manner. Maybe she did understand.

SEVEN

Conversation with Lucas had been surprisingly easy. Carly folded the last of Noah's laundry and put it away. Gram was already in bed, and Carly had kept her evening to herself. Gram would have read something into Lucas's invitation that simply wasn't there.

The baby slept soundly, his little mouth working in his sleep. Carly yawned and turned out the light. She slid between the sheets and sighed with contentment. It had been a long day, but at least she wasn't alone in this quest now. Lucas's help had changed everything. Her grief had left her feeling so alone in spite of Gram's presence, but she felt like she had an ally now.

Her eyes drifted shut, and she settled deeper into the mattress. It seemed only moments before she awoke with a start, but after looking at the clock on her bedside table, she realized she'd been asleep for three hours. It was after one, and yet her heart pounded as if she'd been running. What had awakened her in such a state? Had she been dreaming of finding Eric? But she couldn't remember anything.

A thump came from overhead, and her mouth went dry. Was someone in the attic? She tried to tell herself it was a squirrel or a raccoon, but the movements she heard through the ceiling felt more deliberate and hushed, as if someone was trying to be quiet.

She flung back the covers and reached for her phone. Without stopping to think about it, she called Lucas's number.

He picked it up on the third ring. "Detective Bennett."

She held the phone close to her mouth and whispered, "Lucas, it's Carly. I think there's someone in the attic."

"I'll be right there."

The call ended, and she laid the phone down and went to the door. She eased it open and looked down the dark hallway toward the door to the attic stairs. Was it a trick of the dark, or did it stand open a few inches? She laced her fingers together and tried to calm her breathing so her heart rate would resume its normal rhythm. What should she do? She had to let Lucas inside, but she didn't want to leave her grandmother and Noah alone with a possible intruder.

She went back to grab her phone and texted Lucas the door code to get in. *I'm staying near the baby and Gram. I have a baseball bat.*

After texting him, she grabbed the baseball bat from the closet and went to stand guard at the door again. When she reached the hall, she heard the door creak open downstairs. Relief weakened her knees, and she exhaled. Lucas was inside, and he'd be here shortly.

She peered through the darkness toward the stairs and saw his shadowy figure taking the steps two at a time. He came noiselessly down the hall toward her, and she stepped out to meet him.

"He's still up there?"

"I didn't hear him go past in the hall."

Lucas was dressed in running shorts and a tee, probably his sleeping attire. He held his finger to his lips, gun ready in his hand, and crept toward the attic stairs. As he neared the door, it flew open and a figure rushed Lucas. A shot boomed into the quiet night.

Carly gasped, and her limbs felt heavy and frozen. Though she needed to stand guard over her baby, she desperately wanted to go to Lucas and make sure he was all right.

"Turn on the light," Lucas called.

She reached out and felt along the wall to the switch plate and flipped on the lights. She found Lucas crouched over a figure on the floor. Black covered the figure, from a black ski mask over his head to black shoes.

"Is, um, is he dead?" Her voice quavered, and she cleared her throat.

He peered closer at the figure and pulled off the ski mask. Blonde hair spilled out, and he gasped. "This is a woman, not a man." He pressed his fingers against the woman's neck. "She's dead. She charged at me with a knife." Lucas pointed to the weapon in the woman's hand. "I need to call this in. Stay with Noah just in case." He moved down the hall to contact the police.

Her grandmother's door flew open, and Gram stumbled out in her flowing bright blue robe. "What's happening?"

Carly was so used to seeing her grandmother strong and in control that Gram's quivering chin and fearful mouth filled her with sympathy. She rushed to embrace her grandmother. "It's okay, Gram. There was an intruder, but Lucas came as soon as I called."

Gram pulled away and looked at the body on the floor. "W-were there shots? Is she dead?"

Lucas put his phone away. "She's dead, Mary. Everyone okay?"

"We're fine," Carly said. "I'm going to check on Noah and make sure he's not awake and frightened." He wasn't crying, though, and nothing much awakened him, so she wasn't surprised to find the baby still sleeping.

She touched his warm little hand, then went back to the hall and pulled the door shut behind her. "He's still asleep. Who is that woman?"

"No idea yet. I can't touch the body any more until help arrives. They'll need to do an investigation since I discharged my weapon. I may be on leave for a bit."

"That's not fair! You were responding to a home invasion."

"Standard protocol. It will be fine."

The thin wail of a siren came from outside. Help had arrived, but the only help they'd really needed stood calmly in the hallway, looking like a superhero in jogging shorts.

It had taken over an hour for Lucas's adrenaline-driven heart rate to return to normal. The lingering stench of blood wafted down the stairs to where he stood waiting to hear of any evidence. Mary's house swarmed with forensic investigators and detectives, but after discharging his firearm, he had to turn his gun over to his boss and let others gather evidence.

The coroner, Peppi Perez, came down the stairs to where

Lucas stood. In her forties, she was tall and angular with perpetually pursed lips that made her look like she'd caught a whiff of a foul odor. She was good at her job, and Lucas had always respected her.

He nodded. "Peppi." He shouldn't be talking to her until he was cleared, but the scene was chaotic, and he thought he could get away with it.

She bobbed her head in return. "Lucas. She's dead of course, but you knew that. We'll get her out of here to the morgue shortly, and I can perform an autopsy." She patted his arm as she passed. "I know it's hard, but it sounds like you had no choice."

Discovering the intruder was a woman had been a shock, but it had been dark, and she'd worn a ski mask. It was only when he pulled it off and the woman's blonde hair spilled out that he'd realized he'd killed a woman. The realization had rocked him back on his heels.

He'd fired his weapon in the line of duty only one previous time, and he'd regretted it. A young man in his early twenties had charged at him while waving a gun. Looking back, Lucas wished he'd tackled the guy and tried to wrestle the gun away. Instead he wounded the man. It had been his first experience with the investigation following an altercation like that. He had never wanted to have another. Yet here he was. He'd caught the glint of the knife in her hand and known he had to fire.

Peppi exited the area, and he wandered into the living room, where Carly sat holding her baby. Mary was in the kitchen making coffee and tea as if it were a social occasion. Still, the officers would appreciate some caffeine at two in the morning. He felt awkward in his jogging shorts and tee with no shoes. He'd sprung into action the second he got Carly's call.

Little Noah's delicate eyelids fluttered as he slept, and he smiled as if he dreamed of puppies or something fun. "He doesn't appear to be traumatized."

Carly smiled and shook her head. "He slept right through all the commotion."

She'd gotten dressed before she came downstairs, and she wore yoga pants and a tee that read *RADAR*. The woman *really* liked palindromes.

Her gaze went past him, and her smile faded. Lucas turned at the sound of footsteps from the foyer. Vincent Steadman, bald head gleaming in the overhead light, stepped into the living room. Lucas and Vince had been partners for five years, and Lucas trusted him like a brother.

"Any ID on the woman?" Lucas asked.

"Yeah, we found her pickup with her driver's license in the glove box. Name on the license was Debby Drust."

A Debby ought to be nice and friendly, a next-door neighbor or a woman in the next pew over in church—not someone who would break into a house with two defenseless women and a baby inside.

Lucas nodded. "We know anything about her yet?"

"Registration came back to Dimitri Smirnov, same address in New York as the one on the deceased's license. The interesting thing about Dimitri is he's connected."

"Russian mob?"

"You got it."

The Russian connection right after Carly had found a priceless Fabergé egg couldn't be ignored. He focused on

Carly's pleading expression. One word, even to his best friend, could blow up on them. That egg was worth more money than he could ever imagine. Once that information made it into the investigation's file, the news would get out. There would be no way of containing something that sensational.

He tore his attention away from Carly's chocolate-brown eyes. He should tell Vince and swear him to secrecy, but he couldn't bring the words out. Lucas would have to delve into this situation on his own, even with the conflict of interest.

He had no doubt he'd be cleared of any wrongdoing, but it might take some time. He could get into big trouble by sticking his nose into the investigation, but it couldn't be helped. It was a miracle the captain hadn't insisted he go to the hospital like standard operating procedure.

He realized Vince was staring at him with a lifted brow, and Lucas gathered his composure. "What's this Dimitri guy into? Drugs, trafficking, the usual?"

"Yeah. Heavy into meth and heroin. He's suspected of committing a string of burglaries and murders along the Eastern Seaboard as well, but no one has been able to lay a finger on him. Not yet at least."

"And the Drust woman? What's the connection other than an address?"

"We don't know much about her, not yet. Women can make excellent cat burglars when they're slight and quick. You say she was in the attic?"

Vince looked to Carly for corroboration, and she nodded. "I heard noises in the attic and saw the stair door ajar, so I called Lucas. I was terrified because of my baby and my grandma."

The baby stirred at his mother's words, and his blue eyes

opened for a moment before he gave a yawn and closed them again. Lucas couldn't explain his fascination with the baby when he normally would have been oblivious. Maybe because the kid was Eric's and the little guy was fatherless. Sometimes Lucas had felt fatherless, even though his father hadn't died until a few years ago.

Carly stood with the baby in her arms. "Is it okay if I put him back in his crib? I want to get the mess cleaned up too."

Vince stood aside. "Sure. We're done upstairs."

When the sound of her footsteps on the stairs faded, Vince clapped his hand on Lucas's shoulder. "You doing okay, buddy? You'll need to stay out of this for now."

Lucas gave a jerky nod and turned away. He might not meddle in the review of the gunfire, but there was no way he could stay out of why the Russian mob would come calling.

Lieutenant Bernard Clark gestured from the entry. "Let's get to the hospital, Lucas."

Lucas nodded again and went with him. They'd draw his blood, and he'd have to go to the station to report what had happened. This would be a long night.

EIGHT

The Russian mafia had invaded her house.

The last two days since the shooting had been stressful. Every cell in Carly's body wanted to take Gram and Noah far away from the danger lurking. But she couldn't do that without explaining *why* this had all happened. Right now she had to trust Lucas's assurances that he'd protect them. And he'd done just that the other night. What if next time he was gone? But maybe the police would catch that Dimitri and there wouldn't be a next time.

Carly couldn't wrap her head around the facts as she made up the beds for her sisters, who were due at any time. The fresh scent of the line-dried sheets lingered in the air, making her wish she could climb into bed and pull the sheets over her head. She wasn't ready to face the day that was coming.

Her sisters' presence here would only bring more complexity to what was going on. The thought of working so hard to make sure they were happy caused her to exhale and shake her head. She loved them so much, but they were so demanding. They always had been. And maybe it was partly her fault for catering to their every request.

With the beds made, she checked on Noah, who was still

napping, then went down the stairs to the kitchen. She found Gram baking chocolate chip cookies in a flowing turquoise dress that nearly touched her painted toenails. The aroma made Carly's mouth water.

"Have a cookie, Carly Ann."

Carly snagged a warm cookie from the cooling rack, then popped it into her mouth. She licked the chocolate from her fingers and tipped her head. "Was that a car door?"

It was one of her sisters, wasn't it? She wiped suddenly slick palms on her shorts. If it was the mob again, they wouldn't announce their arrival by slamming a car door.

Through the screen door, she spotted Amelia getting out of a white Escalade. Nothing but the best for Dillard. He was a commercial real estate investor, and appearances were important to him. Even driving from Jacksonville to Beaufort, he was dressed in a suit and tie. He tipped up his head to study the grand old mansion, and Carly knew he was counting their share of the place when Gram was gone. They might be safer with him here. He was an avid gun collector and always carried a pistol.

Carly pasted on a smile and stepped out onto the porch to welcome them. "You made good time."

Jacksonville was a three-hour drive. It was only noon, and Carly wished she'd planned for lunch. She'd assumed they wouldn't get here until early afternoon. There were cold cuts in the fridge and leftovers from last night's pot roast and tomato pie, but she didn't think Dillard or Amelia would be impressed with those offerings. Maybe she could suggest they go to a restaurant.

She hugged Amelia, who folded herself into the embrace and gave a quick squeeze before she let go and stepped back quickly. As the middle child, Amelia tried to avoid conflict, but Carly was well aware of how both sisters kept their guard up when they were around. Amelia wanted her independence just as strongly as Emily did, but she'd always been more diplomatic about it. When they were together, she'd smile and hug, but months would go by before they spoke.

"You look good," Carly said.

She and Amelia shared the same dark brown hair and eyes, but while Carly had hers in a ponytail or messy bun half the time, Amelia changed her hairstyle as frequently as Carly changed Noah's diapers. At least it seemed that way. Today she had a face-framing bob with little wisps that stuck out in an attractive way. She wore white cropped pants with a red silk shirt and strappy sandals that probably cost more than Carly would spend on ten pairs of shoes.

They were so different, but Carly loved her fiercely.

Amelia pushed a lock of hair out of her eyes. "Thanks, you do too. You dropped your baby weight fast."

"It doesn't take long with Noah nursing so often."

Amelia wrinkled her nose. Carly shouldn't have said anything about that. Amelia would probably never have a baby—not if it meant gaining weight and nursing.

She turned toward the door. "I've got the two of you in the Honeysuckle Suite. It has an attached bathroom."

It was one of only three bedrooms with baths attached. Emily might squawk, but Dillard would complain even louder if he had to traipse down the hall to a bathroom. Carly watched him wrestle two large suitcases from the back of the SUV and roll them toward the house.

"A little help here," he called. "There are two more just like this."

They must have packed enough for an army. Carly went down the wide stairs toward the drive. "We do have a laundry room, you know."

The glance he shot her from under his blond brows held animosity. "We came at your request, but we need all our things. You realize I can't stay, right? Amelia's help will have to be good enough."

"I appreciate that." Biting back the words she wanted to say, she lugged a suitcase down the sidewalk toward the porch.

"Let me help you with that."

She turned at Lucas's deep voice. He grabbed the suitcase by its handle and lifted it off the brick to carry it to the house. "What are you doing here?" she whispered.

"I'll tell you later," he whispered back.

He wasn't even breathing hard as he carried the biggest suitcase of the three up the stairs, into the house, and to the second floor, where they found Amelia and Dillard milling around the old carpet.

Dillard's appraising glance around the room raised Carly's hackles. It wouldn't be his decision what they did with the house—it would be whatever Gram wanted. She was not about to let anyone—not Dillard or her sisters—steamroll her grandmother. They were here to steer her vision to fruition. Gram's money was riding on the decisions they would all make, and once Emily arrived, Carly would make sure everyone understood that.

Lucas set down the suitcase. "Could I speak with you for a minute, Carly?"

"Of course." She followed him out into the hall, and he motioned her down the steps before he spoke. "Have you ever met Debby Drust?"

"Not that I know of. Why?"

"According to some records, she attended some maternity classes at the same time as you. But she never had a baby. And her address is in New York, so she's not even local."

Carly absorbed the news. Had Debby been stalking her? The watchful expression in Lucas's hazel eyes made it clear he felt the same way.

"Do you have a picture of her?"

He whipped out his phone and called up a photo. "She looks like she's in her forties. Not the usual childbearing age, wouldn't you say? Not that it's impossible, but you might have noticed her."

Carly studied the picture of the attractive blonde. "I remember her. She sat by me in a couple of classes and asked me where I lived. When I mentioned living with my grandmother, she peppered me with questions about Gram's family. I finally moved to the other side of the room after the break on that last day, and she didn't show up."

His eyes narrowed. "She was fishing for information. Carly, I think someone knows about the egg, or at least suspects it's out there. You might be right and Eric's death had everything to do with it."

And they were all in danger.

Why on earth was he hanging around?

The tantalizing aromas of shrimp and grits made Lucas's mouth water. He held little Noah while Carly cooked the dish. He'd left hours ago, then come back when he'd learned more information about the Drust woman.

Okay, maybe that wasn't the full story. His protective instincts had flared at the way Dillard was treating Carly. And her sister wasn't much better. When Lucas arrived this time, he'd seen Amelia holding Noah in a precarious way where his head bobbled around. When the baby put his wet fingers on her face, she'd nearly screamed as she thrust him toward Lucas.

The baby made a few soft sounds, and Lucas jostled him up and down until he settled. Why didn't the baby have Carly's brown eyes? Weren't brown eyes dominant? He jerked his attention back to Carly instead of focusing on inane internal questions.

Carly's pink cheeks made her brown eyes sparkle, and her forehead was a little damp from cooking in the kitchen. "Whew, getting that air-conditioning can't come soon enough. Thanks for braving the hot kitchen with me and for holding Noah. I can take him back."

He eased the baby into her arms. "Sure thing. Why isn't your sister in here helping out?"

She shifted Noah on her shoulder. "Amelia doesn't cook. She hates for her hair to smell like food."

"You fixed shrimp and grits. Her breath will smell like garlic."

"And Dillard will give her mints. She wasn't always such a diva. Dillard has certain standards."

"He's a dirtbag," Lucas spat out and scowled. "Expecting you to haul heavy suitcases around is ridiculous."

She shrugged. "Sometimes husbands have certain standards, and we wives like to please them, especially if it's something easy."

There was a certain note in her voice that caught his attention. "Was Eric demanding?"

She kissed the soft down on Noah's head. "Not at first. But he listened to his mother a little too much. According to her, I didn't fix the best lunch for him, and I organized the kitchen wrong. When we first married, he was appalled at the thought that I would even fix him lunch. He liked grabbing it with the other officers. But her constant harping wore him down. I don't fault him for it."

Lucas didn't know what to think of that. He hadn't met Eric until their late teens, and he hadn't been around Eric's mother much. Lucas's dad had never been that way with Mom. Instead he'd catered to her every request and treated her like a hothouse flower. But she had been damaged and frail. Taking care of Mom had consumed all his dad's attention, and Mary's as well. As long as he could remember, Carly's grandma had walked across the backyard with casseroles for the family and hugs for him and Ryan. Their childhood would have been very different without her calming presence in the midst of chaos.

He snagged a chocolate chip cookie to help hold him until dinner, and the sound of an engine caught his attention. It sounded close. "I think someone's here."

"It's probably Emily." Carly sounded resigned and excited all at the same time.

He followed her through the dining room to the living room, where the rest of the family sat sipping tea out of Mary's blue Polish mugs.

Carly glanced out the big window to the red Nissan parked behind the Escalade. "It's Emily!"

Mary held out her arms, and Carly deposited the baby into them before rushing toward the door with a smile and bright eyes. Lucas stood where he was and watched the body language. When Carly reached her, Emily stood with her arms to her sides when her older sister hugged her. The only smile was a forced one.

Emily's tight red dress didn't lend itself to bending and stretching to grab luggage, and she'd likely break an ankle trying to drag them in heels high enough to give her a nosebleed. She'd gotten streaks in her brown hair, and it curled around her pointed chin.

Carly's face fell, and she bit her lip before she went around to the trunk to help with the luggage. He should go help so she wasn't lugging them by herself. He could already see how this interchange was going to go. He stepped quickly out the door and walked to the drive to grab two bags.

Emily finally smiled when she saw Lucas. "Are you still living next door, Lucas? I haven't seen you in ages." Her flirtatious smile came, and she took a step closer as if to hug him.

He skirted her and went to the trunk. "Yep, still here."

This family was a mess. While he and Ryan might have occasional disagreements, he never doubted his brother loved him. And he'd do anything for his little brother. Was there no sense of family support in the Tucker family? It had to break Mary's heart to see her granddaughters behaving like cautious enemies.

He carried the luggage up the steps and paused in the entry for Carly and Emily to catch up. "Which room?"

"The first one on the left at the top of the stairs," Carly said.

Emily dropped her leather bag on the stand along the wall. "You put me in the Rose Room? I want the Honeysuckle Suite. Did you give it to Amelia instead?"

"Emily, she's married. It makes more sense for them to have it."

"What about the Lavender Suite? It has a bathroom too."

"Noah and I have that one."

"And you've had it for months! There's no reason you can't change."

Was she for real? Lucas stared at her angry face. She might have been beautiful with the perfect skin that needed no makeup, but the petulant twist of her mouth and the angry slant of her eyes erased anything attractive in her angular face. He willed Carly to have a backbone and stand up to her sister, but she stood there biting her lip like she was considering the request.

"Absolutely not," he said. "Don't be such a dimwit, Emily. Carly has a ton of stuff for the baby, and all her things are there. She *lives* here now. What kind of sister would come in here and try to throw her and the baby out of their room? I'm taking these to the Rose Room, and you can live with it. If you don't like it, there are many nice hotels in town."

Bags in hand, he tromped up the steps and tried to ignore the stunned expressions he left behind. Stunned or not, he was sure he saw a glint of relief in Carly's eyes.

NINE

Sunday night every muscle in Carly's body ached from the constant running around as she made sure her sisters felt loved and cared for since their arrival. By the time she had researched Russian immigrant life and crawled between the line-dried sheets, her bedside clock read nearly midnight. She set her copy of *Plot and Structure* on the nightstand to read later, when her brain was less weary.

Her eyes refused to close, and she lay on her back staring at the ceiling. A faint light swept across it from someone in the drive. Both of her sisters were here, so who could be out there this time of night?

She sprang out of bed and grabbed the baseball bat she'd put by her bed as well as her phone, then rushed out to the hall. She tiptoed toward the steps. No light shone around the edges of Emily's closed door, and the familiar rhythm of waves from her sound machine came faintly to Carly's ears.

Her heart thudded in her chest as she stood at the top of the stairs. Should she go down or call for Lucas? Dillard was here and usually carried a gun, but she wasn't inclined to trust his ability. But would the Russian mafia announce their presence in a vehicle with lights in the drive? Not likely. If not a criminal, then who was out there? Even from here she could see the way the headlights illuminated the entry hall at the bottom of the steps.

She eased down two steps and paused to listen. The head-lamps went out, and the bottom of the stairs went dark. With the bat in one hand and her phone in the other, she slipped down two more steps.

A sound behind her made her jump, and she nearly tumbled down the stairs. Emily stood close behind her. Her dark hair was secured on top of her head, and she was panting. "What's wrong?" she whispered.

"Someone pulled in the drive," Carly whispered back.

"Maybe they were just turning around."

It was a possibility, but Carly grabbed her sister's fore-arm at the sound of footsteps ascending the porch steps. "Someone's out there."

"We should call the police. Or Lucas. He's right next door."

Carly didn't want to bother him again if she didn't have to, but it looked like she had to. She nodded and pulled up his number on her phone. Before she could touch Send, the door-bell rang.

"An intruder doesn't ring the bell." Emily went past her on the steps.

Someone pounded on the door. "Hey, Mom, you up?"

Relief weakened Carly's knees at the familiar voice. What was Dad doing here at this time of night? He lived in Cali-fornia, a continent away from South Carolina. If he wanted to come for a visit, why hadn't he called? Her thoughts scrambled to where to put him. While there were plenty of bedrooms in the huge house, none of the others were made up for guests.

Her feet touched the oak floors, cooled by the night breeze coming through the open windows. The chill chased away the rest of her fear. How long had it been since she'd seen Dad? At least two years. He wasn't the warmest of fathers, and he rarely bothered with his girls from his first marriage. He'd had a daughter with his second wife, but again, Carly didn't know her half sister well. Nor her stepmother, for that matter.

"It's Daddy!" Emily opened the door and flung her arms around the man standing there.

Carly flipped on the porch light, and their dad blinked in the sudden illumination. He hadn't changed much. Still handsome in spite of being nearly fifty. Gray sprinkled the sides of his thinning dark hair, and he wore shorts and a Hawaiian shirt. He'd gotten his boho look from Gram most likely. He didn't come to see his mother any more frequently than he saw his girls, though Carly thought he called her more often.

He embraced Emily. "Hi, Peanut. I didn't know you were here." His gaze went over her shoulder to where Carly stood. "I'd hoped you were still here."

Warmth surged into Carly's chest. He'd come to see her? He'd *wanted* to see her? A smile curved her lips, and she took a step toward him until a figure moved into view behind him. The young girl had to be Izzy. Was she out of school already? It was only mid-May.

Her father released Emily and pulled Izzy to his side. "You haven't seen Izzy in a while."

"Isabelle." The girl's lip curled in disgust, and she jerked her arm out of his grasp.

She was about fifteen now, and Carly remembered all too well how her sisters had been at that age. And the first order of business was making sure she didn't call her sister by the name of Izzy.

Carly stepped out of the doorway and turned on the entry light. "Come on in." She'd need to ready two rooms, not just one. The enormity of everything hitting her all at once was enough to make her want to tell them to get their own rooms ready, but she couldn't do that. How hard would it have been to call before they showed up?

She closed the door behind them and locked it again. "It will take me a little while to get rooms ready."

"No problem. Just get a room ready for Izzy. I can take a nap in the recliner before I fly out tomorrow."

Carly looked at her sister, then back at her dad. "You're not staying?"

"I have to fly to Italy on business. I'll be gone a month, and Izzy needs a place to stay."

Her father was an attorney and traveled frequently. Carly often thought he used his job to escape responsibilities at home.

Isabelle stalked off to the living room and threw herself onto the sofa. "I can't believe I have to stay in this dinky little town!"

Carly trailed her with her father and Emily in tow. "Where's your mom, Isabelle?"

She shrugged but her blue eyes glistened. "She left with a new boyfriend, and I don't know where she is. She doesn't answer her phone."

Carly gasped and put her hand to her throat. Her dad was dropping Isabelle off like an unwanted puppy and taking off?

———

Lieutenant Bernard Clark handed Lucas his gun. "You've been cleared of any wrongdoing in the discharge of your weapon."

Lucas holstered his firearm with a strong sense of relief. "That was fast."

Bernard shrugged his brawny shoulders. His hair had been tamed by his hat and was a sleek cap on his big head. He'd always reminded Lucas of a resting lion with his wild blond hair and massive build. His retirement was coming up in six months, and the whole squad would hate to lose him.

"No more questions?" Lucas asked.

"It was straightforward. Finding out the deceased's connection to the Russian mob helped."

The tantalizing aroma of good coffee drew Lucas to the counter along the wall. He poured himself a mug of coffee from the beverage bar. No burned sludge here. Bernard bought his own gourmet coffee and brought it into his office. He used a Cuisinart coffee maker and had real cream in the small fridge nearby, all paid for with his own money. Even the mugs were good-quality ones that he personally washed at the end of the day.

"Bring me one, too, if you don't mind."

Lucas poured a second cup and added a generous dollop of cream before carrying it to his boss. Once he handed it over, he dropped into a chair and blew into the coffee. "Speaking of the mob, anything new on the investigation?"

"Not much yet. We found out more info on the deceased. She's Czechoslovakian and moved to Russia with her parents when she was ten. Original spelling of her last name was Druzd, but she Americanized it when she came here at age twenty. Her connections with Smirnov go back to Russia. Detectives found her prints at two burglaries in Queens they suspected Smirnov of orchestrating."

"And the murders connected to Smirnov?"

"She's a possible suspect for them, too, but we have no real evidence beyond her prints. For all we know, she handled getting inside and let him in to do the deed."

Lucas took a sip of his coffee. "But why would she be rummaging around in Mary Tucker's attic? Beaufort is a world away from New York." Had the investigation turned up anything about the Fabergé egg?

"We have no idea. Mary claims not to have anything of incredible value up there but antiques. All told, her granddaughter thought the items might bring in twenty grand. Hardly enough to interest a drug dealer who could bring in that in an hour."

So Carly had kept quiet about the egg too. What did Lucas do here? It was a dilemma he needed to discuss with her.

He drank the last of his coffee and stood. "I'll get out of here and let you get back to work. I want to take a look at the case notes."

Bernard was already lost in his computer files again. Lucas went down the hall to his own office and started to enter, then changed course and headed outside. The first order of business needed to be persuading Carly to officially tell the police about the egg. It was safe in the bank.

He drove his pickup to her house and frowned at the strange vehicle still in her driveway. He'd noticed it an hour ago when he left. Looked like a rental car from the airport, but she hadn't mentioned any impending visitors.

He parked in his own drive and went across the lawn to the Tucker house, dodging under the angel tree in the front. As he neared, he spotted Carly on the porch with little Noah on her lap, cooing at the cat. Was she crying? Her eyes were red, and he was sure he heard sniffling. Probably her sisters again.

He picked up the pace and headed up the steps. "Hey there."

She kept her face down. "Good morning. Gram's got coffee and tea inside."

Her husky voice was a dead giveaway. Lucas settled on the Adirondack chair beside the swing. "What's going on?"

She lifted a blotchy face. "My dad showed up at midnight last night. He waltzed in here to tell me to take care of my half sister, Isabelle. No phone call, no request, just a demand." She dabbed at her eyes with a burp cloth. "It's silly to be so upset, but it just brought home what a doormat I am. I didn't argue or even get mad. Dad hasn't bothered with any of us girls since he remarried. He took off after Mom died and never looked back. This is only the third time I've laid eyes on Isabelle. He's never bothered trying to integrate his two families at all."

She dabbed her face again. "It's probably just baby blues. I should want to help—and I do. After all, she's the sister I don't really know. Maybe she will love me when my other two don't."

"What's up with those sisters of yours anyway? They're spoiled brats."

"I did it." She glanced at him with reddened eyes. "Dad's desertion hit us all hard. I wanted to make it up to them, and I did too much. They were never held accountable for anything, and it shows."

"Surely it took more than that. They're downright nasty to you."

She looked down at her hands. "Something happened, but I've never talked about it. I'm not ready yet, not when someone might overhear."

Did that mean she might tell him if they were alone? He wasn't sure why he cared, but he did.

TEN

She'd completely humiliated herself in front of Lucas. If there was one thing Carly hated, it was to cry in front of someone else. Especially someone who was always strong and in charge like Lucas.

She dabbed her face with the burp cloth again and inhaled. "I'm not normally such a wimp. I only got four hours of sleep last night and very little the night before. I'll be okay with some rest." She managed a watery smile. "Maybe I'll nap with Noah this afternoon."

Pepper settled beside her just beyond Noah's reaching fingers. While Noah adored the cat, Pepper was very leery of that tight grip. Noah let out a volley of coos directed toward the feline, but Pepper ignored the plea.

Why had Carly even hinted that something had triggered the estrangement between her and her sisters? It wasn't something she liked to think about, let alone talk about. She'd tried so hard with her sisters, but nothing she did was ever enough. How did someone earn love anyway?

Her eyes filled again, and she blinked away the moisture. "Any more news on the woman who broke into the house?"

He shifted on the chair. "That's why I'm here. We're going to be stymied in our investigation if I don't at least tell my partner and my supervisor about the egg."

Her pulse kicked into overdrive. "But you can't do that!"

"I realize you wanted to keep it a secret from everyone, and you can still stay mum about it with your sisters and your grandma. But my team is hamstrung by not knowing why a Russian mafia group from New York might be interested in you."

"What if it's not the egg at all?" Was she grasping at straws? Only something of huge value like the egg would bring people that powerful to her home.

She slumped against the back of the swing. "I don't know what to do."

"The egg is safe in your deposit box. And we need to get to the bottom of what happened so your family is safe. You don't want more break-ins. The next one might end with one of your family members dead instead of the burglar."

The careful way he spoke told her how important he considered this. She shuddered at the thought of more people knowing about the egg, but it was clearly necessary.

She inhaled and lifted her gaze to meet his. "Why are you helping me anyway, Lucas? You've made it clear you don't really like me."

It had been obvious when she dated Ryan. His criticism of her so many years ago had contributed to her breakup with Ryan. Lucas had confronted her after a fight with Ryan over her sisters, and it had led to her breaking off their relationship. Yet he'd come to her aid when she asked last week. Maybe it was because he was a police officer and felt obligated, but he was a bigger man than most when he'd put aside his personal feelings and been there for her.

He held eye contact. "I don't dislike you."

He didn't explain further and got up. "I need to head back to explain all this to Vince and Lieutenant Clark. I'll try to keep it under wraps as much as I can. But even if it gets out, Carly, that can only help alleviate the danger if Smirnov and his buddies know they won't get it by breaking in here."

"But they might break into the bank."

"I'll ask for enhanced security at the bank."

She managed a smile. "Any chance we can move it to Fort Knox?"

He chuckled, a deep sound that sent a tingle into her chest. "I probably can't make that happen without the whole world knowing about it. Are you going to call in an expert?"

This was all spiraling so fast. She'd hoped to find Gram's birth family as a surprise, but she would have to tell her family what was going on. Everything would probably explode. The contents of the chest had been left to her by her great-grandmother, and her sisters would have a fit. It would trigger them in the worst way.

And she still had Isabelle to worry about. She and Dad still weren't awake, but he'd be up anytime to catch his flight. Maybe she could at least wait until he was gone to reveal everything to Gram and her sisters. The last thing she wanted was for him to be in the middle of everything too. It was going to be hard enough keeping everyone else calm.

Lucas paused on the top step. "I can see the wheels turning."

"The family has to know. It's bound to come out, and they

will be furious if I've kept it from them when the rest of the world knows."

"I don't think it'll get out of my office. We're used to keeping things quiet."

She lifted a brow. "I've seen plenty of leaked reports from police agencies across the country on big stories. This is beyond big, Lucas. And there will be a race to find the surprise that should be inside the egg. I'd like to be the one to find it."

He came back up the step he'd descended and dropped back into the chair. "Tell me again about the surprise thing."

"No one knows what it looks like for sure. There are no pictures, but in the imperial archive, it's described as a gold hen holding a sapphire pendant loosely in its beak. The hen is taking the sapphire out of a nest in a gold basket. The hen and the nest are studded with dozens of rose-cut diamonds."

He let out a low whistle. "It sounds incredibly valuable."

She nodded. "And put back where it belongs, the fully reunited piece would bring an unbelievable price. I can't even estimate how much. But really, the first order of business should be to authenticate it. I have someone I'm going to contact."

Saying it all out loud made her all the more determined to find the surprise—not for the money but to see such an incredible piece whole and in its glory. But how would she do that?

———

"What if you wait to tell the family for a couple of weeks while you and I look for the surprise?" Lucas was as shocked to hear the words out of his mouth as Carly.

COLLEEN COBLE

Her jaw dropped, and her mouth formed an O. "Why would you do that?"

He didn't know the answer, not really. The breeze blew in across the salty bay and stirred the moss on the angel trees in the yard. Mary Tucker had always been a special woman to him and Ryan. She'd made their childhood bearable. If he could do something to help her and her family, he'd do it in a heartbeat. But was this only about Mary? Staring into Carly's face, he wasn't so sure.

She wasn't about to get past his defenses.

He cleared his throat. "I care about your grandmother. And honestly, the egg is intriguing. Who wouldn't want to reunite the egg with the surprise and give the world back a treasure like that? I think we all have a little of Indiana Jones in us. At least I do."

"So do I. The unknown treasure is out there waiting for us." The light of her smile chased away the shadows in her eyes. "I'll take you up on your offer. For now, I won't tell the family. I'll be praying the news doesn't get out, and we can wait until I find Gram's sister and the surprise."

Noises came from inside the house, and she looked that way. "Sounds like my dad and everyone else are up. I'd better go fix breakfast."

"They're all adults. Can't they fix their own? You're not their servant, Carly."

A tiny frown furled her brow. "I know, but they all expect it. It's what I've always done."

He nodded at Noah on her lap. The baby was putting his fists in his mouth, and he thought he was probably hungry.

"You've got a perfectly good reason to let that job fall to some-one else."

"But if I don't do it, Gram will. And that's a lot of people to feed."

He glanced at the time on his phone. "The bakery is open. I'll go get some muffins. That's good enough."

"You don't have to do that," she protested.

"I know I don't, but you need to use your brainpower on the puzzle we have to solve."

She shook her head. "I'm not sure I'm up to the challenge, but I really want to try. I've always been fascinated by history. I taught history in high school for a few years before I got into flea markets."

He rose. "It's amazing how you recognize valuable collect-ibles. I wouldn't know a Fabergé egg from a toy Cinderella carriage. How'd you get into that business anyway?"

"When I met Eric, his grandmother had an antique store, and I helped out by going to flea markets. I found I had a nat-ural aptitude for finding treasures for the store in the most unlikely places. The search for valuables hooked me. When she died, I decided to take a booth on the road to flea markets myself and was making a nice living at it. It supplemented our income enough we could afford a bigger house and I could eventually quit teaching." She shrugged and shifted Noah to her shoulder. "Eric was happy at first, but his mother thought I was gone too much. Among her many other complaints."

"You were gone a lot?"

"About five months of the year I was gone on the week-ends, but Eric came with me when he wasn't working. That interfered with his mom's desire to have us come to Sunday dinners, though. Just before he died, I started thinking about writing a historical novel. He wasn't any fonder of that idea. He thought a nine-to-five job would suit our lifestyle better."

The screen door opened, and Emily poked out her head. "Are you going to fix breakfast? Everyone is up."

Lucas answered before Carly could. "I'm heading to get some muffins right now. Your sister didn't get much sleep after your dad and sister arrived in the night. There's probably cereal in the kitchen if you don't want to wait."

Emily's eyes went wide, and she retreated into the house. Lucas headed for the steps again. "I'll be back as quickly as I can. Take a nap with the baby, and we'll explore the attic again when I get back."

Her family would drive anyone crazy. It might be better for Carly if they didn't come around much.

ELEVEN

The silence was deafening.

Carly found everyone in the living room staring at the floor. What on earth had happened while she was outside talking to Lucas? Noah was sleeping on her shoulder, so before she investigated, she carried him upstairs and put him in his crib. She took the baby monitor with her and shut the door before going back to brave the prowling lions in the den.

Things were no better when she got back to the living room. Dillard and Amelia sat on the love seat, but they looked far from lovey-dovey. Her sister practically clung to the sofa's arm, and Dillard scowled as he looked at his phone. He couldn't go back to Jacksonville soon enough for Carly.

The breeze through the open windows did little to carry away the stench of Emily removing the polish from her nails. Her mutinous expression told Carly she was doing it to distract herself from what was going on. There was no sign of their grandmother or the family members who had arrived in the night.

She couldn't decide if she should ask questions or hope whatever it was blew over. Maybe silence was the better choice. A noise from the kitchen alerted her, and she went that way.

Her grandmother stood at the coffee bar grinding coffee. Dad and Isabelle were at the breakfast bar, and they weren't talking either.

"Good morning," Carly said. "Did you sleep well?"

Isabelle shrugged. "The sheets smelled weird and kept me awake."

Carly forced a smile. "That's called fresh air. We hang the sheets on the line in the backyard."

"You don't have a dryer?"

"We do, but we hang out clothing and linens when we can. It's better for them, and it makes them smell like sunshine and fresh air."

When her sister didn't answer, Carly looked closer and saw her lips quivering. Moisture hung on her lashes, and she swallowed hard. This situation had to be difficult for her, being carted clear across the country and abandoned with people she didn't really know. None of this was her fault—it was their father's.

Carly focused her attention on their father. "Dad, you can't do this to Isabelle."

Her sister's chin jerked up, and she stared at Carly. Was there a glimmer of hope that she had an ally in Carly? She gave Isabelle an encouraging smile. She was used to going head-to-head with their father, who had neglected all his girls for most of their lives. He'd been an absent father even before Mom died. His work had come before any of them.

Her dad didn't answer, so Carly glanced at Gram for help, but her grandmother didn't seem to be paying attention as she poured water into the coffeepot. Carly was on her own.

"Dad," she prodded. "Seriously, you need to cancel your trip. This is too hard on Isabelle."

He sighed and finally looked at her. "I can't do that, Carly. It's too important."

"You can't show up here without so much as a phone call and expect everyone else to cover for you. It's wrong." She tried to pick her words carefully. Isabelle had enough trauma from yesterday without making her feel she was unwanted.

"You don't want Isabelle here?"

She could have slapped her father's smug face. "Of course we want her. That's not the point. It's clear this was not her idea, and you gave her no choice. You yanked her out of school before the year was up and flew clear across the country to leave her with people she doesn't know."

His jaw hardened, and his brown eyes narrowed. "This is my mother's house, not yours. This decision has nothing to do with you."

Carly bit back a remark about preparing their rooms last night. Who did he think did the majority of the work around here? Gram looked good for her age, but she was slowing down, and they all knew it. Which was why no one had made breakfast yet.

Gram turned, her peacock skirt swishing around her ankles. "I'm delighted to see you and Isabelle, Kyle, but Carly is right. You didn't even call. This is unacceptable."

"It was a sudden trip."

"So sudden you couldn't call from the airport while you were waiting to board?"

"We barely made the flight. We threw clothes in the bags and I drove as fast as I could to the airport."

Gram folded her arms across her chest. "You at least need to stay and help her get settled in. What about her schoolwork?"

Her expression softened when she turned her attention to her youngest granddaughter. "Isabelle, when is your school out?"

"Not for two more weeks," Isabelle said in a shaky voice. "I have my tests still to take."

"And how long will you be gone, Kyle?" Gram asked.

He shifted and looked away. "A month or so."

"So you're expecting your daughter to miss the very important last few weeks of school? At her age it impacts her GPA. That's very selfish."

"It can't be helped, Mom. There's a crisis at headquarters."

There was always a crisis. Gram was handling it far better than she could, so Carly bit her tongue. This situation didn't seem to be the underlying cause of the tension she'd left behind in the living room, so what was going on?

"You're not going anywhere until you make arrangements for Isabelle to finish her school year. How do you intend to do that?"

"I'll handle it when I get back."

"You'll handle it now, son." Gram pointed at the phone in his hand. "Right now."

It was only six o'clock in California, but he sighed and picked up his phone. "I know the school principal. I'll see what I can do."

It was something at least. Even Isabelle looked relieved.

"I've got muffins," Lucas announced from behind her. "And I smell the coffee. Perfect timing."

At least it was a distraction.

Someone had brought in seafood for lunch, and the smell permeated the hall outside Bernard's office. Lucas stepped through the open door and shut it behind him. He dropped into a seat beside his partner. "I have some information about what the Russians might have been after."

Vince and Bernard wore identical expressions of interest. Bernard nodded. "So you said. What's going on?"

"It stays in this room. The danger will increase exponentially if word gets out."

"You know that's impossible," Bernard said.

Lucas leaned forward. "The lives of the Tucker family depend on it, boss. This news is huge. Give me two weeks of it under wraps. I'll keep the two of you informed, but I won't put it down in our reports. If I haven't made progress in two weeks, you can inform the rest of the force. This is the find of the century."

Bernard's blond brows rose. "Okay, this better be true, Lucas. Spill it."

"Carly found a priceless Fabergé egg. It's been missing since 1922. Prior to that it had been held in the archive of the provisional government's inventory in Russia, supposedly in the Armory Chamber of the Grand Kremlin Palace."

"Never heard of such a thing," Bernard said. "Worth a few bucks?"

"The last one sold for thirty million. This one is likely worth more, much more. The surprise inside is missing, and the Russians are probably looking for that too."

He told the men about Mary's heritage and how it might lead to more information about who knew of the egg's existence and who might be after the treasure.

"Sounds very Indiana Jones-ish to me," Vince said. "Crazy stuff. You're certain it's genuine?"

"I'm sure of nothing other than Carly believes it. It explains the intruder the other night."

"Has Carly gone through everything in the attic? Maybe that surprise is still up there somewhere."

"She hasn't gone through everything," Lucas admitted. "She's going to do that, but it would make sense that Mary's birth mother would have split it between the two girls. The egg would be worth even more with the surprise inside again."

"Where's the egg now?" Bernard asked.

"In a safety-deposit box."

Vince frowned. "Is that safe enough? If the Russian mafia is on its trail, breaking into the bank would not be a problem for them."

"I thought of that too. Could we stake out the bank for two weeks? I know it's a lot to ask, but think of the contribution to history if we can solve this, Lieutenant."

He wanted to add that it would be a great ending to a long career for his boss, but that didn't have to be spoken. Bernard would have to realize the impact something this big would have on his reputation.

Bernard gave a slow nod. "You're got two weeks, Bennett. I can't authorize spending that kind of money for longer than that. But wow, if we can take down the Russians and deliver the egg to the world in one operation, it would be huge."

That was an understatement. Lucas nodded and rose. "I'll do my best."

He left the other men and headed for his truck. Carly needed to search the attic, and it would be faster if he helped her. He didn't expect to find the surprise up there, but it was the logical place to start. The rest of the family would question what was happening up there, and he had no easy answers. Hopefully Carly had a ready explanation to offer.

The whole family was a mess, but his own home life had been only marginally better. Ryan was supposed to start the remodel on Monday. It was going to get chaotic with all the sisters there. And the scowling dad. Kyle's presence hadn't added anything but more stress to Carly.

He was beginning to see she might have been carrying a heavier load all these years than he'd realized.

TWELVE

No one wanted to talk to her, but she had to figure out what was going on.

Carly inhaled the aroma of Noah's head, then set him on the floor in the living room to roll around on a blanket. Pepper lay just beyond his reach, and the baby squealed and tried to reach for the cat.

Her father was upstairs showering for his trip, and Isabelle had retreated to her bedroom once Dad had managed to arrange for her to finish her classes online. Though that detail had been taken care of, she'd burst into tears when it was clear she would be left here in the care of her grandmother.

Carly grabbed her mug of coffee and settled on the floor beside Noah before staring first at Amelia. "What is going on? No one is talking. Are you mad at me or at each other or both?"

Amelia narrowed her brown eyes at Carly and said nothing. Carly turned to stare at Dillard. Maybe he'd speak up. He had his keys in hand, so she suspected he planned to head back to Jacksonville today.

Emily cleared her throat. "Why are we even here, Carly?

The work on the house hasn't started yet, so there's nothing for us to help with."

"Of course there is. We begin by clearing the furniture out of the downstairs, which is where Ryan will begin the remodel. He starts on Monday." She'd told them all that already, so what was this about?

Amelia crossed her arms. "And how are we supposed to live upstairs? No kitchen for weeks, maybe several months. Nowhere to sit. I'm not needed here, not yet."

"You can start on the exterior anytime, Amelia. You and Emily can work together and decide on a color scheme. That would include trying on paint colors and doing computer design work. And Emily can direct what changes she wants to see in the house. Doors changed, walls removed, that kind of thing."

She glanced around the living room with fresh evaluation. The rose wallpaper was worn and peeling in places, the oak floors needed to be refinished, and the layout would likely need to be adjusted to be more conducive to groups staying in the house. The kitchen and dining room definitely needed major overhauls. The thought of handling it alone was overwhelming.

Emily moved restlessly. "What's the point? You're going to get everything like always."

Ah, the real crux of the matter. It always went back to Mom's will. Carly fingered the platinum cross around her neck. "Gram plans to leave the house to all of us. She plans for the three of us to share in the profit made by the bed-and-breakfast as well."

"That's unlikely to amount to much," Dillard put in. "By

the time your grandmother pays for the upgrades needed, it will take forever to recoup the costs."

He wasn't wrong, and Carly saw both of her sisters harden their expressions. This was going south too fast. "So you plan to walk away and leave all this behind?" She waved her hand around the living room.

"You're the oldest and the favorite granddaughter," Emily said. "And you have Noah as well. You've been living with Gram and have had plenty of time to sway her to leave you everything."

Before Carly could answer, the doorbell rang and she spotted Lucas on the porch. She scrambled to her feet and rushed to the entry. She squashed down her emotion and pushed open the screen door. "Come on in."

His hazel eyes narrowed, and his gaze darted past her to the living room. She was sure he didn't need an explanation about why she was upset when he saw the tension in the family. He nodded when she gave a slight shake of her head. The last thing she wanted was for him to demand an explanation. It would only make a terrible situation worse.

"I thought I'd come help you move things around in the attic. I had some time."

A reprieve. At least she wouldn't have to go back to the living room with fists ready. "That would be great." Her voice quivered, and she cleared her throat. "I'll see if Gram will watch Noah. He'll be awake for another hour or so."

And she didn't dare ask one of her sisters to watch him. Their dislike of her was likely to spill over to her baby, harsh as that sounded.

"I'll watch him."

She turned toward Isabelle, who stood red-eyed at the bottom of the steps. She'd showered, and her blonde hair was still wet on her shoulders. She'd put tiny gold hoops in the four holes in her ears.

"Are you sure?"

"I like babies. I've done a lot of babysitting since I turned thirteen. He's cute, and it will give me something to do." Her blue eyes widened as she moved closer to the wide opening from the entry into the living room. "You have a cat? My best friend has one, and they are lit! Mom wouldn't let me have one, though."

Carly wanted to ask about her mother, but now wasn't the time. "His name is Pepper, and Noah loves him. You can come get me if he needs his diaper changed or is crying."

Isabelle frowned. "I don't need help changing diapers. That's the first thing you have to learn as a babysitter. My friends call me a baby whisperer. They never cry for me. Babies are like dogs—they can sense if you like them. It's all about your energy around them."

Carly's early estimation of Isabelle took a shift. Maybe she wasn't the spoiled brat she'd seemed when they arrived last night. What fifteen-year-old wouldn't be upset to be dragged across the country in the middle of the night without any warning?

"Thank you. I'll be in the attic if you need me. He won't need to eat for at least another hour."

Even an hour away from the tension in the living room would be welcome.

The missing surprise was still missing, but Lucas hadn't expected to find it.

After two hours of opening every drawer in the furniture in the attic and poking through every piece of clothing, Lucas and Carly found nothing to indicate the surprise from the Fabergé egg had ever been with the items she'd inherited.

Carly's dark hair had come partly loose from her ponytail, and she sat on the top step of the attic and exhaled. "I'm not surprised. If the surprise had been with the egg, it should have been somewhere in the chest. You even checked for a false bottom or side."

He propped one foot on the rung of an old chair and nodded. "I checked all the drawers for false bottoms. I don't think it's here—which means our next logical step is finding the family that adopted your grandmother's sister. Do you think it's time to clue your sisters in on the search for her? Maybe it would defuse the anger I sensed downstairs."

He hadn't brought it up yet, but maybe enough time had passed that she'd be calm enough to discuss what he'd walked in on. The way her sisters treated her was a puzzle to him. There seemed no good reason for them to be so angry with her.

She uncapped a bottle of water and took a swig, and he did the same to give her time to decide if she would answer. Or not. Why should she trust him with the truth of what was clearly an unsettling family situation?

She twisted the cap back on her bottle and set it on the attic floorboard. "They've been mad ever since I turned twenty-five."

So her sisters had been this way for five years. "What happened when you turned twenty-five?"

She lifted the platinum chain from around her neck to show him the dainty cross dangling from it. He'd noticed it before, but what did it have to do with her sisters?

"This belonged to Mom. It was never off her neck when we were growing up. After she died, we wondered what had happened to it, but none of us dared to ask Dad. Then he remarried and took off to California, and we forgot about it. The day after I turned twenty-five, I got a box from him. This necklace was in it along with a note from Mom. She knew she was dying, and she left the necklace to me."

"But why did he keep it from you until you turned twenty-five?" And an even bigger question was this: How could a necklace have the power to disrupt the entire family dynamic?

"In the letter Mom said she didn't want me to have it until my sisters were old enough to understand. Her mother had given it to her when she married, and it had belonged to her mother. It was supposed to pass down to the oldest daughter. Which was me."

He nodded. "Makes sense."

"I think my sisters could have accepted it if it had been only the necklace, but there were also some bonds that matured when I turned twenty-five as well. The payout was for fifty thousand dollars. I was married then, but I planned to split the money with my sisters." She looked down at her hands, and she swallowed. "The money was in our joint banking account, and I had written out checks for Emily and Amelia before going to a flea market. Eric was working so he didn't go."

Lucas tensed, already sensing how this was going to go down. "He spent the money?"

Her hands twisted in her lap, and she nodded. "He put a down payment on a new house."

He blew out a breath. "Wow, just wow. And your sisters didn't take it well?"

"I never told them. I didn't want them to hate Eric. They didn't know I'd planned to share it—they only knew I'd gotten an inheritance from Mom and they hadn't."

"So why did she leave the money only to you?"

Her face went pink, and she bit her lip. "When the girls were thirteen and fifteen, they found some cash our mom had saved. It was in a baggie in the kitchen drawer. Two hundred dollars was a lot of money to them. It was a lot to our mom too. They took it and went clothes shopping. Mom had a fit about it, and she didn't think they'd put the money in the bonds to good use. I always believed she would have wanted me to split it with them once I was sure it wouldn't be frittered away."

"But Eric's actions prevented you from doing that."

"It was too late to change. The money was gone, and Eric thought he was doing the right thing by trying to use it for our future."

Even now she was making excuses for him. Maybe she hadn't been the poor wife he'd thought. "Did he know you planned to split it with them?"

She nodded. "I'd told him, and we argued about it. We could have gotten the house without that big down payment, but cutting that much off the mortgage made the payments easier. When I left on Friday morning for the weekend, I thought he understood how important it was to me to share with my sisters. By the time I got home Sunday night, it was done."

"How'd he close on a house without you?"

"I'd signed before I left, and he was handling the last of the closing. So it was too late to change when I got home."

He had to have planned it all along. The papers would have reflected the down payment, but maybe she'd just signed where directed. "How did your sisters find out about the money she left you?"

"They saw the necklace and asked Dad about it. He told them."

Everyone had thrown her under the bus. This was a long-standing disagreement that wouldn't be easily mended. "And now your grandmother is wanting all the sisters together. It won't be an easy time."

She redid her ponytail and shook her head. "They think they'll do the work and Gram will leave everything to me. But she won't. And even if she did, I'd make sure they got their part."

"What happens when they find out the trunk's contents were left to you alone? They'll hear about the egg."

"I'll split the money with them."

He wanted to tell her not to give in to their tantrums, but he didn't want her to think he was like Eric. But until her sisters treated her with respect, he didn't think she owed them a thing. Not one thin dime.

THIRTEEN

She had to tell Gram about her birth mother.

As Carly searched the attic with Lucas, that knowledge had crept into her heart. She always tried to be strong—to go it alone because her family depended on her. But she didn't have the right to do this alone. Gram was intimately involved and deserved to know about it.

Lucas's deep voice broke into her introspection. "Ready to go downstairs and face your family?"

She forced a smile and wished she could stay here a little longer, but Noah would be ready to nurse and go to bed any minute. Isabelle really must be a baby whisperer. There hadn't been a peep from him.

She reached for the file folder of papers she'd pulled out of the chest earlier and held it up. "I'm going to tell Gram."

Lucas's dark brows rose. "About the egg?"

She shook her head. "Not unless you think I should. It's just that I know my sisters. When they realize the egg's value, they'll be bombarding me to get it appraised and sold. Dillard will be leading the charge."

"It's your property," he reminded her.

He had to know her inner fairness code wouldn't let her

keep it all to herself. It was too much money for one person anyway. "Once the media gets wind of it, things will turn into a circus. We won't have the quiet space to investigate her past."

"Slugs will come crawling out from every rock claiming to be her family in hopes they can get their hands on some of the money."

She wrinkled her nose. "Ugh. That's the last thing we need."

His phone beeped with a message, and he glanced at it. "Vince has a lead on your grandmother's birth family. He texted me a phone number and address. The woman, Anna Martin, seems to be related to the Balandin family. The documentation is murky. Feel up to a road trip? She's just up near Savannah. Tybee Island."

A road trip with Lucas sounded immensely appealing. Getting away from the stony glances and stares of her sisters would be a welcome reprieve. "When?"

"Tomorrow after church? Is Noah a good traveler?"

"He's a stellar traveler." It touched her that he realized she wouldn't want to be gone long from her baby. And she couldn't be gone long. He nursed about every three hours. "He usually pops off to sleep right away." A trip to Tybee Island would be a pleasant hour-and-a-half drive along a lazy road. "Too bad we couldn't go by boat."

He lifted a brow. "We could. Ryan and I have a boat. We're so busy we don't get to use it often, but we keep it ocean ready. Could the baby handle a boat ride?"

"He's never been on one, but the rumble would probably put him right to sleep."

"I'll meet you down at the waterfront at one."

"I'll bring lunch." She started for the steps at the same

time a thin wail filtered to her ears. Noah was hungry and ready for bed.

She'd have a couple of hours to talk with Gram and broach the subject of her birth family. Carly's palms grew moist at the thought of telling her family about the packet of papers in her hand. At least the egg was safely stowed at the bank and wouldn't be discovered. That was one secret she could keep a little while longer. The hullabaloo that would ensue at its discovery would echo through the art world.

She paused long enough to stash the file before going down to the living room, where she scooped up Noah, who was red-faced and angry, out of Isabelle's arms. "He's ready for a nap."

Isabelle appeared calm and unruffled by the crying baby. "He didn't make a peep until just now."

"You did a great job." Carly jiggled the baby in her arms. "Where's Dad?"

The slight smile fell off Isabelle's face. "Gone."

Without saying goodbye. His quick visit cemented his supreme disregard for his girls. He hadn't cared about seeing any of them. All that mattered to him was using Gram and the rest of the family. At least they didn't still live with him like poor Isabelle. What a terrible father.

"I'll be right back." She carried the squalling baby up the stairs.

What kind of father would Eric have been? She'd never had a chance to tell him about Noah, but she suspected he'd have been angry at first. She'd been talking about a baby for nearly two years, and he kept postponing the question. It was a mystery how she'd gotten pregnant on the pill, but clearly God had plans he hadn't let them in on.

Noah was her chance to experience unconditional love. She settled in a rocker and fed him. The sweet aroma of his skin soothed her, and she ran her hand over the downy softness of his hair. The love a parent felt for their child was like none other. Even if he'd initially been upset, Eric would have come around. Who could resist Noah with his blue eyes and gummy grin? Eric would have taken one look at his son and been as smitten as she was. She blinked suddenly blurry eyes. If only he'd had the chance.

An image of Lucas holding Noah sleeping on his chest came to mind. Even a stranger had been unable to resist the baby's charisma.

Noah's eyes drifted shut and she transferred him to his crib, then turned on the noise machine. She grabbed the file folder, then tiptoed out of the room.

Now to talk to Gram before she told her sisters. Gram deserved to hear the truth in private in case it was upsetting. Carly hoped she'd be excited at the thought of finding a twin sister.

The house felt curiously empty when Carly descended the steps. The living room held only Gram, who sat sipping a cup of tea in her favorite blue Polish mug. Her peacock skirt draped around her ankles and covered most of the chair where she sat. The aroma of lobster bisque drifted from the kitchen and reminded Carly that she hadn't had lunch yet.

"Where are the girls?" Carly asked.

"I had them take Isabelle shopping. They were only too glad to get out of the house before you came down and put them to work." She pointed to the sofa. "Have a seat, Carly Ann."

Carly perched on the edge of a sofa cushion. "You think I was wrong to tell them what needed to be done here?"

"Of course not. They needed to know their marching orders. I'm surprised you waited as long as you did."

"Were they still mad?"

"Over their hissy fit, I think." Gram took a sip of her tea and released a satisfied sigh. "How are things in the attic—about ready for the flea market?"

"Not even close." Carly leaned forward. "Um, Gram, I found something very unexpected up there. I actually found it a week ago, but I was going to keep it quiet until I learned more. I think you need to know about it, though." She handed over the papers. "I think it's best if you read it for yourself."

Her grandmother's blue eyes revealed her curiosity as she took the papers. "What is this, Carly Ann?"

Carly's pulse skipped, and she shook her head. "Read that top little note—the one in the spidery handwriting."

Her grandmother read in silence before reading the birth certificate under it. She gave a quick gasp and held her hand to her throat. She lifted her gaze to Carly's. "This seems to indicate I might be adopted?" Her voice quivered. "Why didn't my parents tell me?"

"I don't know. There's a note to me from Gramma Helen. She said she was leaving it to me to decide what to do. I think that's why she left all the mementos in the chest to me." Carly gestured to the documents. "Those are adoption papers, Gram. Your name was changed from Mary Balandin to Mary Padgett. Did you see the picture?" She got up and retrieved the picture from the file folder. "This is you and your twin sister, Elizabeth."

The pink washed from Gram's cheeks as she stared at the picture. "Twins. How old were we?"

"It doesn't say, but I think the babies appear to be only a

few weeks old. Not older than a couple of months." Carly took the adoption papers and studied them more closely. "This is dated July 2, same as your birthday. Gramma Helen must not have known your exact birthdate so she used the date of your adoption."

"I-I can't believe it."

Her normally vibrant grandmother seemed as though she might faint. Carly had never seen her so pale. "Do you need to lie down?" she asked.

Gram shook her head. "No, no. It's just such a shock. A *twin*. I can't wrap my head around something so astounding. I've hankered for a sibling all my life. Can we find her?"

"I'm trying. Lucas is helping me, and he's found a possible relative. We're going to take a boat trip to Tybee Island and talk to her. It might be nothing, but we have to try. I'd hoped to find your family and surprise you with it for your birthday, but it's more complicated than it first seemed. The name Balandin is not common. I didn't have the resources to try to track down the family until Lucas offered to help."

Gram didn't take her attention from the picture. "It's very good of him." Her eyes were wet when she finally met Carly's gaze. "What if my birth mother is still alive? If she gave us up for adoption, maybe she was quite young. Sixteen, seventeen. She'd be in her eighties, but she might still be living."

"The thought crossed my mind."

The hope in Gram's face tore Carly's heart wide open. What if they couldn't find her sister or her mother? What if they were both dead? It was possible. Gram was nearly seventy. Accidents, illness—something could have carried off both sister and mother. Still, there might be an aunt or an uncle left. A niece or a nephew. Gram would welcome any family with open arms.

Not that she lacked family right here in her own home, but this sudden crossroad had opened up, and it had to be a thrilling sensation to think she had unknown family out there.

Carly intended to find them no matter what. She wouldn't give up no matter how long it took.

The screen door opened, and the rest of the family spilled into the foyer. Isabelle's cheeks were flushed, and her blue eyes were bright. Getting out into the sunshine had been good for her. Even Emily and Amelia were smiling. At least until they entered the living room and saw the papers spread on Gram's lap.

"What's going on?" Amelia asked.

Carly flinched at her sister's strident voice. Why did it always have to be this way? "I found something interesting in the attic."

"Not just interesting. Earth-shattering," Gram said. "Look here, girls. It appears that I was adopted, and I have a twin sister out there somewhere. Carly is going to find her for me."

"Carly the paragon. Carly the superhero." Amelia's tone grew shrill. "Why can't you see through her, Gram? She wants you to leave everything to her. She probably planted those documents."

The blood rushed away from Carly's head, and she felt faint. Could her sisters really *hate* her? She staggered to her feet and rushed up the steps to her room before she let the tears fall.

FOURTEEN

Carly looked beautiful in her red sundress, but her brown eyes were shadowed today. What had happened after Lucas left the house yesterday? She hadn't had much to say when they boarded the boat, and he bit back the questions hovering on his tongue. If she wanted to talk about it, she would do so without his prying.

The wind teased strands of dark hair loose from her ponytail, and the warm breeze pinked her cheeks. Somehow he managed not to stare as he navigated the boat out of the harbor and south to Tybee Island. They motored past grand old homes sheltered by live oak trees laced with moss. Raucous music blared from a boat of teenagers they passed, and he caught a whiff of a shrimp boil somewhere along the shore.

Once they were out on open water, the sounds fell away and the silence felt more intimate and friendly. Just as Carly predicted, the baby fell asleep in her arms, and she shuffled him to a more comfortable place on her lap. The fluorescent green vest with its head rest surrounded his little face and tufts of light hair, but he didn't seem to mind it and snoozed through the movement.

"How'd it go with telling your grandmother yesterday?"

"It took her a minute to believe it. Once she did, she wanted me to find her birth family as quickly as possible. If she had her way, we'd come back home with her family aboard. She immediately started wondering if her birth mother could be alive." Carly turned serious brown eyes his way. "Do you think it's possible?"

"Depends on her mother's age when the twins were born. It wouldn't be surprising if she was a young mother. If that's the case, she might be as young as maybe eighty-five or eighty-six."

"Or already in the grave. I tried not to get Gram's hopes up. Or my own for that matter."

He itched to ask her why her ready smile was missing, but he turned his head and looked out over the blue water. The sea spray left the taste of salt on his lips and in the air. Why had he let so much time go by without getting out here on the water? Busyness was no excuse for not taking some downtime for something he loved.

Gulls soared overhead, and a dolphin splashed off the starboard side. Unease crept into his sense of peace, and he glanced at Carly, who sat crying silently.

It shocked him into asking the question he'd been holding back since he saw her. "What's wrong? I could tell something had upset you the minute you boarded the boat."

She swiped at her cheeks with the back of her hand. "The usual."

At least she didn't tell him it was "nothing" like many women might have. "Your sisters."

"Until last night I didn't realize they actively hated me. They think I planted the documents so I'd look like a hero when I found Gram's birth family."

Her family's audacity left him breathless, and he couldn't

find adequate words to express his disgust. "That's cold, even for them," he said finally.

She nodded and tucked a loose strand of hair behind her ear. "I didn't sleep much. I don't know how to fix it, Lucas."

Hearing his name on her lips gave him a strange thrill, which was weird. It wasn't like he'd never heard her speak his name. He shook off the sudden sensation. "Did you try to talk to them about it?"

"No, I went to my room. I was too hurt to discuss it. No one but Isabelle was up before I left. She told me she was sorry I was upset. I nearly invited her along today, but Ryan came over to talk to Gram about starting the remodel tomorrow. One look and she was smitten." Carly gave a slight smile. "I didn't want to disrupt her hero worship."

"Ryan tends to have that effect on females. He did the same with you once upon a time."

A smile, this time a genuine one, tipped her lips up. "A long time ago in a land far away. I was young and dumb. It never would have worked."

"Why not?" Lucas tensed as he waited for her answer. Crazy that it mattered after all this time.

"He's still unmarried. He wasn't the settling down kind. After we broke up, I found out he'd been meeting my best friend for coffee. He'd asked her out, but she said no. That shook me up, though."

That news didn't really surprise Lucas. He'd suspected Ryan dated more than he admitted. The only women he mentioned were ones he'd gone out with at least three times. It was hard to say how many he'd taken out to dinner, never to call again.

He turned the boat a bit. "Maybe we're both a little

damaged by our home lives. Seeing Dad deal with a depressed wife for so many years left its mark. Mom could seem so happy and normal, but then the tide would turn and she'd take to her bed, maybe for days. She wouldn't eat, would hardly talk."

"I had no idea, Lucas. I'm sorry. That had to be hard. Who cooked your meals, did the laundry, that kind of thing? Your dad didn't seem the Mr. Mom type."

"Oh, he wasn't. I did those things some nights, if you can call what I cooked meals. It was mostly canned spaghetti and grilled cheese sandwiches. Anything that could be warmed in the microwave." He shrugged. "But I was the oldest, you know? I had to take care of Ryan. At least twice a week your grandmother brought over casseroles and cookies or cake. She was an angel to us."

Her eyes widened. "That's why you ran interception for Ryan when he dated me. I get it now."

True enough. He'd always looked out for his little brother, and he always would. And he couldn't deny his beautiful neighbor was beginning to intrigue him more and more.

———

Lucas had arranged for two bikes at the marina, and though Carly had balked at the idea at first, he'd been right. It had been a short but exhilarating ride along the waterfront to the address. Lucas had taken the cargo bike with the bucket in front where Noah was secure in his car seat and little helmet, and they arrived with the baby awake but happy.

She put down the kickstand and went to unstrap Noah. He gave her a dimpled smile and waved his small fists in the air. "You liked that, didn't you, sweetheart? I'll have to get one of these for home." The fresh air and sunshine were good for him—much better than being in the back seat of a car. She removed the helmet and picked him up.

With the baby in her arms, she turned to face the house. The white cottage was as cute and quaint as could be with the palm trees waving above the steeply pitched roof. A blue door under a white stoop added a welcoming touch. Her heart did a staccato pump in her chest as she stared at the house. Were answers inside, or was it going to be a dead end?

She'd wanted to call first, but Lucas had insisted surprise would be the better option. He was a detective, so he should know, but she felt uneasy about landing on the woman's doorstep with no warning.

Lucas's warm hand came down on her shoulder. "Relax. The baby is bound to win her over. He's got all the right moves. Dimples too."

She chuckled. "You have a point. Maybe I'd better turn him around so he can slay her with his cuteness."

Noah loved to walk facing forward, so he kicked his legs when she moved him around. Supporting him with both arms, she walked toward the entrance. As they neared, she noticed the door stood slightly ajar. And something about it struck her with trepidation.

She stopped, and Lucas nearly ran into her. "Lucas, I don't feel right about this."

He surveyed the slightly open door. "Someone forced open the door."

The gouges around the latch might have subconsciously clued her in to the problem. "What should we do?"

"I want you to go across the street to that café." He pointed it out. "I'm going to call the local police before I go inside."

Leaving him didn't feel right, but she had the baby's safety to consider, so she reluctantly retreated across the street to the Sandy Bar, a low-slung restaurant with a blue roof and cute beach decor. She couldn't bring herself to go inside, though, and instead settled at a white iron dinette. The aroma of crab cakes made her stomach cramp, but not in a good way. She was too frightened for Lucas's safety to be hungry.

She watched him talk a few moments on the phone before he drew out his pistol from its holster on his belt and advanced to the door. He nudged it open with his foot and disappeared inside. She felt like throwing up when she couldn't see him any longer. What was he seeing inside the home? She prayed for him and whoever lived inside.

It seemed an eternity he was hidden from her sight. Sirens blared in the distance and two squad cars screeched to a halt in front of the residence. Lucas reappeared and she finally exhaled. At least he was all right. He spoke with the officers, and his grim expression did nothing to alleviate her anxiety. Something had happened inside.

She finally broke down and ordered iced tea as she waited for him to join her. One sip of the sweet beverage braced her, and she guzzled more of it down. He finally turned and came her way, and she started to stand but he waved for her to stay where she was.

He reached the table and sank into a chair beside her. "It's bad, Carly, real bad. I found Anna Martin dead in the kitchen."

Dead. Carly put her hand to her throat.

"Looked like she was shot by a .44 sometime late last night.

The place is torn apart too. The intruder was looking for something. Very methodical and expert."

"The Russians again?"

His hazel eyes met hers in an unflinching stare. "Maybe. Someone knew what they were doing. I'll have to tell the detective here about the break-in at your house."

He couldn't be serious. She parted her lips but couldn't speak at first. She swallowed and tried again. "Lucas, you'll have to tell them about the egg."

"I don't think we have a choice, Carly. This has grown and someone innocent has died. I hate to break your trust, but if we kept this to ourselves, we would be hamstringing the investigation. What would be the first thing on your list to do if you knew this news would hit the papers?"

"I'd really need to get it verified."

"So maybe it's not really a missing egg?"

She hated to disrupt his hope, but she shook her head. "I'm relatively sure of it, Lucas, but we need proof. But backing up, I'd say I need to tell my family first. After last night, it won't be easy." Her voice thickened at the thought of facing more vitriol, but Lucas was right.

This was too big to contain now. A killer had struck, and her family could be next.

Her arms tightened around Noah. Their safety was more important than a priceless Fabergé egg. No amount of money would be worth the loss of her family. The poor woman inside had already paid a final price.

FIFTEEN

It was a long, quiet ride back to Beaufort. Carly started to speak several times, then lapsed into silence. What could she say? Finding those documents had been the fuse that lit all of this trouble. If she'd never found that folder, Anna might still be alive.

The family was gathered around the dining room table when she and Lucas entered. She'd told Lucas he didn't have to come, but his jaw flexed and he said, *"I'm not leaving you alone to face this."*

And she didn't have the heart to argue. Knowing she had someone in her corner stiffened her spine and lifted her chin.

Her grandmother was the first to see her, and she started to rise. Carly shook her head. "I think you'd better stay seated, Gram. There's a lot to tell you. Too much."

Her gaze swept around the table. Amelia and Emily looked a little shamefaced, but maybe it was Carly's inherent optimism that made her think they might regret their harsh words. Isabelle sprawled in her chair and stared at her phone as if what the older siblings had to say had no bearing on her life. But it affected them—all of them. At least Dillard had gone back to Jacksonville.

"Isabelle, would you take the baby?" she asked.

Her sister looked startled, but she put down her phone and held out her arms. Noah was a heavy weight in Carly's arms, and she laid him in Isabelle's arms. Should she sit or stand? Stand, Carly decided. The weight of what she had to say would come across better if she stood.

"I found something else in the attic. I'd tried to keep it secret because its discovery will change everything." It had ended everything for Anna, and Carly choked on her next words and lost her train of thought. Feeling cold, so cold, she shivered.

Lucas moved close enough for Carly to feel the heat of his body warming her up. He set his hand on her shoulder. "Want me to tell it?"

A lump formed in her throat, but she shook her head. "There was a garish red egg wrapped in a Russian shawl in the chest. At first glance I thought it was a child's toy, but it was far more than that. I saw white porcelain through some chipped paint and decided to clean it up."

The family's attention was focused completely on her, and she pushed herself to get it all out. "As soon as the paint was gone, I realized I held one of the missing Fabergé eggs."

No one gasped like she had. No one flinched or showed any emotion, but then, they wouldn't know what that meant. "Fabergé eggs were created for the wife of the tsar of Russia. In 1885 Tsar Alexander III gave the first one to Tsarina Maria Feodorovna. Records show a total of fifty-two eggs created, but some are missing. The chest held one of the missing eggs, the Hen with Sapphire Pendant."

Emily gasped. "It's worth a lot of money?"

"I don't even know how much. Millions. Fabergé eggs all had what was called a 'surprise' inside. The surprise in our egg is missing, and I'd hoped to find it before news of this got out. Media will be camping on our lawn when they hear about this. It will be nearly impossible to search for the surprise once it all comes to light."

"Then why are you telling us, sugar?" Gram asked. "The contents of the chest belong to you. You didn't have to reveal it now."

"I know," Amelia said. "Russians broke into the house, right? So someone knows."

Carly gave a jerky nod. She met Gram's gaze in an unflinching stare. "They killed the woman we were going to see, Gram. They trashed the house looking for something—maybe the surprise. If she had it in her possession, they found it."

"The woman we thought might be a relative?" Gram asked.

Carly nodded. "Lucas found her. We never had a chance to talk to her."

He squeezed her shoulder as if to tell her she'd done a good job. "The egg is in a safe place, so no one breaking in here will find it. But everyone needs to be vigilant. While Carly won't announce this to the media, it may leak out. I hope not, because it will put you all in greater danger."

"But why?" Isabelle asked. "If it's safe, it's safe."

"What do you think your sister would do if the killer kidnapped one of you and demanded the egg in return?" Lucas asked.

"She'd give it to them," Gram said. "And they'd probably kill us all to make sure there were no witnesses."

At least Gram got it. Carly's mouth was dry as she thought

about how bad this could get. How did she get them out of this mess? Give the egg up willingly? But how did she do that when she didn't know the shadowy assailant out there or how to reach him? Her family was precious to her, even if her sisters didn't believe it. She'd willingly give the Russians everything she owned to protect them.

Right now that didn't seem to be an option.

———

Lucas loved his job, but he didn't want to be in the office right now—not when so much was riding on finding the Russians who had murdered an innocent woman. He scrolled through the list of names possibly associated with the Adams family. If Eric thought he was being followed after contacting the son, he likely hadn't been mistaken. Now that the news about the egg was likely to come out, there was nothing to be gained by skulking around Roger in hopes of not drawing his attention. He either knew of the egg or had some reason to be interested.

A printout of Roger Adams's rap sheet proved interesting. Shoplifting, a DUI, and one count of robbery told Lucas that the man wouldn't be above breaking into Carly's shop space where Eric had been killed. Would he be capable of murder, or did that crime need to be dropped at the feet of the Russian mafia?

His door opened and Vince stepped in. He held a donut box and offered one to Lucas, but he shook his head. "Thanks, but I just had an omelet."

"Too healthy." Vince dropped into his desk chair on the

other side of the room. "Lieutenant Clark wants an update. I sat around outside the bank all day yesterday thanks to you. Nada. I doubt anyone knows the egg is there."

"Someone knows it's out there." Before Lucas could explain, their boss stepped into the room and shut the door behind him.

Bernard selected a maple nut roll and settled in a chair with his boot propped on a knee. "Whatcha got from the weekend?"

"We've got worse than a robbery." Lucas told the men about the Martin woman's murder.

The smile vanished from Bernard's face, and he put both boots on the ground, then tossed away the rest of his donut. "I wasn't sure you were right, Lucas. I should have known better than to doubt you. Have the police on Tybee Island come up with a suspect?"

"I haven't checked in this morning yet. I'm racing against the clock to try to find who's behind this before they make another move against the Tucker family. Carly told her family about the egg last night. Once we knew about the murder, we wanted them on alert." He handed Bernard the list of Roger Adams's crimes.

Bernard smoothed one blond brow as he studied the paper. "Could be implicated." He passed it to Vince.

"I think it's the Russians." Lucas told the men about how methodically Anna Martin's house had been searched. "They meant business. If we found a connection to the Balandin family, I'm sure they could've done the same. They are probably looking under every stone for the surprise. I think they know Carly has the egg."

Bernard pulled out his phone. "I know the chief there. Let me see what they've found out."

Lucas continued to look for other family members while his boss placed the call to Tybee Island PD. He listened with half an ear while he scanned the list of crimes in the county. One entry caught his attention, and he leaned forward. A home invasion at a property in Bluffton that was owned by Grace Adams Hill.

"Did you notice the name on this home invasion?" he asked Vince. "Maiden name is Adams."

"Along with a thousand other people. It's hardly note-worthy, Lucas."

"But it's possible she's related. I think I'll run out there and talk to her."

Bernard ended his call. "Interesting chat with the chief. Neighbors heard a disturbance just after midnight. The woman next door reported seeing an Asian man fleeing in a dark van."

"Asian?" Lucas exchanged a glance with his partner. "That's not what I expected."

"The neighbor got the license plate, and they picked the guy up. He's in a cell right now, and I told him you might want to interview him if he thinks it's a good lead."

This took precedence over a home invasion, and Lucas rose. "Let's head out there now."

"Maybe you'll be able to determine if the murder was related to what we have going on here."

Lucas didn't believe in coincidences, so he had high hopes of some kind of answer. "I'll drive," he told Vince.

He and his partner got into Lucas's pickup. "I don't know

why you drive this flashy thing," Vince grumbled. "Everyone in town knows it's you when you pull up."

Lucas started the engine and pulled out into traffic. "It doesn't seem to stop them from answering questions."

He'd found that the unusual appearance of his Jeep pickup could open conversation and leave witnesses more willing to talk. The bright blue color made people smile, and Lucas would take any goodwill he could get when getting to the bottom of a crime.

It would take an hour and a half to get out to Tybee Island, and he thought about taking the boat again, but by the time he got out to the marina and did a safety check, he could be halfway to the island. They could make a stop at Bluffton on the way back. It wouldn't be much out of the way, and they could kill two birds with one stone.

He glanced at his partner. If only he could change out Vince for Carly. His partner would likely want to listen to jazz on the drive or talk about the Braves during the whole trip. Carly was an excellent travel companion. She didn't try to take control of the radio, and she wasn't a chatterbox.

Hopefully, the only drama she would have today would be Ryan's crew starting the demo on the downstairs. Was it safe for the baby to be in all that dirt and dust and commotion? When they stopped for coffee, he would tell her to go to his house if she needed to escape.

He wouldn't complain if he got home to find Noah and her there. At least the killer might not know where to look for Carly.

SIXTEEN

It was going to be a chaotic day. Carly walked cautiously over the debris of what remained of the wall between the living and dining rooms. The palindrome tee she'd picked out this morning perfectly summed up what she expected: *WoW.* The future of the house looked exciting, but she was less sure about what life with her family held.

Isabelle moved out of the way as Carly went to the fridge for a bottle of water. "Where's the baby?"

"Sleeping, though I wasn't sure he'd drop off with all the racket. I turned on the sound machine and shut the door to keep out the noise and dust." Carly glanced around. "Where is everyone?"

"Emily stepped on a nail, and Amelia freaked out. They rushed to an urgent care." Isabelle lifted her blonde hair off her neck. "You have a crazy family."

Carly started to tell her it was her family, too, but the teenager went to the toaster and popped in some bread. She was beginning to think the girl was the most even-tempered of all her sisters. Too bad they hadn't had more time with her.

"Hear anything from Dad?" she asked Isabelle. Her stomach rumbled at the scent of browning bread. She needed to get some breakfast, but cooking in the chaos didn't sound like fun.

"He got to Rome okay. That's all I know." Her voice quivered, and she reached for the butter when the toast popped.

What did Carly say to comfort her? They'd all been faced with his inattention their whole lives. It probably wasn't anything new to Isabelle either. "You're really good with babies."

"I like them." When she turned to face Carly with the plate of toast in hand, her blue eyes held no trace of tears. "One good thing about being here is that school starts three hours later for me. I have most of the morning before I have to hop on the computer. Is there anything I can do to help you?"

The loud clatter of a board falling made Carly wince. "Sounds like the house is falling down."

"At least you'll have air-conditioning when it's over. I don't know how you live here without it."

"You've never heard of the history of Beaufort and how the houses were built. Let's take a carriage ride around town after Noah wakes and before it gets hot."

Isabelle eyed her. "Why are you being so nice to me?"

"Why wouldn't I be nice? You're my sister."

"You never came to see me."

Carly didn't want to blame Isabelle's parents, so she thought through the minefield of what to say. "It's a long flight, and everyone is always busy. I'm glad you're here now, though." Isabelle's smile was almost too slight to see, but Carly caught it. Maybe this situation would end up being a blessing from God. "I could use your help boxing up the items in the kitchen and moving them upstairs. The destruction will move in here in a couple of days."

Heavy boots walked through the debris in the living room, and she turned to see Ryan step into view. A leather tool belt wrapped around his waist, and the heavy tools tugged it lower on his hips. The red bandanna around his head made him look like a pirate—and entirely too handsome, though Carly believed she was immune to his immense charm now. Isabelle was a different story, and the stars in her eyes twinkled when she stared at Ryan.

"Your crew is making good progress already," Carly said, handing him a cold bottle of water.

"Thanks." He uncapped it and took a swig. "The demo goes fast. I wish I could say the same for the remodel. You'll have to live with dust and noise for months."

She wrinkled her nose. "Did you have to remind me?"

He grinned. "I'm trying to head off complaints about how long it's taking. You'll have your hands full keeping your sisters happy."

He'd always seen the dynamics of her relationship with her sisters. "I'll do my best."

"I found something in the wall I thought might be interesting." He yanked a paper out of his back pocket and handed it to her. "Looks to me like a Padgett family tree."

"The house has been in Gram's family since it was first built, and she moved in here with Grandpa when they were first married." Carly unfolded the paper and spread it out on the kitchen table to have a look. "Gram is going to love seeing this."

She started at the top and traced the family tree down to Gram and to Dad, then her and her sisters. No surprises there. She stared at a small star next to Gram's name. It was the only name with that emblem on it. What did it mean? She examined the rest of the paper for a hint of what the star might mean. Nothing.

"There's stuff on the back too," Ryan said. "Just some writing, I think." He turned toward the living room when one of the workers called for him.

She turned it over to find spidery writing sprawling across the back. And a handwritten star at the top of the text. It took a second of reading for it all to soak in. Next to the star was a name—Elizabeth Durham. It listed her as a sister to Gram with the same birthdate. This must be the legend explaining the star on the front.

Gram's twin.

Carly couldn't believe it was all laid out. Was this the surname of Gram's twin after adoption? It appeared to be since the surname was different from the name Balandin they'd seen on the paperwork in the chest. Durham was a common enough name, so it might still be hard to track down, but it was a great start.

This could be a game changer for their search. She couldn't wait to tell Lucas.

———

Hopefully, this stop would prove more useful than the last. By the time Lucas and Vince had arrived in Tybee Island, the police had released the suspect. After talking to the arresting officer, Lucas found the guy's alibi plausible, and he would have released him as well. Witnesses vouched for his whereabouts at the time of the murder, and it had clearly been a false arrest.

He chatted with the detective for a few minutes, too, and discovered the police believed the victim had walked in on the burglar.

The Grace Adams Hill home was on Island Slipper Drive in Bluffton, and the views from inside had to be spectacular with the river on one side and the golf greens on the other, especially with the brilliant blue sky overhead and the slight breeze stirring the tops of the trees.

Lucas parked in the circle drive and got out. "This probably won't take long. I doubt this home invasion had anything to do with Carly's situation."

Vince grunted as he got out of the truck and followed. "I tried to tell you."

The sidewalk curved around the front of the house through beautifully manicured flowers and shrubs to the front porch of the two-story. Two carpenters worked on replacing the front door and jamb. They stopped and stepped out of the way when they spotted Lucas and Vince.

"The owner is around back working in her garden," the younger man said.

Lucas thanked him, and the men went around toward the water. Lucas expected to find the woman weeding flower beds, but instead she was bent over in a vegetable garden. She appeared to be picking bugs off leaves and tossing them into a bucket.

She straightened and saw them. "Can I help you?"

Lucas guessed her to be in her fifties. Her curly dark hair, sprinkled with gray, was up in a bun, and her cheeks were flushed with the heat. The skin that showed around her tank top and shorts was red, and he suspected she'd be hurting later today.

Both men got out their IDs. "Beaufort police, Ms. Hill. I wondered if we might ask you a few questions," Lucas said.

She pulled off her gloves. "Of course."

Lucas glanced at the bucket of soapy water beside her. "You're washing bugs?"

"I'm ridding the plants of potato beetles. I don't like to use insecticides." She nodded toward the expansive deck with its comfortable chairs and outdoor kitchen. "Could I offer you some tea or lemonade?" Without waiting for an answer, she headed for the outdoor cooler.

"Lemonade sounds great," Vince said.

Ice clinked in glasses, and Grace brought them to the men. "I made it just this morning from my own lemons."

The sweet tartness hit Lucas's tongue. "Best I've ever had."

She settled on a sofa and gestured to the lounge chairs. The men perched on the edge of their seats. "Well, you didn't come here to talk about lemons and gardening. Is this about the break-in? It was an odd burglary. The thieves busted into my safe but didn't take my bonds or wedding rings. They ransacked boxes in the basement, of all things. It didn't appear that they took anything. I was away on a business trip and came home to the mess."

Lucas exchanged a glance with Vince. "Any idea what they might have been looking for?"

"No idea. All that was in that basement room were old files from the orphanage where my grandmother worked a long time ago. In Savannah."

Bingo.

"Was your grandmother Natalie Adams?"

Grace's brows arched. "How did you know that?"

"It's a long story about twin girls separated at birth and adopted by two different families."

Grace leaned forward. "How fascinating. Can you tell me anything else?"

"Have you ever gone through the files?"

She wrinkled her nose and shook her head. "Not those dusty old things. My daughter has, though. She's working on a novel and thought the orphanage was interesting."

"So you don't know if the burglars took any of the files?"

"I think they are all still in the basement, except the ones my brother has."

"Would that be Roger Adams?"

"Yes, he's my older brother."

Lucas already suspected Roger could be behind Eric's death, so he had to pick his questions carefully. "Has your brother ever looked through the files you have?"

She shook her head. "He's wanted to, but we're not friendly and haven't been for a good twenty years."

"Does your estrangement have anything to do with the files?"

"It's more to do with Roger being such a jerk. When Mom died, he thought he was in charge and could determine who got what. Mom assigned him as executor and he took whatever he wanted, even the things that used to belong to Grandma. I wanted some mementos, but he objected to almost everything. It was so traumatic that we haven't spoken since."

Lucas finished the lemonade and rose with the glass in his hand. "Thank you for your time."

She hopped off the sofa and took the glass from him. "Glad to be of help. You've made me wonder if Roger broke in to get those files. I don't know how to find out."

"I'm sure the detective in charge of the break-in took fingerprints. Maybe their investigation will bring back some answers."

She followed them down the steps. "I doubt I'll be that lucky. I should give Roger a call."

Lucas stopped and turned back to face her. "It would be best if you didn't. There are some very bad men looking for anything to do with that adoption. I'd hate for you to draw their attention."

She frowned. "You hadn't mentioned that. Do you think they could have broken in here?"

"It's very likely. Could I get Roger's address and phone number? Your daughter's too. She might have noticed something in the old orphanage files."

"Of course." She went inside and came back with a business card she handed to him. "Here is Roger's. He lives on the island, and my daughter lives with me. She'll be home in about an hour." Clouds drifted across the sun, and she hugged herself and shivered. "And here I thought it was a simple burglary. Should I hire security or move to a hotel for a while?"

He glanced at the card. Roger was an auctioneer. "I think the burglar found what he was looking for, but it wouldn't hurt to be careful."

She looked relieved. "Thank you for coming."

Lucas waited until they were in the front yard to say what he was thinking. "Vince, I don't like this. She's lucky she wasn't here."

SEVENTEEN

Roger's auction business was located in a pole barn that sat near the street in a quiet part of Tybee Island. Behind the building, Lucas pointed out a small ranch house. Cars were in the lot, so he assumed Roger was working, and he parked his truck close to the door.

As he and Vince approached the entry, a man rushed through the front door and brushed past them.

The older man's face was red and his lips were pursed in anger. He glanced at them as he went toward his car, an older model blue Taurus. "I advise you not to do business with that shyster."

Lucas exchanged a glance with Vince, whose brows were raised. Not a good first impression. They headed for the entrance and stepped into a large, open space that smelled of a mixture of oil, dust, and old wood. The room held everything from old car parts to furniture and kitchen items. Lucas wasn't sure where to look first, then he spotted a man with thick white hair and a white beard.

The detectives walked to intercept him. "Roger Adams?" Vince asked.

"Who wants to know?"

The men flipped out their IDs. "Police detectives."

Roger barely glanced at them as he continued to write on a paper attached to a clipboard. "What's this all about?"

"Eric Harris." Lucas wanted to catch Roger off guard, and Eric's murder was mostly old news for people.

"Yeah, he called me once, but I never met the guy."

"Can you tell us the details of your conversation with Mr. Harris?"

Roger moved to the next pile of items: boxes of car parts. "He asked about my grandmother's work with an orphanage a long time ago. I didn't know much about it, though."

"Did Mr. Harris say why he was asking about her?"

"He was trying to find records of an old adoption."

"He made a note that you'd asked about old belongings he might have found. What was that all about?"

Roger swept his hand around the cluttered space. "I sell old things for a living. I didn't want to waste an opportunity to get business."

"Your sister said you have some files from the orphanage. Have you seen anything about an adoption?"

Roger bent over and moved a box. "Not much. I tried to find out a bit about it and thought I'd found someone related to the Balandin family, but it turned out she was just a cousin and didn't know anything about them."

His cagey actions and reply aroused suspicion, and Lucas studied his expression when Roger rose without meeting their gazes. "Was that person you found Anna Martin?"

"Yeah. So what? It was a dead end."

"She was murdered by a burglar."

Roger's eyes widened and unease flickered in his gaze. "You're kidding. Any idea who killed her?"

"Not yet. You weren't looking for anything specific that Mr. Harris might have found?"

Roger finally stared at him and lifted a brow. "Like what?"

"You tell me."

"I got nothing to say. It's all old history. Look, I got a client coming any minute, and the last thing I need is to be found talking to cops. Scram, why don't you?"

Lucas shrugged and handed him a card. "If you think of anything, give me a call."

Roger didn't look at the card but stuffed it into his shirt pocket. "Sure."

Lucas and Vince headed for the exit. "He knows more than he's saying," Lucas said when they got outside. "I'll bet he ran across something in the files about the egg, and he's been curious ever since. I suspect his lead to Anna Martin alerted the Russians to her connection to the Balandin family, so they decided to search her house. Unfortunately, she walked in on them."

Lucas glanced at his watch. "It's been long enough that Grace's daughter should be back. Let's go see if she's seen anything of interest in the files."

The men drove back to Grace's house, and a white sedan was parked in the drive. They went to the front door and rang the bell.

Grace answered the door. "I was just telling Jessie about your questions. She's happy to talk to you about the files. Come with me."

She led them through the entry to the living room, where a woman in her late twenties sat with a box at her feet. Papers were strewn on her lap and across the sofa. She looked a lot like her mother with dark curls and a heart-shaped face.

She looked up with a smile when she heard them enter. "Mom told me about your questions, and I was pulling some papers for you. Have a seat and we can talk about it." The men settled on chairs across from her, and she pulled out a wrinkled paper. "I had these in my car, so the burglar didn't get them. It was an interesting time back then. My great-grandmother Natalie was a nurse at a small orphanage in Savannah. There are so many heartbreaking stories."

"How long did your great-grandmother work there?"

"Twenty years or so?" She glanced at her mother for confirmation, and Grace nodded. "My great-grandfather died when my grandma was two, and my great-grandmother went to work there for her kids. There were four of them."

Lucas leaned forward. "We're particularly interested in twin girls who were left at the orphanage about seventy years ago. Last name of Balandin."

"I read something about that adoption. It's sad, really. Some of the information is missing. Uncle Roger has some of the boxes from back then so I don't have the full story, but there's an old diary of Granny's that talked about a Russian girl who came in. She'd been working at one of the big plantations and had gotten pregnant. No one realized it, and she delivered twin girls in an old smokehouse. Another employee told her about the orphanage, and she brought the babies there. Granny was working that day and said it broke her heart at how much the mother wanted to keep them." She shook her head. "So sad."

It sounded right. "Can I see the diary?"

"Here it is." She handed over an old leather journal. "It's marked with the yellow sticky note."

Lucas flipped to the page and read the entry. "Your granny said she wished she could adopt the girls to keep them together. So she knew they'd have to be split up."

Jessie nodded. "On the next page, Granny mentions the mother left some belongings to help the girls find each other. An old egg and a pendant. I never found anything like that, though."

Lucas read the entry, then shut the diary and handed it back. "No idea who adopted the babies? And would you mind copying the pages that mention the twins and the egg?"

"I'll make a copy before you leave." Jessie rose. "I'm not sure how you even figured out Granny's name. You've got more information than we do about that."

No help there, but it confirmed they were on the right track. Lucas stood. "You've been very helpful." He handed her a card. "If you find out anything else, please call me."

Carly would be very interested to hear about the pendant. And to read those pages.

———

The chaos in the house drove Carly to the backyard, where the aroma of the sea breeze blew away the stench of dust and old wood. She unfolded Noah's play yard and placed him inside. He stared at the moss blowing from the limbs of the live oak tree and kicked his feet. "Time for some exercise, little man."

He was growing so fast. It pained her that he would never

know his father. Eric wouldn't even be a dim memory. There would be no pictures of him holding his son as a baby. All of that had been erased by his death.

She and Lucas hadn't talked about Eric's death in several days. The murder of Anna Martin and the break-in here had pushed away that concern, but she was more and more convinced the same man had targeted her husband and deprived Noah of a father.

She swiped on her Kindle, and it opened to the middle of *Anna Karenina*. Reading the Russian novel had fired her imagination, and she was beginning to get a better idea of the book she wanted to write. Her phone rang, and she winced when she saw Opal's picture on the screen. Her mother-in-law called every two weeks or so with a request to see Noah, and Carly had to sit through a visit, enduring veiled and constant criticism. She forced a smile before she answered the phone. "Good morning, Opal."

"I'm going to be in Beaufort today and wondered if I could stop by and see the baby." Opal's usual tone was saccharine sweet with claws masked. Today it was more like the bite of a lemon.

"We'll be around, but the place is chaotic since the renovation on Gram's house started. We can sit out in the yard to get away from it, though."

"Renovation? You said nothing about that the last time I was there."

"It was a decision Gram hadn't mentioned to me until it was nearly ready to start."

"I see. Well, I'll see you in about an hour."

"Okay, see you then."

A movement caught her eye, and she smiled when she saw Gram exit the back door and head her way. The tinkle of Gram's bracelets announced her arrival. "There you are." Gram corralled her billowing red skirt and bent over the play yard to smile at Noah. "Hello, little man. Are you glad to see your grammy?"

Noah kicked and cooed at the attention.

"You can get him out if you want. I think he's glad to see you," Carly said.

Gram lifted him out and settled on the grass with the baby on her lap. He promptly tried to grab her bracelet but couldn't make his fingers work well enough, so she put a bangle in his palm. "The racket inside is enough to make anyone crazy. They are breaking for lunch now, though."

"Would you mind watching him a minute? I want to do something with my hair. Opal is coming."

Gram wrinkled her nose. "Mercy, that's all we need today." She let Noah clench her finger. "I'll watch the little man."

The hammering and commotion had ceased, and Carly was glad for the reprieve when she stepped inside and went through the debris to the stairs.

She moved to a mirror and put her hair in a ponytail before turning to the door. A slight sound caught her attention. The shifting or shuffling on the floor came again, but she couldn't make out the direction of the noise. And there shouldn't be anyone here to be moving around. Her sisters hadn't come back from their run to urgent care, and Isabelle had gone to the library, where she would jump on the stream for class. The workers were on lunch break, so she had to be the only one in here.

Goose bumps rippled down her back, and she poked her head out of the door. "Anyone there?" Everything in her wanted to rush for the stairs and get out of here, but she told herself she was overreacting.

She whirled and looked around her bedroom. The closet door stood open slightly, and she knew she'd closed it after getting dressed this morning. She backed away and lifted her phone to call Lucas as she ran down the steps.

It was probably just the house shifting during the reno. She rejoined her grandmother and Noah, and Gram frowned. "Carly Ann, your expression looks like you ate a pickle."

Carly forced a smile. "Just weird noises in the house."

A shout for help came from the house, and Carly turned and ran back the way she'd come. She rushed inside to find Ryan on the phone calling for an ambulance. "What's happened?" she asked when he ended the call.

"One of my workers has been stabbed."

"A construction accident?"

He shook his head, his eyes grim. "He was in your closet, Carly. There was no good reason for him to be up there. We aren't working on anything on the other floors yet. Someone knifed him up there."

She gasped and took a step back. Another intruder?

EIGHTEEN

Seeing flashing red lights on his own street wasn't something Lucas would ever get used to—and this was the second time in a week it had happened. The ambulance had parked in the driveway, and two police cars were in the yard. He spotted Ryan with his construction workers talking to an officer by the porch.

Where were Carly and Noah? Lucas got out and ran toward the porch. One of the other officers spotted him and motioned him over. Lucas reluctantly switched directions and went to speak to him.

"What do we have?" Lucas knew the basics. A worker had been found bludgeoned and stabbed in the house.

"Vic is Charlie Kostin. He works for your brother."

"What's his condition?"

"Team is working on him, but it doesn't look good. Knife hit his liver. They're trying to stabilize him before transport."

"Who found him?"

"Your brother. He was in the closet of Carly's bedroom."

"What was he doing there?"

The officer shrugged. "Your guess is as good as mine."

"Where's Carly? And is everyone okay?"

"She's in the kitchen. No one else is injured."

Lucas thanked him and started for the porch again when his brother called his name. He turned to find Ryan coming his way. His wide eyes and pinched mouth showed his worry.

"Do you know what happened here?" Lucas asked him. "What was Kostin doing upstairs in Carly's room?"

"We were on lunch break. No one should have been inside. I didn't notice him missing until we started working. His truck was still here, so I started to search for him and heard a moan. He's in bad shape."

Lucas winced at the thought of Carly being faced with something like that. "How long has he worked for you?"

"He's a new hire. Started this morning."

Kostin. "Russian?"

"Maybe Russian heritage. He's American, though. He claimed to be born in New York and worked construction there for some years. Recently moved here. He had several job offers, but I got him."

He could have been searching for the egg.

Lucas didn't want to jump to conclusions, but it made sense. Maybe Carly would have noticed something she'd only tell him. "I'm going to go find Carly."

"She's on the back deck with Mary and Noah. Her sisters aren't here."

Lucas nodded and headed around the side of the house to the backyard. Carly and Mary sat on a double swing with an overhead canopy. Noah slept on Mary's shoulder.

Carly spotted him, and the anxiety in her face intensified. She stood and rushed toward him. "I was hoping you'd come. I called and left a message on your phone." She made a move as if to fall against his chest, then caught herself and clenched her hands in front of her. Her slim shoulders trembled, and she tightened the ponytail on her head.

He stifled the inclination to embrace her. "Vince told me there'd been an incident here, so I came right away. Did you see anything?"

She shook her head. "I tried to stay out of the way of the workers. I went to my room to touch up my hair because Opal is coming. I heard some noises and got spooked. If I'd looked around, maybe he wouldn't be in such bad shape."

"Or maybe you would have been attacked instead."

A decision began to harden in his mind. Ryan might not like it, but it seemed the only solution. Lucas steered her toward her grandmother because he suspected Mary would be the one to make the final call on what he had planned.

Mary appeared as serene as ever, though an unusual frown line creased her brow. Her updo had loosened from its crystal clips, and several white strands of hair trailed along her jawline. "Now that you're here, maybe Carly will quit worrying."

Carly sighed. "Gram, someone attacked the man. It could be you next. Or one of the girls. There have been too many intrusions into the house. We're not safe."

"What's going on here?"

Lucas turned behind him to see Opal Harris walking toward them across the grass. Eric had resembled her with her blue eyes and blonde hair. Her focus went to Mary holding Noah.

Mary smiled. "There's your grammy, Noah." She handed him to Opal when she reached the group.

With the baby in her arms, Opal again demanded to know

the cause of the police presence and chaos, so Carly explained. Opal's eyes widened at the news of the attack. "You and Noah should come stay with me."

"I can't do that. My sisters are here and I need to help oversee the renovation," Carly said.

"You're putting my grandson in danger. It's very foolhardy. Eric would insist on keeping him safe."

"I totally agree," Lucas said. "I have a solution." He turned to look at the Bennett house soaring above the trees surrounding it. "We have plenty of room in our house for all of you. Until we know things are safe, I want you all to move in."

"We couldn't impose like that," Carly said immediately.

"It's not an imposition. You'll be close enough to oversee what's going on over here, but you'll be away from any intrusion into the house."

"Out of the question," Opal said. "Eric would want you at my house."

Carly turned toward her. "You don't have enough room for all of us, Opal. And you're too far away for us to oversee things."

Lucas wasn't deluding himself over how difficult it would be to have a houseful of women in their all-male household. Neither of them had ever lived with a woman other than their mother. He'd seen enough of the Tucker girls growing up— and enough of their behavior lately—to realize histrionics were likely to be a daily occurrence.

But he couldn't stand back and let anything happen to them. Someone was very determined to get hold of that egg. The only way to thwart him was to get to the bottom of all of this.

Mary put her hands on her hips. "Lucas is right, Carly Ann. Thank you for your generosity. We're happy to accept."

Carly shot a glance at her grandmother, and her shoulders slumped. "Okay, but it won't be easy. For anyone."

An awkward silence ensued after Mary rose and turned toward the house. "I'm going to go pack. I'll tell your sisters to do the same. Enjoy your visit with Noah and Carly, Opal."

Lucas saw the longing in Carly's gaze as she stared after her grandmother. "You'd better pack too, Carly. I'll sit here with Opal and Noah."

Carly's smile lit her eyes with relief. "It shouldn't take too long." She headed for the house behind Mary.

Opal narrowed her eyes his direction. "I should warn you about Carly. She's not good wife material."

Lucas stared at her. "I'm merely protecting her, Opal. You should try doing that for once instead of constantly criticizing her."

Red bloomed in her cheeks. "I can see she's already caught you, Lucas." She lifted her chin. "I'm going to take Noah for a walk around the block. You don't have to babysit me. I know better than Carly how to care for a baby."

He watched her stalk around the end of the house. No wonder Carly wanted to escape.

His phone dinged with a message from Carly. *I want to go see Kelly tomorrow. If she knows what's going on here, maybe she can get some traction on Eric's death too. I am more and more convinced it all has to do with the same man or group.*

He hadn't thought much about Eric's death this week with the urgent situations slamming into them daily, but she wasn't wrong.

He texted back. *I'll go with you. In the meantime, let's get things packed up and moved over.*

———

The pandemonium was worse than Carly had expected.

It wasn't her sisters—when they got back from a long wait at urgent care, they were more than thrilled at the thought of being out of the chaos of the house remodel. It would allow Ryan and his team to attack the house renovation at one time instead of in pieces too. And maybe it would all be done sooner.

The problem was her own emotions. She cared too much about what Lucas thought. She'd found herself thinking about him in the oddest moments. There was danger in that direction. Her marriage hadn't been the happiest of years for her. Or for Eric. She needed to focus on raising Noah.

At least that was what she usually told herself. Being around Lucas all the time would be way too much distraction for her peace of mind.

But there was no stopping it now. Nearly all their personal belongings had been moved over. While she answered the police's questions one more time, Lucas had Ryan's workers help toss things into baskets and suitcases and haul them to his house. By dinnertime they were all in suites upstairs.

And his home was gorgeous. She'd never seen the full renovation, and the quality of every room was a marvel. Her suite was huge, and the bathroom had a big soaking tub plus a walk-in shower. The tile work was beautiful, and she suspected no one had used this bathroom since the work was done. Her feet sank into the thick oatmeal-colored carpet, and the bedding matched with its neutral colors. The windows looked out on the bay, and she paused a moment to admire the view.

She made sure Noah was sleeping in the crib in the corner, then grabbed the monitor and exited into the hall. She closed the door behind her and headed for the stairs. From the top of the staircase, she could hear her sisters chattering about the house. For the first time since they'd come, they sounded happy and excited. Maybe this could be a new beginning for them. Being in this beautifully redone historic home, maybe they finally saw Gram's vision.

They were clustered around a baby grand piano in the music room. Isabelle's hands rested on the keys, but she hadn't started playing. Amelia and Emily sat on a sofa in a seating area framed by a plush rug. Gram was in a high-back chair reading a book. Behind the sofa was a wall of bookcases. Where the quarter-sawn oak floors could be seen, they gleamed with a fresh refinishing.

Carly lifted her phone and snapped a quick picture of the peaceful, happy family. It was a scene that might not come again soon.

Carly moved to the piano. "Everyone settled?"

Isabelle nodded. "Do you think Lucas would mind if I play the piano?"

"I can answer that." Lucas's deep voice spoke from the entrance into the room. "No one has played it since our mom died, but we've kept it tuned. I'd love to hear it again."

Carly shot him a grateful smile and noticed he'd showered and changed. His dark hair still looked damp, and he wore shorts and a tee. His feet were bare, which made him somehow more approachable and appealing. Major was on his heels. The golden retriever sniffed the air, and she knew he scented Pepper sleeping on Isabelle's lap.

It was going to be a full household. Did Ryan even know yet?

Isabelle's fingers moved into position on the piano. "Any favorites?"

"Anything you'd like," Lucas said.

That was a dangerous statement. Carly expected her sister to pound out a rock song, but instead "Brahms' Lullaby" rippled from her fingers.

Lucas smiled and came to the piano. "My mom used to play that every night. You play beautifully. How long have you been taking lessons?"

"Since I was three. I love the piano."

Carly watched the interaction between her little sister and Lucas. She had a lot of regret that she had missed Isabelle's true nature in her first introduction to her. The girl had a lot of heart.

Major tensed when he spotted the cat, but Lucas set his hand on the dog's red head. "Stay."

"Should we keep Pepper upstairs?"

"Major will get used to him." Lucas released the dog, and Major went to sniff at Pepper, who hissed and assumed attack-mode posture with his back up and his tail whipping. The dog yelped and slunk back against Lucas's leg. "Pepper showed him who was boss."

Isabelle finished the song and moved on to another classical piece. Noah made waking sounds through the monitor, and Carly turned toward the door.

Lucas stopped her. "I'll get him. Come, Major."

The dog gave a last soulful glance toward Pepper and

followed Lucas. It felt wrong to Carly for someone else to answer Noah's cry, but she forced herself to stay put.

She walked over to join the rest of the family in the seating area. "Everyone settled?"

"My room is gorgeous," Amelia said. "The designer knew what they were doing. I hope our house turns out this beautifully."

Emily gave an annoyed toss of her hair. "Are you saying you don't think I'll know how to do it this well?"

"You usually do more modern spaces," Amelia said. "Think you can rein that in and decorate with restraint and elegance?"

Carly wanted to hold her hands over her ears and scream at them to stop. Did they have to bicker all the time? "Emily has wonderful taste. She's trained in every style of design. We're lucky to have her."

Emily straightened and her eyes widened. "Thank you, Carly. I'll do my best."

Carly had elevated the warmth between them, and she prayed her sisters were beginning to thaw.

NINETEEN

He was getting good at this baby stuff.

Lucas hadn't let Noah's head slip even a little bit. He patted the tiny bottom on his chest, and the baby's head bobbed up off his shoulder to look around. Noah started making those noises again that Carly called coos. There was no denying the kid was cute.

He glanced around the room, which was neat and orderly. Carly had put everything away. Had she realized he'd given her the best room up here? He and Ryan had identical masters on the first floor, and the second floor held another five suites. Each had its own bathroom, but this room was the upstairs master with its spacious bedroom and luxurious bathroom.

Once her sisters saw it, the bickering would probably begin.

He carried the baby out into the hall and down the staircase. Carly exited the music room, and he jerked his head for her to follow him into the kitchen. He'd like to stay away from her sisters as much as possible, though Isabelle wasn't like the others. She seemed to have lost her initial hostility and teenage angst. Maybe the extreme circumstances with her father had brought it all out.

"Hello, sweet thing," Carly said.

"You talking to me or Noah?" He regretted the joke as soon as he said it. Stupid thing to say.

Red flared in her cheeks, but she managed an uncertain smile. "Um, has anyone ever called you a sweet thing?"

"No, as a matter of fact, they haven't. I was joking, of course." Like it could have been anything else.

"Anything new on the investigation?"

Good idea of hers to change the subject. "The doctors don't think Kostin will make it."

She winced, and tears filled her eyes. "I was afraid of that."

"Ryan just hired him. Honestly, Carly, I suspect he might have been part of the group trying to find the egg."

"I've wondered if I should call the media and release the news about the egg and that it's in a safe place. It might stop the attacks."

"Or intensify them. What if someone kidnapped a family member—even Noah here—and demanded you give them the egg in order to have them returned unharmed? I don't think releasing the full information would work. You're safe here."

"Unless they decide to up the ante and do what you just described anyway."

That was Lucas's worst fear, and it could happen. He had to track down the culprits and get them in jail before they could harm Carly or her family. "I have some news. I talked to the family of the nurse who is mentioned in the letter from the orphanage. Her diary indicates the mom was from Russia and gave both girls something to help them find each other—an egg and a pendant. Sound familiar? The great-granddaughter copied some pages from Nurse Adams's diary as well as a picture just like the one in the attic. I'll get them for you."

Carly held her hand to her mouth, and her eyes went wide. "That's amazing. So the items were intentionally split up as we thought. We need to find out what happened to Gram's twin. I about forgot to tell you what happened today. One of Ryan's workers found a family tree hidden in a wall they tore down. It was an illustration of the Padgett family tree, and it mentioned Gram's twin. And it gave her adopted name: Elizabeth Durham!"

His pulse kicked. "That's huge news! We might be able to track her down."

"I hoped it would be the key." She moved closer and stroked her son's cheek. "I'm still sorry about Charlie Kostin. I've been praying for him. Maybe he'll make it yet."

"You prayed for him?"

She nodded. "It's so hard to discern God's will, isn't it? When Eric died, I thought it was punishment for all the ways I'd failed as a wife. I thought maybe God took him to glory to save him decades of being married to me."

Lucas frowned. "That's crazy talk. You couldn't have been such a terrible wife."

"I don't know." She broke eye contact with him and lifted Noah from his shoulder. "We'd started fighting all the time. It was like living with a stranger toward the end. I know he wasn't happy."

With Carly so close, her scent wafted to him—something flowery and light. He missed the weight of the baby on his chest almost instantly.

Noah nestled against her, and she kissed the top of his downy head. "I think we humans are constantly searching for unconditional love, and I'm beginning to think it's a fool's hope. Everything is conditional. We only keep our jobs if we perform them well. If we fail at marriage, we get divorced. It's the same kind of thing. We're never going to make someone happy all the time."

He realized he'd done a 180-degree turn on his initial view of her. "Maybe it was a part of learning to live together and compromise with each other. It's impossible to think there's never conflict in a marriage. You learn to work through it."

Her gaze met his again. "Says the man who's never been married."

He grinned. "In my line of work, I see a lot of good marriages and a lot of bad marriages. Marriage takes work, and I've never had the time to put into it. You can't go off to work and assume the relationship will roll along without maintenance."

"We went our own way so much of the time. He wasn't interested in my flea market business, and even when he'd come with me on the weekend, he spent most of his time in the hotel watching TV or wandering the town where we stayed. And I couldn't be part of his work. He wasn't allowed to talk about cases or anything like that. So I was shut out of what transpired in his everyday world."

More reinforcement of how difficult it was for a police officer to make marriage work. Maybe it hadn't been Eric's fault. Lucas didn't believe it was Carly's fault either. Maybe it was no one's fault but the circumstances.

———

After the house was quiet and everyone was sleeping, Carly studied the short sentences on the copy Lucas had gotten from the Adams family.

A Russian girl came to the orphanage today. Sofia Balandin had been working as a kitchen worker at one of the many plantations. She spoke English very well and said she'd been in the Savannah area for five years, ever since she emigrated with her parents from Russia. She had twin girls with her and said she'd delivered them in a smokehouse. Another employee told her about our orphanage, and she had to give them up or lose her position. She cried and it broke my heart to see her pain. She left the picture and some trinkets for the babies. I must find adoptive parents.

The bare-bones account fired Carly's imagination. While no one judged her when she was pregnant with Noah, she understood the challenges of being a single mom. It had to have been overwhelming to a young immigrant girl with little money and few resources in 1955.

The events unfurled in her mind like scenes from a movie. Carly suspected Sofia had to have known the egg and the surprise inside were valuable, though back in the fifties, the value wouldn't have been anywhere near what it was today. The way she'd disguised the egg with red paint indicated that she had tried to protect it.

Gram would love to read a story about her birth, even if it was mostly fiction. Before Carly could reconsider, she opened her laptop and called up her Scrivener app. She'd sketched out a couple of scenes before, but not like this. The words poured out in a torrent that caught her up and swept her away with it.

Sofia Balandin hid behind some flour sacks and prayed the distant laughter from the new episode of *I Love Lucy* had masked her movement to the pantry. Her back had been a misery most of the day. The room was airless and so hot she struggled to breathe. Outside in the dark, Andrew, the plantation owner's son, moved through the downstairs whispering her name.

Sofia had been foolish enough to answer his call once nearly eight months ago, and she'd paid for it dearly. She should have told Mrs. Larson about the attack, but she'd been certain she would take the blame, not Andrew.

Her hand drifted to her swelling belly. The *ditya* would be born soon, and what was she to do? She'd seen Mrs. Larson eyeing her dress earlier in the day and had wondered if she would guess her condition. If she did, Sofia would be thrown out. She couldn't go home, not with Mama gone. Papa would kill her. His Russian pride would never be able to handle having an unwed, pregnant daughter. He had his own struggles with the need to hide from the KGB.

When the echo of Andrew's whispers faded, she eased out from behind the flour sacks and tiptoed in her bare feet to the door. What was she to do? She entered the kitchen and glanced around. The sleek new Formica counters gleamed in the moonlight streaming through the windows.

"Sofia." The whisper was soft but clearly Angelica, not Andrew.

The pain in Sofia's back intensified, and she moved toward the sound of her friend's voice. She found Angelica, her hair in pin curls, by the back door. "Did you see him leave?"

"Yes, he's gone. I saw him go to his bedroom and shut it. Did he catch you?"

"No." A groan emerged from Sofia's throat, and she doubled over with the pain.

"Sofia, what's wrong?"

"My back," Sofia whispered.

"Oh, Sofia, it might be the baby. My mother always said her back pain was the worst." Angelica supported her and practically carried her out the door, taking care not to let the screen slam. "The smokehouse will muffle your cries. You mustn't let Mrs. Larson know you're pregnant."

A circle of pain encased Sofia's middle and settled in her back. It was getting worse. Was this really the *ditya*? And what was she to do once she delivered? Maybe she should have spoken with Andrew and let him know she was carrying his child. She'd been fearful to do that in case he told his mother and she ended up standing outside the Savannah mansion with nowhere to go. Her employers would do everything in their power to make sure the story of Andrew's behavior didn't get out into the city's society.

Angelica got her inside the smokehouse and shut the door behind them. She bustled around finding old flour sacks to cushion the hard stone floor for Sofia. The *ditya* was coming.

Hours later, Sofia held not one but two babes, both girls. They were so beautiful, though tiny. A month early. She didn't know whether to pray they would survive or beg for God to take this problem from her hands. Tears blurred her vision, and she wanted only to sleep and wake up to find this had been a dream—a nightmare so overwhelming couldn't be true, could it?

Angelica leaned against the stone wall and stared down

at Sofia. Her friend was five years older and stout enough around the middle that Andrew paid her no mind. She'd been so kind to Sofia, but even she couldn't solve this problem.

Sofia closed her burning eyes. "I don't know what I will do."

"There's an orphanage in Savannah not far from here. I'm going to borrow a truck and take you there. We might be missed, but the punishment won't be nearly as severe as if they find you with the babes."

Sofia opened her eyes. "You are a good friend, Angelica. I have no choice. Could you fetch my knapsack? I wish to leave the girls small mementos."

"I will be right back with your knapsack and the pickup."

She hadn't been able to bring herself to sell the egg and the surprise, knowing she would get only a few meals from their disposal. But her girls might uncover their Russian heritage through the items. Maybe someday they would be reunited.

It was Sofia's greatest prayer.

Carly blinked and realized it was after two. She closed her laptop and stretched out on the bed, but pieces of the story filtered into her dreams all the way to morning.

TWENTY

Carly's pulse jumped when Lucas parked outside Kelly's condo, and she wasn't sure why she was nervous. Noah had slept the whole way, but he stirred when she lifted him from his car seat. Lucas grabbed the diaper bag and the baby gift, and they went to the door with Carly's heart trying to jump out of her chest.

"You okay?" he asked. "You seemed quiet on the drive here."

She marshaled her thoughts. "I can't figure out why Kelly acted like she didn't want us to come. She only agreed when I told her I had a gift for the baby. I always thought I had a good relationship with her."

"Hmm, that is strange."

"It made me wonder if she knows something about Eric's death that she doesn't want to share yet. Maybe they're close to an arrest, and she doesn't want to discuss it."

"I think I would have heard from Robinson if that were true." He shifted the gift to his other hand and knocked on the door.

It took a few seconds for the door to open. "Good morning." Kelly stepped out of the way to allow them to enter, but she didn't smile and didn't meet Carly's gaze. The small entry opened to a hall that veered right into a tiny kitchen connected to a living room or left into the bedroom area.

Kelly led Carly and Lucas into the living room, where a candle filled the air with its apple scent. She gestured to the sectional sofa. "Have a seat. Caroline is asleep, and I'm not sure she'll awaken before you leave."

Her auburn hair curled around her head in a new shorter style, and she wore a trace of makeup that enhanced her green eyes. Her smile finally emerged, but was it forced or was it Carly's imagination? And why would she sound hopeful that they wouldn't get a chance to see the baby? It was all very strange.

Noah stirred and opened his eyes. His yawn turned into a squeak, and Carly settled him on her lap with his face turned toward Kelly. She put his plastic keys in his hand, and he clutched them in his tiny fingers.

"He's darling," Kelly said.

"Thank you. He's such a good baby." Carly leaned forward. "A lot of things have happened this past week." She launched into the break-ins and the murders, and Kelly's eyes widened as Carly laid out the events one by one. "I am more convinced than ever that Eric was killed by someone searching for something. Have you heard how the investigation is going? There might be evidence they've uncovered that would help with the new murders as well."

Kelly's frown deepened. "I haven't talked to anyone at the station. Honestly, I've tried to stay out of it. I made the decision not to go back. My hours can be so unpredictable, and as a single mom, it's hard to find day care at odd times. I have enough money for a few more weeks, but I'm looking around for another job."

Carly felt deflated. She'd been so sure Kelly would want to help find Eric's killer.

"Don't worry about it, Kelly," Lucas said. "We'll swing by and talk to Chief Robinson when we leave here."

"I'm sorry I'm not more help." Kelly crossed her arms over her chest and tipped up her chin. "Having a baby changes everything."

"It does," Carly said. "You have to do what's best for Caroline. When another person depends on you, your perspective changes."

Kelly bit her lip and glanced at her watch. Carly couldn't figure out why she was so nervous and on guard. It didn't make sense. She took the NeverMore Books gift bag from Lucas's lap and handed it to Kelly. "This is for Caroline."

"It's very nice of you." Kelly opened the bag and pulled out three picture books.

She stared at the top one, *I Prayed for You,* and her lips began to tremble. "Th-thank you."

Was she crying? Carly was mystified by Kelly's reaction. She shuffled Noah around and realized he'd lost his toy somewhere. She patted the cushions and glanced around on the floor. "Do you see Noah's key ring?"

Lucas joined in on the search, but Kelly jumped to her feet. "I think I hear Caroline." She rushed out of the room like she couldn't wait to get away from them.

Carly stood in case the rattle was hidden in the folds of her tee or shorts, but nothing dropped out.

"Maybe it fell under the sofa." Lucas dropped to his hands and knees and ran his arm under the brown tweed furniture. "I think I got it." He pulled back his hand, but instead of a toy, he had a real key ring. "That's not it."

He laid the keys on the coffee table, and Carly gasped when she recognized the key ring. It held the keys to the lake cottage she and Eric owned. He claimed to have lost them when he was fishing with his buddies the weekend before he died, and Carly hadn't found them when she moved into Gram's. Yet here they were—at Kelly's.

Kelly returned with baby Caroline in her arms. The four-month-old had a tuft of blonde hair that stood straight up. Her big blue eyes fastened on Carly, and she gave a gummy smile. Carly smiled back, but her focus went to the baby's soft blonde fuzz.

Eric had been blond. And his keys had been under Kelly's sofa. Without stopping to think, Carly reached over and grabbed the keys from the table. She dangled them from her finger. "Kelly, Eric's missing keys were under your sofa."

Kelly went white, then red, and she swallowed. "I-I . . ." Her voice trailed off, and she looked panicked.

"Is Eric your baby's father?" Carly heard her own words from a far-off place. This couldn't be happening. Any second Kelly would laugh at her question, and they'd all be friends again.

Kelly pressed her lips together before she gave a shaky nod. "I never wanted you to know, but maybe it's best. I never intended to hurt you."

Carly's ears roared and she felt faint. She barely noticed Lucas taking her upper arm and leading her to the sofa. He plucked Noah from her hands and pushed her head between her legs. "Breathe."

She wasn't sure she could breathe past the pain in her chest. Her marriage had been totally over, and she hadn't even been aware of it.

———

Something about Kelly had been bugging Lucas through the entire visit.

While Carly recovered from the unwelcome realization that her husband had been unfaithful, Lucas juggled the baby while he tried to figure out what was bothering him. He mentally ticked off what he saw in the condo. Small but comfortable. New furniture, the kitchen looked remodeled, and the carpet smelled like it had just come from the factory too. Through the open door beside the sixty-inch television, he could see into the master bedroom. The carpet in there matched the carpet out here, and the bed and bedding looked freshly purchased too. And through the glass door to the small patio on the other side of the TV, he saw new outdoor furniture. All the items had to have cost a fortune.

Kelly was on maternity leave and didn't plan to go back. Where had she gotten the money for all the renovations? While she'd get maternity pay for part of the time, it wasn't enough for her to live on once she quit. Yet she hadn't seemed overly concerned about finances.

Carly lifted her head, and her ashen face had begun to regain its color. He touched the top of her dark hair. "You okay?"

She nodded and reached for the baby. "I need to feed him."

Kelly stood awkwardly by the dining table with her baby in her arms. "You can use my bedroom. There's a comfortable rocker in there."

Carly usually covered herself with a thin blanket and stayed put, but she rose and went into the other room. Lucas thought she needed some time alone to gather her composure. Kelly's face didn't have much more color than Carly's, but Lucas didn't feel sorry for her. However, he did want to know where she'd gotten the money. He waited to speak until Carly took the baby into the bedroom with her and closed the door behind them.

Kelly's baby was cute, though not as cute as Noah. That little mite was beginning to work his way into Lucas's heart. He took a couple of steps closer to Kelly and gestured around the space. "Looks like you've been doing some remodeling. New carpet, new kitchen." As he continued to name the new items he saw, her cheeks flushed and she looked away from his stare, which was more confirmation to him that something didn't pass the sniff test.

"A little bit."

"You have a sudden windfall?"

She seemed scared and pressed her lips against the baby's hair. "That's none of your business."

"True enough, but something about all this doesn't feel right. Let's talk a minute about what's going on." He didn't want to tell her about the egg, but maybe dangling some intrigue would make something slip. "We suspect there are valuables with the items left by Mary Tucker's mother. You were seeing Eric. Did he mention finding anything of value?"

She licked her lips and shook her head, but her gaze didn't meet his. She was lying.

"I think he did, Kelly. Maybe he even found it and gave it to you to help with baby expenses. He knew you were expecting, didn't he?"

"He was mad about it. They said—" Her face went white and she shut her mouth.

"Who said what?"

"Nothing. It doesn't matter."

The door opened, and Carly returned with Noah. His blue eyes were drowsy.

"I'm going to get to the bottom of this," Lucas said to Kelly. "It would go easier for you if you told the truth."

She looked away and said nothing, but he could sniff out her fear and guilt. There was a lot Eric's partner wasn't saying. Kelly was in a position to explain most of what had been going on with him in the last few months before his death, and Lucas intended to get it out of her.

He gestured to the furniture. "All this cost money. So does staying home with your baby. Where did that money come from? You might as well tell me. Your bank records will reveal the truth."

Tears flooded her green eyes. "He gave Eric money to let them have a look at the things Carly inherited from her great-grandmother."

"Who is 'he'?" he demanded.

Her lips quivered and she swallowed, then shook her head. "I don't know."

"How much money are we talking about?" Carly asked.

Kelly pressed her lips against her baby's head. "A hundred thousand dollars."

Lucas exchanged a long glance with Carly. That much money meant the mysterious *he* knew about the egg. Nothing else in the attic could warrant that much.

Carly shifted the sleepy baby to her other arm. "Eric let them rummage around in my workshop?"

Kelly shook her head. "He changed his mind two days before he died."

"And *he* killed Eric?" Lucas asked.

"I don't know for sure, but it makes sense."

"Has *he* been in contact with you since then?"

"I haven't answered calls from any unknown numbers. I'm afraid."

Lucas didn't offer Kelly any reassurance. When you lay down with dogs, you got up with fleas.

He grabbed the diaper bag and followed Carly to the door. Neither of the women spoke as they made their departure from the condo. This was a blow Carly hadn't been prepared for, and likely Kelly hadn't imagined it would all come out. And it wouldn't have if Lucas hadn't found those keys.

His hand slid into his pocket. The keys. Could there be something in the cottage that would help them figure this out?

He waited until they were out in the sunshine. Once Carly got Noah into his car seat and came around to slide into the passenger seat, he pulled out the keys and handed them to her. "Where is the cottage?"

"Not far from here. Lake Moultrie." Her brown eyes narrowed. "Are you thinking what I'm thinking?"

He started the engine and put the truck in Drive. "Yep. It's not far out of our way. Let's swing by there and see what we can find. You haven't been there since Eric died?"

She shook her head. "I couldn't find the keys. I meant to have the locks changed, but it had been Eric's bachelor pad, and it was more of a hangout for him and his fishing buddies. I never felt it was my space."

No wonder they'd had a struggling marriage. So many parts of their lives unshared. What had Eric been thinking? Maybe that was the problem—he hadn't been thinking of *them*. Only of himself as a single guy. Lucas had seen that problem often enough in his buddies. If he was honest, it might even be the reason he'd steered away from a serious relationship. He knew a good marriage was hard work, and he wasn't sure he had the focus to pull it off.

He drove out of town for now, but he planned to return to find out more. Soon.

TWENTY-ONE

The cottage had never looked welcoming to Carly. It was a low-slung ranch with fading white paint and no landscaping to soften the block foundation. A half-dead palm tree cast a bit of shade over the spotty grass in the front yard. In the distance came the rumble of boats out on the lake.

Carly grimaced as she approached the stoop with Noah in her arms. Lucas had the key out, and he unlocked the door. Stale air rushed to greet them when she stepped into the small foyer off the living/dining room that opened into the kitchen.

She noticed white cabinets lining the kitchen wall and frowned. "The last time I was here, the cabinets were still worn pine."

Lucas walked into the main area and glanced around. "When was that?"

There was something sad about walking through these rooms Eric had loved and realizing he'd never again sit on that worn sofa with his boots propped on the chipped coffee table. He'd never build a fire in the blackened fireplace or dart out the back door with his fishing pole in hand to head to the lake, which could be glimpsed through the trees lining the weedy yard.

It was all gone. The grief she'd felt had been replaced by a huge sense of betrayal.

"Carly?"

She looked up to realize Lucas had been talking to her. "Sorry. What did you say?"

"When was the last time you were here?"

"Um, about six months before Eric died. So it's probably been about a year." She walked through the tiny space to the kitchen. Gleaming white paint covered the pine cabinets, and new brass pulls and handles had replaced the old wooden knobs. The Formica counter in a fresh blue color was new too.

"He never mentioned he was giving the kitchen an update."

"Maybe he didn't want to tell you he was spending money on the cottage when you disliked it."

That didn't sit well with her. "I wouldn't have argued against it. Eric spent a lot of time here. He never once complained about the state of the place." She glanced around. "Though they are small, inexpensive updates. Paint and a new counter don't cost much." The worst part of it wasn't the money—it was that he'd most likely done it to make Kelly happy.

Dread congealed in her belly as she turned and went to the main bedroom. She yanked open the drawers in the chest, and just as she'd feared, two of the drawers held female underwear and tees.

They weren't hers.

Lucas's broad shoulders loomed in the doorway, but he said nothing as she examined the rest of the room. The closet held more women's clothing, and the bathroom drawer contained makeup. None of it was hers.

Her eyes burned, and a boulder formed in her throat. Kelly

hadn't been a careless fling that had resulted in a baby—she'd been having a full-fledged affair with Eric. How long had it gone on?

Noah sucked at his fists and kicked his feet, and Lucas stepped to her side to take him. "I'm sorry, Carly."

No one had to tell him what all this meant. She swallowed and gave a stiff nod. Words wouldn't make it out of her throat just yet.

Lucas's phone vibrated, and his footsteps faded as he went down the hall. His voice was faint, and she was thankful for the alone time to try to process all she'd learned today. She never would have dreamed Eric would be a cheater. Had he been planning to file for divorce? Kelly had told Lucas that Eric knew about her pregnancy.

How would he have reacted if he'd known both of the women in his life were pregnant at the same time? Would he have chosen her or Kelly? She'd never know now.

Lucas's footsteps came back toward her, and she swiped the moisture from her face and turned to face the door. This was something she would have to live with. She held out her arms. "I can take Noah. Thanks for the space."

He handed the baby back to her, and she inhaled the scent of Noah's soft head. If nothing else good had come from her marriage, her baby was here in her arms. That was enough.

"I had some interesting news," he said once the baby was situated. "I had my partner take a look at Kelly's finances. A deposit of a hundred thousand dollars went into her bank account two days before Eric's death and another one of the same amount just last week. We traced both deposits back to a shell company affiliated with an official high up the food chain in Russia."

"Part of the Russian mafia?"

He shook his head. "A businessman named Ivan Bury. He lives in Moscow. We've found no connection with organized crime. But get this—he's put out a bounty on finding any of the Fabergé eggs."

"Why would he give Kelly money?"

"I suspect Eric asked for it to be that way to hide it from you. He wouldn't want to put it in your joint account because you'd ask questions. This way the two of them could use it for whatever they wanted." His hazel eyes narrowed, and he ran a hand through his short, dark hair. "Has she ever asked you about your flea market finds and what Eric was working on for you?"

She thought back over the past few weeks and winced. "I mentioned going through Gramma Helen's things. Maybe she asked or maybe I volunteered the information. I can't remember, but I think I mentioned finding an old egg. That was before I stripped off the paint."

"She's a police officer. We're good at steering conversations in the right direction. I suspect she took those calls all right. I'll bet she called him herself and negotiated that second payment because she'd found out about the egg."

Carly shifted Noah to the other shoulder. "What do you make of it?"

"The egg was stolen from the Kremlin. I'm not sure how it came to be in the hands of Mary's birth mother, but we know about the looting that went on during the Russian Revolution. Maybe Ivan is a collector. There's no way of knowing. I did some research, and there are some who believe the egg was sold to get money for the new government. It supposedly made it to the Kremlin, so it seems a logical possibility. If he's a collector, maybe he got a whiff that it was out there."

It was a good premise for her novel, and she tucked it away in her head. "I wish I knew how it ended up in the chest."

"I intend to find out."

Staring at his determined face, she felt a glimmer of hope that he'd be able to do just that. "We'd better get back."

———

His house held more people than Lucas could ever remember.

When they got back from the trip to the lake cottage, he heard the sound of the piano floating from the music room, and he spotted Amelia in there with Isabelle. Emily was moving cushions around in the living room, and though he didn't mind if she wanted to mess with the decor, it seemed a bold move for a guest to make.

Carly went straight up the steps to change Noah's diaper, and Lucas went to the kitchen. Mary was always a good person to talk to when his thoughts were a jumble. The aroma of Italian sauce made his mouth water. They hadn't eaten since breakfast other than a couple of handfuls of nuts and a granola bar Carly had brought for snacks.

"Lasagna?" he asked.

Mary adjusted the apron around the waist of her red-and-black paisley skirt. "I hear that hope in your voice, and yes, it's lasagna. And cheesy garlic bread with salad. I even made chocolate cake for dessert."

"I knew there was a good reason to invite you to stay."

She batted her eyes at him. "I know the way to a man's

heart. Now if you were about forty-five years older, we might get somewhere."

He laughed. "You're one of a kind, Mary Tucker."

He slid onto a stool at the breakfast bar and contemplated how much to unload on her. She had a lot of wisdom, but he didn't want to tell her something worrisome—or details Carly would rather keep quiet.

She pointed a set of tongs his way. "Bless your heart, you'd better tell me what's ailin' you."

His mouth watered as she layered the lasagna noodles with the sauce and cheese for a minute. Eric's infidelity was Carly's news to share, but he could tell Mary his suspicions. "I've found evidence that there may be two groups of people after that egg. It ups the danger to everyone, and I'm not sure what to do about it."

"You've done everything humanly possible, Lucas. Not one of us will leave this earth until the good Lord decides it's our time. It's fine to take precautions, but I wouldn't want any of us to be paralyzed by fear. Have you made any progress in finding my twin sister?"

"Not yet. We know the couple who adopted her were named Durham. It will take a while to track down the right Durhams, but it's a good start."

"Elizabeth Durham. Such a lovely name. I can't wait to meet her and see if we look alike or have the same interests. But it doesn't matter a hill of beans to me if we are very different. A sister!"

He wanted to caution her that Elizabeth might not be alive, but he didn't want to dampen the glow in her blue eyes. "Durham is a common enough name. I hope we can find her."

Footsteps clattered on the wooden floor, and he turned to see Carly approaching with Noah in her arms. The baby kicked his feet and smiled when he saw Lucas. Lucas smiled back and took Noah's hand when Carly was close enough. The baby's fingers curled around his in a tight grip.

"I didn't think you'd fall back asleep after that car ride, little man," Lucas said.

The baby kicked his feet again and seemed excited to see him. Even though it was probably Lucas's imagination, his chest warmed and he took Noah from Carly. "I'll take him in case you need to help Mary."

As he lifted the baby from her arms, he saw the anguish in her eyes, and he wished he could lift that weight from her. She'd taken a terrible blow today.

He shuffled the baby to one arm and took a gulp of his water.

Mary studied her granddaughter's expression. "I'm fixin' to put the lasagna in the oven, and the garlic bread is ready to be toasted as well. Have a seat, Carly Ann, and tell me what Lucas isn't saying. I could tell the minute you came into the room that something has upset your apple cart. You're pale and your eyes are red. What has happened?"

Lucas choked on the water in his mouth, and he met Carly's gaze. Her dark eyes narrowed as though she thought he'd spilled part of it, but he shook his head to reassure her. Carly slid onto a seat beside him and handed the baby a new set of plastic keys, the "key" to unlocking Eric's secret.

"We saw Kelly's baby today."

"And?"

"She's Eric's child."

Mary's eyes widened, and she took a step toward Carly, who held up her hand. "I'm okay, Gram. It was a shock, but the bigger surprise was that the large amount of money she's been spending has come from a Russian businessman named Ivan Bury. He's put out a bounty on finding any of the Fabergé eggs, and Lucas suspects Kelly might be trying to help him find my egg. And it all started with Eric. We don't know what Eric found in the chest. Did he see the egg and suspect its value was great? Or was there something there that led him to reports of the missing egg? If so, he might have discovered the bounty Ivan Bury had on the egg and contacted him. Kelly asked a few questions when I called her after finding Eric's note, but I'd thought it was just idle chitchat. Now I don't know."

Mary's lips twisted with disgust. "Pillow talk. I can't believe Eric would do this. Her baby is a little older than Noah, right?"

"Yes, six weeks older."

"Scum," Mary said darkly. "Total scum."

Lucas couldn't disagree. Everything he thought he knew about Eric had changed the instant he'd realized what Kelly was hiding. "I'm going to go back and see her. Once she knows we've tracked where the money came from, she might spill what she knows."

"I wonder if she realizes how much danger she might be in," Carly said. "People have already died. If this Ivan Bury thinks she could incriminate him, he wouldn't hesitate to eliminate her."

Lucas would have liked to think they could wrap this up quickly, but having two separate groups to investigate muddied everything. And he still needed to find Mary's twin.

TWENTY-TWO

How had life gotten to be such a mess?

Carly put Noah into his crib after dinner and forced herself to go back downstairs. Living with her sisters had been tense and uncomfortable. Her initial dreams of mending fences with them had gone nowhere with her focus on the danger swirling around them.

Her phone rang when she went into the kitchen to make tea, and she checked the screen. Her pulse jumped when the name Willard Auction House came up. She'd sent an email after dinner with her number, but she hadn't expected to hear anything for a few days.

She answered the call. "This is Carly Harris."

"Ms. Harris, sorry to call you so late. This is William Taylor with Willard Auction House. I just opened your email and examined the pictures you attached. Is the egg in a safe place?"

"Yes, it's secure." Though she had asked for the expert to call her, now that she was about to reveal everything, it felt wrong. Once her egg was shown to the world, it wouldn't be hers any longer. It had to be authenticated, though, and she didn't want to waste Lucas's time if it was found to be a fake.

"That's wonderful news. Can I see it tomorrow? I can get a flight to Savannah first thing in the morning and be there by eleven."

"I could meet you in Savannah if you like."

"I'd rather keep the egg secured and let me see it there. I don't want to take any chances with it."

"You think it's real, don't you?"

"There's no way of telling until I examine it, but the pictures are very compelling." The man's voice vibrated with anticipation. "This will be an exciting discovery if it proves to be the Hen with Sapphire Pendant. Where shall we meet?"

"I'll send you the address of its location."

"A bank vault, I hope?"

"Yes, that seemed the safest. And the police have put extra security on it."

"Wise. Very well, I'll see you at eleven. Thank you for contacting us."

Carly ended the call and exhaled. Tomorrow she would know if the egg was real or some elaborate fake. No part of her believed it was a copy, though. She recognized real gold when she saw it. And the markings matched those of other Fabergé pieces.

Still smiling, she went to the music room. Amelia and Emily were on either side of Isabelle. Her sisters were all in exercise clothes, and their faces were red like they'd just done a routine or yoga. Isabelle's face was pink and blotchy and her eyes were wet. There was no sign of Lucas or Ryan, and she couldn't blame them for wanting to disappear from the drama that surrounded her family.

This was her problem to fix. Carly took a step closer to her youngest sister. "What's wrong, honey?"

Isabelle bunched her hands at her sides. "I called Mom and she kept trying to get me off the phone. Some guy in the background told her to hang up. Why wouldn't talking to me be more important than listening to him?" Her voice trembled. "Doesn't she even care about me? She didn't want to hear about school or what Dad was doing. She kept saying she'd call me later, but she always says that and then never does."

Carly remembered how things were when Dad left after Mom's death. "I know how you feel. It's hard, but grown-ups don't always act right."

"At least you're here with us," Emily said. "When Dad left, we had Gram and Carly. Imagine how you'd feel if you were stuck at home without anyone now that Dad has run off again. He's good at avoidance."

Fresh tears ran down Isabelle's cheeks. "He doesn't really care about me either, does he? How will I even figure out life with no one who loves me?"

Carly narrowed her eyes in a warning glance at Emily and Amelia. "It's just his job. He loves you, Isabelle. He loves all of us." The words felt hollow as they rolled off her tongue.

"That's what you always said to us too," Amelia said. "At some point you have to realize people are who they are. You can't change your parents, Isabelle, and it's not your fault. You can't take on blame for something beyond your control."

"And how you react is the only thing in your control," Emily said. "People are going to disappoint you all the time. You have to take charge of your own life and go after what you want. Your future belongs to you. Look at where Amelia and I have gotten, and we had a mother die and a father desert us. You can overcome all that."

Carly stopped and stared at her sisters. Her mouth went dry, and she thought back over all the assumptions she'd made about the relationship between her sisters and her. She'd blamed herself and had reacted instead of seeing the situation clearly. Why had she done that? Emily was right—her future was in her own hands, not her sisters'.

Amelia frowned and studied Carly's expression. "What's wrong?"

"I've blamed myself for years over how you girls have treated me. Like I deserved it because I didn't do enough after Mom died. And then when Eric used the money without my consent, you blamed me for that. And again, I took the blame because I thought it was my fault. I just found out Eric was having an affair and has another child—one with his partner. I had already begun thinking through whether I'd caused that. I thought maybe it was my fault he'd strayed." She shook her head. "I'm not going to do that anymore."

Amelia's brown eyes widened. "Wait, back up. *Eric* spent the money? And without your permission?"

Carly nodded. "I'd already written out checks to you girls before I left for the flea market. But he'd planned all along to use it for our new house—he did it without permission."

"Why didn't you tell us?" Emily demanded.

"I didn't want you to be mad at Eric."

Amelia clenched her fists. "That's terrible, Carly. You should have seen the signs of his character when he used your money without permission."

Carly started to agree, then stopped. "See how you do that so easily, Amelia? That subtle hint of blame directed back at me? I *should have seen* implies something was my fault. It wasn't. Eric made his own decisions, and they had nothing to do with me."

Amelia flinched, but comprehension settled over her face, and she said nothing as she tucked her chin and stared at her hands in her lap.

Carly saw a long stream of years behind her—years where she'd accepted the blame her family had heaped on her head. It was going to take work for her not to react that way any longer, but she saw it now. And things were going to change.

———

Sleep was as elusive as finding the culprit who was after Carly.

Lucas paced his room awhile before he grabbed a book and headed downstairs to the sunroom. He wasn't sure his guests had discovered it yet, but the spot was his favorite place to think.

He walked through the door and down a step into the space and saw a faint glow. Carly sat with a laptop on the lounge chair, and she looked up. Her somber expression told him she was still upset over the events of the day.

"Couldn't sleep either?" he asked.

She shook her head. "It's not every day you find out the man you married isn't who you thought he was." She closed the laptop. "Um, it might sound silly, but after I read the journal entry about Sofia, I wanted to write about her. I'm working on a novel for Gram—what might have happened. A way to dramatize it all for her."

"That's amazing. I didn't know you were a writer."

Her hair lay on her shoulders and she looked lost and vulnerable. A pink robe covered her pajamas, and she set the laptop on the table beside the baby monitor. She put her feet onto the floor to make room for him. "I've always toyed with the idea. I used to teach history at the high school, and the thought has been simmering awhile. Flea markets aren't the best way to earn a living when you have a tiny infant. I was trying to think outside the box. It's probably never going to be published, but Gram will like it."

She constantly surprised him. He sat on the foot of the lounge chair beside her. "I'm sure you can do anything you set your mind to."

She gave a half smile. "Don't you have to work tomorrow?"

"Yeah." The scent of gardenias wafted through the space. Or was the sweet aroma in her hair? "I'm sure it's been a shocking day."

What did someone say in a circumstance like this? It had to have rocked her world. Maybe he didn't have to say anything. Being with her might be enough comfort.

She tucked her hair behind her ear. "I didn't get a chance to tell you. There's an expert from Willard Auction House coming from New York tomorrow. He's eager to examine the egg. I'm supposed to meet him at the bank at eleven."

"Good news. At least we'll know for sure if it's everything you think it is."

"He sounded very optimistic and excited."

"He must be if he's coming here so quickly."

"He read the email today and was ready to get here tomorrow." She looked down at her hands. "I'm not sure what to pray for. I'll be thrilled if it's real, but it also means the attention on our family will intensify."

He couldn't argue against that conclusion. This would hit the news soon, and who knew what would happen? "What's the guy's name?"

"William Taylor."

"Vince and I will meet you at the bank. I don't think he'd try to take it, but I want to make sure you and the egg are safe."

"Thank you. I was going to ask if you'd like to be there."

A shadow crossed his line of vision, and he saw Ryan heading toward the back door. Late night. Ryan turned his head and waved. A few seconds later he was inside the screened porch.

Fatigue shadowed his brother's eyes, and he leaned against the back wooden wall. "You all are up late."

Lucas glanced at the dim glow of his watch. Nearly two in the morning. "That's the pot calling the kettle black. What's kept you out so late?"

"Just stuff." Ryan shot a quizzical glance toward Carly. "Everyone settled in okay?"

"We are. Thank you for having us."

Ryan shrugged. "That was all Lucas."

"It's still your house too. And we're all thankful to be out of the noise and dust. I'm sorry about your employee. How's he doing? Have you spoken with his family?"

"That's where I was actually—looking for his family. The address he gave me here in town was fake, and none of the other workers have any idea how to get in touch with anyone. The emergency number he gave me doesn't work either. As far as I know, he's still unconscious."

Lucas nodded. "That was my last report too. Vince has

probably discovered the fake address and phone number as well. I was following other leads today so I hadn't heard. I'll check with Vince in the morning."

Ryan yawned. "You mean today."

Lucas grinned and rose. "We'd all better try for some shut-eye. I hope Kostin wakes up so I can question him."

"It's enough to scare me off hiring any new workers, and I need help in the worst way," Ryan said.

The monitor made a noise, and Carly picked it up. "Sounds like Noah is waking. I'd better check on him." She squeezed past Ryan and vanished into the shadows.

Ryan crossed his arms over his chest. "You like her, don't you?"

Lucas considered how to reply for a brief instant. He didn't want to have a deep discussion this late, but he didn't want to blow off his brother's question either. "Yeah, I like her. She's been through a lot."

"What about Eric?"

"What about him? He's out of the picture." He told Ryan what they'd discovered today.

Ryan straightened. "Lucas, she's going to have baggage from this. Be careful. I don't want to see you hurt." He chuckled and passed his palm over his hair. "I never thought I'd say those words to you. You've always had a steel plate around your emotions as thick as a battleship. Just—be careful."

"I said I like her. I didn't say I was thinking about marrying her. Good grief, Ryan. I'm simply helping her solve the egg's mystery, and it's escalated into murder and break-ins. Once this is over, I won't be seeing her so much. We're just friends."

"I've heard that before. What I haven't seen before is the

expression on your face when you look at her. And you invited the whole gang to stay here without talking to me about it. You've always liked your privacy, but you tossed it out the window without a second thought. You're fooling yourself if you think you don't feel something deeper than friendship. Maybe it's just starting, but I think it's probably too late."

Lucas shook his head and started for the door. "You're crazy."

His brother's soft chuckle followed him down the hall to his bedroom.

TWENTY-THREE

Carly wanted to look as professional as possible for her meeting with William Taylor, and she smoothed the wayward strands of hair escaping the French twist at the back of her head. Her feet already hurt, unaccustomed to wearing pumps, and she couldn't wait to ditch the navy skirt and white blouse for shorts and a sleeveless top. The sun beat down on her head as she waited with Lucas in front of the bank.

"You remembered to get the key out of your safe?"

"Of course." Perspiration beaded Lucas's forehead. "We could go inside, you know."

"I wanted Mr. Taylor to be able to spot me easily."

Lucas lifted his phone and studied the picture on it. "Bald guy, big mustache. Should be easy to identify. He's a little late. Wasn't he supposed to be here at eleven?"

She nodded. "His flight could have been a little late." Noah had been fed before she left him in Isabelle's care, but she didn't want this to take all day either.

Or had he lost interest in the egg? Maybe he'd seen a red flag that indicated it wasn't genuine. She rejected the idea— everything in her knew the egg was genuine.

A black Escalade pulled into the parking lot, and a man got

out. He was in his thirties with blond hair and a clean-shaven face. The smile he turned her way as he stopped in front of her spoke of recognition. "Mrs. Harris? I'm William Taylor."

Her answering smile faltered, and Lucas tensed at her side. She grabbed his forearm in a warning squeeze as he started to speak and shook her head. "You don't look much like your picture on the website, Mr. Taylor."

"Call me William. We all have fake pictures online. Privacy, you know."

His explanation made sense, but she wasn't convinced. "Could I see some ID?"

"Of course." He whipped out his wallet and showed her his driver's license as well as his official Willard Auction House card. "I'm eager to see the egg. Shall we go in?"

She glanced at Lucas, who raised a brow before he gave a slight nod. At least he'd be with her and ready to intercept any attempt at theft. They walked inside, and the rush of AC cooled her cheeks. After showing her documentation, Carly and the bank employee went back to get the box while Lucas took Taylor to a private viewing room.

Her pulse elevated as she carried the box into the room. She couldn't wait to see the egg again. Every minute with it out of her hands had been an eternity. She set the box on the table between the two men and lifted the lid to reveal the contents. The opalescent egg gleamed in the overhead lights, and Taylor gasped.

He reached toward the egg, then drew his hands back. "May I?"

"Of course."

He pulled on white gloves and lifted the egg out reverently.

"Extraordinary," he whispered. "Exactly how I imagined it." He turned it around and looked at it from all angles, then pulled out a loupe to look at the details more closely.

The wait was excruciating as he took his time with every detail of the egg. He opened it and examined the inside as well as all the markings before he finally put it gently on the table and exhaled. "There is no doubt in my mind it's genuine. I can't imagine how much it will fetch at auction, but I suspect it will be close to forty million dollars."

Carly inhaled. It wasn't the money—it was knowing the egg held so much value. What might men do to possess it? No wonder there seemed to be two camps after the egg.

"I'm prepared to arrange secure transport for the piece to the auction house and to begin informing the public of its upcoming sale," Taylor said.

Carly found herself shaking her head. "I'm not ready to sell it. Not yet." How did she explain such an irrational answer? If the egg without the surprise was worth so much, what might it bring if they could find the surprise? Again, it wasn't the money, but as she thought about it, she realized she didn't want to give it up. She wanted to see it whole and complete.

Yet she had to relinquish it. She didn't have the means to protect it from thieves. What good would it do anyone stuck in a dark safety-deposit box where no one enjoyed its beauty? It had been in an attic for decades, and it deserved to be seen and admired.

But she'd lost so much this past year, and the thought of the egg being gone made her heart hurt.

The light in Taylor's eyes faded, and his mouth flattened in a grim line. "I see. You don't wish to sell it?"

"I will, just not yet." She glanced at Lucas for support and found him looking as puzzled as Taylor. "What if we had the surprise?" she blurted out. When she saw the shock in Lucas's eyes, she knew she shouldn't have mentioned the possibility. "I mean, the surprise might show up."

"Once the public knows of the egg's existence, someone might realize they have the surprise," Taylor said. "But short of that news hitting the world, I doubt you'll find it by looking. Unless you have some sort of information about its location?"

She knew better than to admit to that. "Let me think about it." The egg felt cool in her fingers as she placed it back in the box and rose to lock it back up. "Thank you for coming. I'll be in touch."

She rushed out to put the egg back in its safe spot so she didn't have to deal with the disappointment he showed. Her sisters would be furious when they learned what she'd done.

Lucas wasn't sure he'd ever understand women. Hadn't selling the egg been the whole point of getting it appraised? They hadn't talked about it on the way back to the house, and he'd suggested they take Noah to the Chambers Waterfront Park. The baby was too little to enjoy the playground, but it was a serene spot to walk in the shade of the live oaks with their hanging moss and to watch the boats glide in and out. The river flowed into open water, and the marina was always busy.

The salty scent of the Beaufort River mingled with the flowers blooming in the gardens. The squeals of children playing and the wind in the palms were a soothing backdrop as he pushed the stroller toward the patio's tables and chairs. Major's nails clicked beside him on the brick path, and Carly, silent with a faraway expression, moved woodenly beside him. She carried the lunch they'd stopped to pick up at Lowcountry Café.

He found an open table near a palm tree overlooking the water and set the stroller's brake. Noah kicked his feet and squealed at the fronds rippling in the wind above his head. "The little guy likes it here."

"He loves to be outside." She opened the bag of food and pulled out the items. "Ooey Gooey Burger and fries. Those are yours. I got a crab cake sandwich, but I'm not very hungry." She set her lunch on the table before she plopped onto a chair and put her face in her hands. "I'm an idiot. Why on earth didn't I let Taylor take the egg?" She lifted her head and caught his gaze. "I love that egg, Lucas. Isn't that stupid? I can't protect it. It would be hidden away in the bank forever. And I *have* to sell it—my sisters will want their cut."

"I thought the contents of that chest belonged to you."

"They do, but it's hardly fair to hog it all to myself when the egg is so valuable."

She was the most selfless person he'd ever met. Her concerns were all based around her family and not on things she could buy with that money. It was life-changing wealth for her entire family, but she wasn't focusing on her own circumstances.

Something stirred in his heart—a warmth that was almost painful. Since his engagement ended seven years ago, he'd guarded against feeling anything for another woman. He didn't want to go through that kind of rejection again, but Carly wasn't Frani. She'd already been married to a cop and had managed the worry just fine. It had been Eric who had failed her—not the other way around.

He saw Noah, and the heat in his chest intensified. The baby had wound his fingers around his heart even faster than Carly. It made the stakes of a relationship higher, but he might be too far gone to pull away now. Ryan had been right all along. Lucas had been fooling himself about his feelings.

Now that he knew, what was he going to do about it?

There would be time to think about that later. Right now he needed to help Carly get clarity on what she was going to do about the egg. "It's not a bad idea to wait until we see if we can find the surprise."

Noah let out a squawk, and she leaned over to hand him his plastic keys. "That's another thing—I shouldn't have said anything about trying to find the surprise. What if he talks about it?"

"It might have been best to keep it to yourself, but we can't worry about that now. Let's see what we can find out about Mary's sister, Elizabeth. At least we have a name, and I'm looking for her in the database. I should get a report back later today."

The wind had wreaked havoc with her hair twist, and she pushed strands of dark hair off her cheeks. "There's that hope, at least. I don't know what I would do without your support, Lucas. You're the only one I can really talk to about all of it. And here I thought all along you didn't like me."

"I didn't know you," he shot back. "And what I thought I knew was wrong. I believed what Eric said." With her big brown eyes fixed on him, he struggled to express what he meant. "I'd known him a long time, and it goes to show how people can be so different from what you think. I never would have guessed Eric to be the straying type."

"What did you used to think about me?"

"You were young when you and Ryan were dating. When you guys broke up, I thought you were using your sisters as an excuse to toss him aside and you had someone else already picked out. I told you that directly, and the next day you broke up with Ryan. When you started dating Eric, I was sure I was right. But now that I've seen the way you put everyone else's needs ahead of your own, I realize that wasn't it at all. You're only now starting to break free of the chains your family has shackled on you. Back then, those chains must have been strangling you."

She looked down at her hands. "It's not wrong to take care of other people."

"Of course it isn't. Being a police officer is my way of caring for others. But your sisters have hobbled you."

"I know. I realized that yesterday. Guilt is never a good basis for any kind of decision."

"You've had nothing to feel guilty about. And you still don't. You can choose to do whatever you want with the egg. It's yours. Make the decision based on what's best for you and Noah."

She caught her bottom lip in her teeth. "Even now I know I need to sell it. It's too beautiful to be stuck in a safety-deposit box."

He dragged his attention away from her utterly delicious-looking mouth when his phone dinged with a message. He glanced at it. "And right on time. Here's the report on Elizabeth I mentioned. We might be getting somewhere."

TWENTY-FOUR

While Lucas examined his report, Carly pushed Noah in his stroller out on the walkway around the water. The trees blocked the heat of the sun high overhead, and the cool breeze off the river evaporated the perspiration on her forehead.

She might as well follow through with her decision. She looked up the Willard website on her phone and placed a call to the auction house. "Um, I spoke with William Taylor today, but I didn't get his phone number. Do you have it?"

There was a long pause before the woman spoke. "Mr. Taylor died two weeks ago. Are you sure that's who you spoke with?"

Carly froze. "He said he was William Taylor." She told the receptionist about her email and his call before describing the man to her. "I noticed he didn't look like his picture on the website, but he said those are all fake for privacy concerns."

"That's not true. The pictures are accurate, but we haven't had a chance to remove Mr. Taylor's information."

"But he had my email message. Would it have been forwarded to someone else?"

"Let me track down your correspondence. Please hold."

Music played in her ear, a light classical piano number. The man had provided ID. Surely he was an employee.

It was several minutes before the music stopped and a male voice came on. "Ms. Harris, this is Brian Schoenwald. We've tracked your email, but no one seems to have received it. I'm not sure how the impersonator got your information, but it's very concerning to us. If the man contacts you again, please inform law enforcement. We will look into it on our end."

"You think you were hacked?"

"We have very tight online security, but there doesn't seem to be any other explanation. I looked at your pictures, and I believe we would be very interested in taking a look at the egg. May I come for a visit myself and evaluate it?"

She wanted to say no, but she'd already made a decision she felt was right. "Yes, but I'd like a few days. I-I have a busy week ahead. Maybe next week?"

"Today is Friday. How about the end of next week, say next Friday?"

"That would be fine." She gave him her phone number and the bank address. "Thank you for your help."

When she ended the call, she glanced back at where she'd left Lucas. He was off the phone as well, so she gestured for him to join her, and he strode toward Noah and her.

He frowned when he saw her. "What's wrong?"

"William Taylor, the *real* William Taylor, is dead. That guy was an impostor." She told him what she'd learned. "He had all the right documentation. How did he even know I'd offered the egg to the auction house?"

His mouth flattened. "It's easy to hack email and monitor electronics. Someone has a vested interest in discovering what you're up to. I'll have Tech go over your computer and phone, but it might have been a remote hack. I'll put some tighter security on your computer, but in the meantime, you shouldn't do anything critical. Use my computer—it's locked down well. There are impressive listening devices out now, though in this case, I suspect someone has rerouted your email. It was a good thing you followed your instincts and didn't let him have it. If this other guy wants it, don't let him take it either. We'll handle security on our end and deliver it to them ourselves."

Her pulse was beating fast at the thought of how badly things might have gone wrong this morning. It was further confirmation that something had to change in the egg's circumstances. "What did your report show?"

A smile lifted his lips. "I think I've found her. There are several Elizabeth Durhams around, but only one who's the right age."

"Gram will be so thrilled! She'll want to go with us."

"And we shouldn't let her until we know the truth. We don't know what we'll find on the other end. Let's go see Elizabeth ourselves first. If it goes well, we can arrange a meeting."

"I hate to keep it from Gram. It feels like we're juggling so many balls and I'm struggling to keep them all in the air. This should be a happy time. Can't we let her have the joy of anticipation?"

His hazel eyes went thoughtful. "I wish we could, but I don't think it's wise, not just yet."

"She's nearly seventy—she knows how to temper hope with

reality. Even if it ends up not being her sister, she can savor the anticipation for a while. But I'll bow to your experience."

"How'd you land on knowing it's important?"

She smiled. "I've had disappointments in life too. Vacations that fell through because of Eric's work schedule, the possibility of moving to a different town for a while, several things. After the disappointment was over, I told Eric I was glad for the chance to be excited about the possibility of those things happening. It gave us an opportunity to dream together, to plan. For every disappointment like that, there's the flip side of hope. After Noah came along, I resolved to try to catch the joy in the small things. I want him to experience that too."

"Joy. That's a word we don't use much."

"I know. It's not happiness, because that comes and goes. It's that inner peace we have when we take every day God gives us and are thankful for it."

"I never know how you're going to surprise me next, Carly. You're an amazing person. Eric didn't know how lucky he was to have you."

She warmed at the tender expression in his eyes. The feelings building between them were unspoken, but she felt them in every meaningful way. She didn't know what the future held for them, but she could anticipate it and take joy from every moment.

———

Lucas placed a package of chicken breasts in the grocery cart as a shadow loomed behind him, and he turned to see Vince holding a shopping basket. "Hey, you must have seen my truck in the lot." He maneuvered the cart off to the side of the meat counter and turned to watch the aisles.

The fluorescent lights shimmered off Vince's bald head as he nodded. "Sure did. I've been checking out Charlie Kostin. He seems okay, Lucas. I talked to the current workers at one of his old job sites, and they knew of him but had never seen him. He showed up here and started the job with Ryan right away. Ryan's employees say he was quiet but pleasant. He didn't share any personal details with them. His move here seemed purposeful, knowing what we know."

"Married?"

"No."

Lucas wasn't surprised by that. Russian organized crime lived by what they called a thieves' code, which was something to be admired in their culture. They left behind any family ties, including wives or children. But the code of thievery also included not working, and this Kostin had been at Ryan's job-site.

If he wasn't organized crime, why was he here? "I think he might have been looking for the item."

Vince picked up a package of ground beef and placed it in his basket. "That's what I thought. And if he was, who stabbed him? Could there be some disagreement with another member who wants it? That doesn't seem likely, and it made me wonder if you have two parties after the same thing."

"That's what I was thinking. You find anything else on Kelly Cicero?"

Vince scowled. "Nothing other than the two big deposits. I get bad vibes from her, though."

"Me too. And Bury?"

"Nothing more than what I told you. We need to get Kelly to talk to learn more."

"Is Kostin still in a coma?"

"He started to come out of it about an hour ago. Not coherent enough for us to interrogate him, but the doctor thinks he might make it. He's far from out of the woods yet, though."

"I think I'll go have a chat with Kelly again. You spoke by phone. Maybe in person I can get her to talk."

Vince shook his head. "She's gone. When I got there to see her, she was packing up a moving van. I asked where she was going, and she wouldn't tell me."

"Did you check with the moving van company to see where she was dropping it?"

"They wouldn't give up that information without a warrant."

"Maybe a neighbor would know."

Vince picked up a package of sausage and dropped it into his basket. "I have a call in to the neighbor down the street. I'll let you know what I hear."

"One more thing." Lucas told him about the expert from Willard's. "Since it was an impostor, I arranged for extra security at the bank. He was disappointed Carly wouldn't turn it over to him. If he doesn't know she found out the truth, he might try to contact her again."

"You could have her call him, set up a sting."

"I'd like to keep her out of danger. This thing is growing tentacles by the minute, and I'm not sure I want her involved in something like that."

Vince stared at him before a slow smile spread across his face. "Whoo boy, she's got you, hasn't she?"

"I never like to put the public in danger." Lucas's voice rose, and he glanced around before forcing a lighter tone. "I think she's a great person, but beyond that, she has a small son to raise by herself. I'd hate to see Noah orphaned."

"Speaking of Noah—I'm still reeling that Eric has another child." Vince shook his head. "How is Carly handling it?"

"She's okay. It was a shock, but I think she knew there were problems in the marriage. I don't believe she's thought through if the kids will want to know each other. I doubt Kelly has either. What a mess."

"You got that right." Vince glanced at his watch. "I gotta go. The wife needs some things to start dinner. Wait until she hears how the mighty has fallen."

"Hey, you're blowing things out of proportion. I *like* Carly. I didn't say I was going to marry her."

Vince tapped Lucas's chest with his index finger. "I know you, man. I've never seen that look in your eyes before, and it's very different from how you looked that night you shot the intruder. Things have changed. Quit fooling yourself and figure out how you'll make it work."

Lucas opened his mouth to retort, but Vince moved toward the front of the store and left him with his mouth agape. He sighed and went to get the rest of his groceries.

He liked being around her, and he'd imagined taking her on a real date and kissing her. But a kiss wasn't a ring and it wasn't some huge commitment. There would be a lot of moving pieces to figure out if things ever went further than that. Taking on raising another man's baby wasn't something he'd ever thought about. He hadn't even wanted to have a kid of his own, dependent on him, with his crazy schedule either.

But he couldn't deny how he felt when he was with Carly. She took all his attention when she was in the room, and he couldn't look away. It wasn't just her external beauty—it was the way she served other people. She was always thinking of how to make others happy and comfortable.

Had she always been that way? Looking back, he realized he'd been around her only in very superficial ways—a smile across the backyard, a wave as he walked past.

His fascination with her was a little scary.

TWENTY-FIVE

Gram's house, smelling of new wood and dust, was un-recognizable. Carly stood in the morning sunshine streaming through the new windows and stared. Noah squeaked in her arms as if he was surprised too. With old walls removed, the large area seemed huge. Ryan's workers had opened up the dining room to the living room, divided by a large overhead beam, and the extra space seemed to go on forever.

Ryan's hazel eyes held a touch of concern. "You're not saying anything. What do you think?"

"It's wonderful, Ryan. I never dreamed it could look like this. Gram will love it." Carly moved in a circle to take in every bit of the view. "Guests will have so much room to gather and enjoy the space. Any surprises that are going to strain the budget?"

"Not really. The place has good bones. Your grandmother has kept up on termite prevention and general maintenance, and it just needed updating. We'd already planned to put in new copper plumbing and a new HVAC system. We have a lot of work to do, but it's going to look great."

Carly had thought it might feel awkward to be around Ryan, but it wasn't. He hadn't made any reference to their long-ago romance and neither had she. It seemed to have happened to other people, ones she no longer recognized. They'd both changed so much and had moved on.

"We're all so grateful to you for taking on the project. You were the one Gram wanted, but I had another quote just to make sure. Yours was fifty thousand less than the other one, so I know you were shooting her a deal because you care about her."

A smile lifted the corners of his lips. "I've always thought Mary was an amazing woman. You're a lot like her, and I'm glad Lucas is seeing what I always realized."

Heat bloomed in Carly's cheeks. "Your brother and I are just friends."

"Even if that's true—and I doubt it—he used to think you were a she-devil. So that's progress."

"He hated me that much?"

Ryan adjusted the leather tool belt hugging the waist of his jeans. "Let's just say he's a protective older brother." He studied her face. "You should have cut your sisters loose years ago, Carly. I'm glad you finally see it now."

She held his gaze even though it hurt. "I know, Ryan. And I'm sorry I hurt you back then." She decided to say nothing about him asking out her best friend.

He grinned. "We weren't right for each other, not really. I'm not sure I'm cut out for marriage. I'll be honest. I wasn't faithful when we were dating. I always had my eye out for a pretty girl. I even asked out your best friend, though she said no. Others didn't, though. You deserve better than that, and I'm sorry Eric was such a heel."

She tried not to show her shock, but he must have heard

the gasp she tried to hold in because his smile vanished. "I-I don't know what to say."

"I'm good at hiding what a heel I can be." He glanced out the window at the slam of a car door. "My crew is here, so I'd better get to work. Glad it all meets with your approval. Have Mary and your sisters come by and take a look too."

"I will." She watched him yank out a hammer from the loop on his tool belt and head down the hall.

The shock of his confession was beginning to fade, but she still felt a little stunned and disoriented. She never would have guessed Ryan would admit he'd cheated on her. And not just asking out her friend. Hearing that right after learning about Eric's infidelity made her question some men's integrity.

She hugged the baby to her and buried her nose in his sweet-smelling hair. She needed to make sure her son became a man of morals and integrity. Taking him to church wouldn't be enough—she'd have to teach him to love God and care about other people. It was a big job to accomplish all by herself, but she had to do it. Other single mothers had raised good men. So could she.

Carrying Noah across the yard, she saw Lucas in the backyard approaching his truck. He spotted her and stopped to wait for her. She picked up the pace and was out of breath when she reached him.

He plucked Noah from her arms and smiled down into his face. The baby kicked his feet and squealed as he reached out his chubby hands to grab at Lucas's nose. "Hey, buddy." Lucas's gaze went to Carly. "You're out early."

"Ryan wanted me to approve the floor plan before they started putting up drywall. Have you seen it? It's amazing."

197

"Looks good. Did your sisters see it too?"

She shook her head. "They weren't up yet. I'm supposed to send them over after a while."

Did he know Ryan hadn't been faithful? The words hovered on her tongue, but she couldn't do it. The secret wasn't hers to tell. If Ryan wanted his brother to know, he'd tell him. Lucas already realized she hadn't been the person he'd thought she was. That was enough.

"Off to work?" she asked.

She held out her arms for the baby, and Lucas handed Noah back to her. "Yeah, Vince tracked down Kelly's new address. She moved to Savannah."

"You're going to Savannah?"

"Not yet. I have to file reports in the office. Boring day but I have to do it. I'll give Kelly a day or two, then go see what I can find out."

"I could talk to her. Maybe she'd tell me."

"I don't think so, Carly. She didn't tell you when we saw her last time, and it's a moot point anyway. I'll take care of it." He tickled Noah under the chin. "See you tonight."

She watched him drive off before she headed to the house. Savannah was only an hour away. She could be there by midmorning. Vince would give her the address.

———

Kelly's new house was a white two-story with dormers and a large porch set back from the road. The moss hanging from the live oaks sheltered the house from prying eyes and made for a pretty backdrop. Carly parked and got out. She lifted her sleeping baby from the car seat and headed for the steps.

A screen door let in the breeze, and as Carly mounted the steps, she heard a baby's wail. The wail increased in tenor to a sound of pure distress, and she quickened her pace. She reached the entry and pressed the doorbell. "Kelly," she called.

No footsteps approached the door, and the baby continued to cry, a heart-tugging sound Carly couldn't ignore. After a second callout to Kelly, Carly tried the screen door, which wasn't locked. She stepped into the foyer and moved toward the sound of the crying baby to her left. Following the wails, she went up the stairs and down the hall to a bedroom where she found baby Caroline. The baby's diaper had drenched her onesie as well as the sheet over the mattress.

She laid Noah in a bouncy seat on the floor, then popped a pacifier in Caroline's mouth for a minute while she cleaned up the baby and the mattress. "There, there, sweetheart," she soothed. The baby's lips worked the pacifier, but the frown lines between her blue eyes didn't ease, and Carly knew she was hungry.

Where was Kelly? Carly left Caroline in her crib for a minute while she picked up Noah and went to find the baby's mother. The master bedroom was empty and so was the other bedroom. Carly went toward the bathroom, which was half open. Her heart bounced against her ribs, and she was half afraid she would find Kelly drowned in the tub, but the bathroom was empty.

She exhaled with relief and went back to Caroline's room, where she managed to get a baby in each arm. Noah still slept but Caroline was restless, and Carly went in search of a bottle. She reached the bottom of the steps and laid both babies on the thick rug in the living room. The burgundy patterned rug was clearly new and fit nicely with the new furniture she'd seen in Kelly's condominium.

"Kelly?" she called again.

She went through to the kitchen and found a can of formula. She prepared a bottle and went back to prop it in Caroline's mouth. Not the best way to feed her, but Carly needed to find Kelly. Maybe she'd fallen and broken an ankle.

With the baby settled, Carly pushed open the screen door and went out onto the deck. Banks of red and white flowers were carefully groomed under the palm trees, and the moss from the large live oaks waved in the wind. She called for Kelly again, and a sound caught her attention. She turned to her left toward a carriage house. A tire swing bumped against a large tree. Was that the sound she'd heard?

She took a step that direction and heard a moan. "Kelly?" She ran down the back steps and across the yard toward where she thought the groan had originated.

As she reached the back of the carriage house, she saw a stream running through the edge of the property. A scrap of bright yellow drew her attention, and she spotted Kelly's shirt. She ran to her side and knelt. "Kelly?" She touched the arm that was flung over Kelly's face, and Carly's hand came away wet and sticky with red. Blood?

Carly moved Kelly's arm. A red stain spread over the front of her shirt. Kelly's face was much too pale, and her lids fluttered but didn't open. Carly rose to go call 911, but Kelly's hand shot out and grabbed hers.

"Carly," she groaned.

"I'll be right back. I need to call an ambulance."

Kelly frowned and her lids fluttered quickly before she managed to get them open. She clung to Carly's hand with surprising strength. "My baby."

"I found Caroline. She's fine." Carly tried to extricate her hand from Kelly's grip, but the other woman clung tenaciously.

"Take care—Caroline."

"I've got her. She'll be all right. I need to get help for you."

"Wrong, so wrong. Knew he'd find me."

Carly froze. "Who found you, Kelly?"

"Knew he'd kill me. Wrong. Sorry. Sorry, Carly."

"Who, Kelly?"

She tried to move. "L-look under me." Her eyes closed again, and her breath eased from between her lips. Her grip on Carly's wrist loosened.

Carly ran her hand under Kelly's back and felt the soft edges of paper. She pulled it out and stared at the small leather folder. She sprang to her feet and sprinted to the back door to call for help. She found her purse and dug out her phone, then dialed 911 and asked for an ambulance. "She's bleeding. I think she's been shot."

"Stay on the line, ma'am. Help is on the way."

"I can't. I have to take care of the babies and get back to Kelly. We'll be in the backyard. Hurry!" Carly ended the call and went to pick up Caroline, who had fallen asleep after emptying the bottle.

Noah was sleeping too. She couldn't leave him, though, not with an intruder out there. How could she manage two babies and get out to Kelly?

She saw a stroller by the front door and retrieved the babies. They were small enough to snug them close together in the stroller. She thrust the folder she'd found into the depths of the stroller, then wheeled it to the kitchen to grab a clean towel for Kelly's wound.

Outside, she found Kelly had moved a foot closer to the house. She was on her belly now with one arm flung out in front of her. Carly rolled Kelly over to her back again so she could apply pressure to the bleeding wound. The front of Kelly's blouse was more drenched than before, and Carly lifted her top to take a look.

The hole in her chest still pumped blood, and she put the towel on it and pressed down as the wail of an ambulance blared. *Please, God, let her live.*

TWENTY-SIX

Carly would be the death of him.

Lucas parked behind Carly's car at the address he'd been given. Police cars and a forensic van crowded the drive as well. A tech rounded the end of the house ahead of him, and he followed. He heard a baby crying and picked up his pace past a couple of gardenia shrubs at the side of the house.

He heard Carly's voice, quivering with distress, before he saw her. She sat on the back deck with two babies in her arms. She rocked back and forth a bit as she talked with the detectives standing in front of her.

He spared a glance toward where gloved techs roamed the area bagging evidence. What had happened here? When Carly called him, he'd been in a meeting and she'd been dumped into voice mail. All her message said was that she'd found Kelly shot in the backyard of her home.

When Carly spotted him, she started to rise but stayed put when he headed her way. He bounded up the steps of the deck and put his hand on her shoulder. "You okay?"

"Fine. I didn't see the attacker. It had happened before I arrived."

Lucas turned to the Savannah officers and showed them his ID. "What do you have?"

"Ms. Cicero was shot with a .44. We found the casing in the grass. We don't know much more yet."

So she'd been shot outside. Had she run from an intruder in the house, or had she been outside for something else? "The ambulance already took her?"

Carly answered with a jerky nod. "When I got here, Caroline was screaming her head off and hungry. I have no idea how long she'd been left, but I think it had been some time because she was soaked through like she hadn't been changed yet this morning." She glanced down at the baby girl in her arms. "Poor little mite. She was very hungry, too, but she had cried herself into exhaustion and fell into a hard sleep after her bottle."

One of the Savannah officers, an older man who reminded him of Denzel Washington, addressed Carly again. "Did you see or hear anything in the house or outside? A vehicle pulling away, a gunshot, anything?"

She shook her head. "But to be honest, I was so concerned about the baby I might not have heard it. She was wailing and the noise might have drowned out anything else. I searched the house calling for Kelly, and when I didn't find her, I went outside."

Lucas focused on the older officer. "Could you tell if anyone had broken in here and why she was outside?"

"Both entries were ajar, and we found moving boxes in the garage with the door open. We think she might have been unpacking while the baby was sleeping." His gaze went to the baby girl. "Do we know who to call to care for her baby?"

"CPS has been called," the other officer said. "They can care for her until we find her closest relative."

"That might be me," Carly said in a low voice. "She's my deceased husband's child."

Both officers wore identical expressions of shock. "I see," the older one said. "Are you willing to care for the baby for now?"

Carly's gaze locked with Lucas's, and he saw the plea in her eyes. She wanted to keep the baby after all that had happened? He gave a slight shake of his head, but it was more to clear his thoughts than to deny her what she clearly wanted. What would she do if he actually said no? They were living in his house, and another baby would add to the chaos. He could only imagine Ryan's reaction.

"Lucas?" she whispered.

"Whatever you want to do is fine. We'll make it work."

Relief lifted her mouth in a smile. "I'll keep her, Officer. Thank you. It's only right. She's my son's sister."

"CPS will talk with you, but you can take the baby for now." He dug out his phone and both officers walked away.

Lucas watched the forensic team for a few seconds. "I have a bad feeling about this, Carly. Kelly seemed to have been working with Ivan Bury, who isn't with Russian organized crime. From what I've learned about him, I don't think he would have killed her."

Lucas turned back to Carly and continued, "She was afraid that day we talked to her. If she wasn't afraid of Bury, who scared her?"

"She came to for a few moments and said something about she was afraid he'd find her."

205

"He? Did she say who that was?"

"No. I asked her, but she lapsed into unconsciousness again, and I ran inside to call 911."

"Maybe she moved hoping to disappear. I'm sure she would have been found quickly. She was probably followed right here to the house. She only moved in two days ago." He leaned down. "Let me take Noah, and we can go inside and pack up what you need. Where will she sleep?"

"They can sleep in the same crib. There's room. I'll mostly need her clothes and feeding supplies. Caroline's on formula."

He lifted Noah to his chest, and they went inside, where more techs swarmed the house looking for evidence. The sooner Lucas got them all home so he could go into the office and find out more, the better.

"What on earth were you thinking?" Emily's dark hair held a trace of drywall dust as she stared at the baby girl in Carly's arms. She'd come racing back from Gram's house when Carly texted her an SOS. "That woman had an affair with your husband!"

All of Carly's family stood in a circle around her, and they wore identical expressions of horror. She hugged the baby to her chest. "It's not Caroline's fault, and besides, she's Noah's sister."

Isabelle stood in a shaft of sunlight streaming through the music room windows. "I'll help take care of her. She's like me, and I've always wished I got to see all of you more often. Noah will want his sister around. Maybe if we take care of her, Kelly will let that continue more easily than my mom did."

Emily bit her lip and looked down but said no more. Amelia looked away, too, and even Gram looked a bit ashamed. Her initial reaction hadn't been any better than the rest.

"Thank you, Isabelle," Carly said. "Would you take her while I get a bottle ready? She'll need to eat quite a bit today. I think she missed at least one meal and was screaming when I got there." The baby had begun to waken and purse her lips, and the hungry cries wouldn't be far behind.

Isabelle held out her arms, and Carly shifted the baby to her. "Lucas is getting her things from my trunk."

Gram took a step closer as Caroline opened her blue eyes. Gram's flowing skirt swished around her ankles. "Is he prepared for the added stress of another baby?"

"He told me I could do whatever I wanted."

Amelia had been working on the exterior of the house this week, and she had a streak of white paint across one cheek. Her gaze lingered on the baby's fuzzy blonde head. "Where would we all be if Carly hadn't shouldered the burden of making each of us feel loved and wanted?" Her low voice trembled, and she stared at Carly. "We haven't been very good to you, Carly. I hadn't realized what brats we'd been until the other day. I'm sorry I blamed you for Eric's actions. Even though I thought you'd spent the money, it wasn't right. It was your money. If you want to take care of this baby, I'll help too."

Emily frowned and picked at a nail before she sighed and chimed in. "I'm sorry too. I should have remembered all you did for us and how giving you've always been. I'll help too."

A lump formed in Carly's throat. Maybe the big blowup had been worth it. "I love you, all of you. I hope you never think I regretted anything I did."

"You gave up a lot for us. Even your boyfriend back then," Amelia said.

"I learned this morning it never would have lasted anyway." Carly nearly turned at a sound from another part of the house, but her sisters and grandmother moved closer in a circle of support.

Gram laid her hand on Carly's arm. "Guard your heart, sugar. This baby will need to go back to her mother, and I worry you'll be devastated if Kelly cuts off contact when that happens."

Even now the thought made Carly wince. Would Kelly take their kindness and throw it back in their faces? Carly had hoped this would open a door between them so Noah and Caroline could be close. "I'll try, Gram."

The noise in the other room came again. "I'll go help Lucas get things into my room. Amelia, would you mind fixing a bottle for Caroline? The instructions are on the can on the kitchen counter."

Amelia nodded, and Carly hurried off to find Lucas. A smile settled on her lips at the way they'd come around to helping her. Maybe their relationship would survive after all.

She found Lucas with his arms full of a box of baby supplies. "Let's put those in my room," she said.

His hazel eyes were frowning. "What did you mean about Ryan?"

Her smile faded. She'd hoped he hadn't heard that comment. It was Ryan's story to tell. "Um, just that we weren't really suited."

"I think there's something you aren't telling me. You said you found out *this morning* it wouldn't have lasted. I know you saw him before breakfast. Did he say something?"

She sighed as he backed her into a corner. Lying never helped anything. "He told me he hadn't been faithful when we were together. That it was better for me that we'd broken up."

Lucas's eyes flickered. "I thought you broke his heart."

"So did I." Better not to say more than that. "It's all water under the bridge now. Please don't tell him I mentioned it. It feels like gossip."

"You answered what I asked." He moved past her toward the bedroom, and she followed.

When she reached the main bedroom, she went to the dresser and pulled out the bottom drawer, which was empty. "I'll put her things in here. Have you heard anything from Vince on how Kelly is doing? Have they found who did this yet?"

"She's in the ICU on a ventilator, Carly." He set the box on the floor by the dresser. "Have you thought about what you'll do if she dies?"

Her hands froze as she reached for the baby clothes. "She can't die. Caroline needs her."

"It's a bad injury. She's lost a lot of blood, and her lung was damaged. The prognosis isn't great."

His reluctant tone told her he hadn't wanted to tell her that. "I don't know. She might have parents who would want Caroline. Or siblings."

"I don't think so. Eric mentioned she was an only child, and her parents are elderly. They live in an assisted-living facility in Florida. It would be life-changing for them to take her."

She moistened her lips. "There's something else. Kelly told me to take a folder she had lying underneath her." It wasn't exactly what Kelly had said, but the intent was clearly there.

"You gave it to the police?"

She shook her head. "I was afraid we'd never see it, and it might be important to our investigation. I haven't looked at it yet. There hasn't been time."

He pressed his lips together. "You're probably right about that, but the local police might need it too. Let's take a look."

She went to her purse and found the leather file fastened with an elastic band. "There's a bookmark." She flipped through the pages to the marked page and scanned down the spidery writing. It was all in Russian, so no real help. She unfolded the paper to study it and froze. "Lucas, this is the provenance for the Fabergé egg and surprise! It documents the egg's existence and its cataloging after the revolution, though it doesn't say how Sofia came to possess it. I suspect it was stolen."

TWENTY-SEVEN

Lucas filed paperwork in his office and tried not to think about the situation at his house. Carly might say she didn't think she'd end up with little Caroline, but it was entirely possible. He took a swallow of coffee. His stomach was hollow, or maybe it was the shock of the day.

What happened if Kelly died? If he let himself fall for Carly, he'd be raising *two* babies fathered by Eric. It was a crazy situation, one he needed to guard against. Any feelings that had built for Carly needed to be firmly squashed. His neatly ordered life couldn't take that much upheaval. Carly's big brown eyes flashed into his mind, and he pushed away the image.

Vince entered the office and closed the door behind him. A waft of garlic came with him. "There you are. Big news, partner. Kostin is awake, and the doctor says we can talk to him. He's likely to be a little confused, but he might say something that opens the investigation for us. You got time to go there now?"

Lucas rose from behind his desk. "I'm with you." He followed Vince down the hall to the parking lot. "I'll drive." He clicked the key fob and unlocked his truck.

"I know."

He and Vince got in and headed for the hospital. Vince smelled of garlic and tomato sauce. Lasagna? Lucas's stomach rumbled at the thought. Dinner would be in a few hours, but he rummaged in the truck for a snack pack of pretzels. He ripped it open with his teeth and offered it to Vince, who shook his head.

Lucas tossed a handful into his mouth while Vince kept shooting questioning glances his way. He navigated the traffic along Ribaut Road toward the hospital. "Why are you staring at me?"

"Trying to figure you out. What's happened? You look like someone just stole your truck." He smacked the dashboard. "But it's right here, safe and sound. What's up?"

"Nothing."

"Spill it, Bennett. You're bad off. You got termites gnawing at your bones."

"Carly took Kelly's baby home with her."

Vince's eyes widened. "To your house? So there's two babies and five women living with you and Ryan? You're not getting any sleep. Come crash at my house if you want."

"It's not that. I can live on a couple hours a night."

Vince studied his face. "You worried about raising both the kids? It'd be like raising twins. Me and Nell thought we'd go bat crazy when ours were little. Crying at all hours. One would start and the other would chime in. Sleep was a rare commodity."

"It's not the sleep." Lucas raked his hand through his hair as he turned into the hospital parking lot. "Two kids by another guy is a hard thing to think about."

"Ah, gotcha. Every time you looked at them, you'd see Eric, right? Little Noah looks like his daddy. That bug you?"

Did it? When Lucas thought about Noah, all he felt was affection. The little guy had wrapped Lucas's heart around him like a blanket. "Noah is different. But *two* of them? I can't handle it."

"Whoa, I didn't think anything made you tuck your tail and run. Carly is the best thing that's ever happened to you, partner. You let her slip away because of this kind of fear and you're crazy."

Lucas shook his head. "Marriage is hard enough without mixing in even more stress. I'll need to pull away, but how do I do that with her living in the house? Maybe work would do it, but I've promised to help her find Mary's twin sister. And there's the egg to think about as well as the investigation into the break-ins and murders." He turned off the engine and pushed open his door. "Maybe I *should* move in with you for a few weeks. Give me some space."

"Nope. I withdraw my offer. I'm not going to be party to your cowardice. You ever think the good Lord brought Carly into your life on purpose? You're a stand-up guy, Lucas. She hadn't had the experience of meeting a man like you. Eric was a sleaze, and Ryan . . ." Vince's voice trailed off, and he looked away.

"You knew Ryan was a player?"

Vince got out and shut his door. "The whole county knows Ryan is like a bee buzzing to the next pretty flower. You've worn shades when you looked at your bro. Anyone with one eye could see he's never going to settle down."

Lucas fell into step with Vince as they headed for the hospital entrance. "He told Carly this morning that he'd cheated on her when they were dating. I never knew."

"Now you do, so you can put any guilt away and focus on how you feel about her." Vince stopped before they reached the door and clamped his big hand on Lucas's arm. "Don't blow this, buddy. Most of us only have one shot at the right woman. If you can't see Carly is the one, you need glasses."

Was Vince right? Lucas had begun to think it might be true, but today's events had knocked him into a tailspin. Maybe he could table all this until he found out if Kelly would make it. This might all be a moot point.

———

The pale man sleeping in the hospital bed looked far from a hale and hearty construction worker. He was in his thirties but looked closer to fifty lying there in the white sheets. Lucas raised a brow and shrugged at Vince as they stood and waited for Kostin to open his eyes. The blinds were drawn and the lighting dim. The machines made noises, and a murmur of voices rumbled outside the partially open door.

Vince cleared his throat, and the man in the bed opened blue eyes that he fixed on Lucas's face. Lucas gave a nod and a restrained smile. "Mr. Kostin, I'm glad to see you're awake. You've had a rough time of it."

Kostin cleared his throat. "Cops, right?"

Vince nodded. "That's right. We wanted to ask about the attack on you. Did you recognize the man who stabbed you?"

Kostin shook his head. "Didn't see him at all. I'd heard a footstep and started to turn but never got the chance." He spoke slowly as if he were still unsure of how to talk.

More pointed questions needed to be asked, but Lucas

didn't want to risk making the man clam up. "You're lucky to be alive. We weren't sure you'd make it. Have you had family visit?"

Kostin did a slow blink and shook his head. "No family."

The silence stretched out until Vince shifted his bulk and folded his arms across his chest. "Look, I'm not going to pussyfoot around. You had only one reason to be on that second floor—you were looking for something. I'd like you to tell me what you were looking for and who sent you."

Confusion clouded the man's eyes, and he raised the head of his bed a few inches. "I don't remember."

It could be true, but Lucas wasn't ready to buy it. "Does the name Ivan Bury mean anything to you?"

"Sounds Russian."

"He is. You know him?"

Kostin's frown deepened. "I don't think so." He rubbed his forehead. "Could you send the nurse in? I don't feel so good."

They were getting nowhere here, so Lucas beckoned for Vince to follow him, and they backed out of the room. Lucas stopped at the nurses' station. "He's asking for a nurse. He claims not to remember much. Has the doctor said if he has memory issues from the injury?"

"It's not uncommon with a trauma like he suffered," the nurse said. "I'll go check on him."

She wasn't offering up any information, but then, Lucas hadn't expected her to. He'd had to try at least. He and Vince went back into the intense sunshine of midday.

"Now what, buddy?" Vince asked.

"Back to the office," Lucas said. "I want to research that Bury guy."

"You can read my printout. Nothing ties him to any crime organization. He seems to be a rich Russian who has a major interest in Russian art. He possesses some of the Fabergé eggs already. Lives in Moscow but travels all over the place constantly."

They drove past the bank, and Lucas spotted the officer staking it out. It seemed all was well there, but maybe they should consider moving the egg. The whole thing with the impostor from the auction house made him uneasy. What would be the guy's next move? The fake William Taylor had held the egg in his hands. He wouldn't walk away.

Lucas parked at the police station, and he went to their office while Vince stopped to speak to Bernard about another case. Lucas dropped into his desk chair and pulled a yellow pad of paper to him. Lists always helped him organize his thoughts, so he grabbed a pen.

- Debby Drust, burglar. How did she know to look for the egg—Dimitri Smirnov? Find him.
- Anna Martin, murdered. Balandin cousin but dead end.
- Elizabeth Durham, Mary's missing twin—FIND HER!
- Grace Adams Hill, home was burgled.
- Ivan Bury, has reward out for discovery of the egg.
- Kelly Cicero, large amount of money transferred to her from Bury. Attacked—needed to silence her?
- William Taylor. Who is he really and how did he get email Carly sent?
- Three possible groups after the egg? Roger Adams, Russian mafia, Ivan Bury.

This case spiraled in so many directions that Lucas didn't know where to look first. About the time one thing came to his attention, another came along before he'd fully investigated the first one. Now that he had a list, he saw he'd left way too many clues unfollowed. There had to be a common thread connecting these events. Where should he start first?

The door opened, and Vince stepped in with Bernard. Lucas spun his pad of paper around for them to review. "I need some direction. Take a look at the events that have happened and see if you can find a common link and suggest where I should look first."

Bernard picked up the pad and scanned it with Vince looking over his shoulder. "Lot of things here. Some of them are out of our jurisdiction."

"But we can find out what's going on with the investigations."

"You left out something," Vince said. "Eric's death seems to be connected too. And he was more involved than we realized since Kelly got all that money and he was supposed to allow someone to go through Carly's workshop."

"You're right." Lucas took back the notepad and jotted down Eric's death. "If I could decide which string to pull first, the others might all unravel to where I could figure this out."

He stared again at the list. "It all started with Eric's death. I think he found that egg and contacted Ivan Bury. That's my gut anyway. Chief Robinson gave me that printout of Eric's calls, but it got pushed aside while I was dealing with all the other problems. I'm going to go through it and see what I can find out."

Maybe Carly could help him. She might recognize names.

TWENTY-EIGHT

Isabelle had been true to her word, and so had Carly's other sisters. They'd all pitched in to help with the babies, and the afternoon sailed by without any real problems. Carly prayed off and on for Kelly, but she refrained from calling to check on her. First off, the hospital was unlikely to tell her anything, and besides, it would take longer than a few hours to see things turn around after such a bad injury.

Gram shooed her onto the back deck while she fixed dinner, and Carly stretched out on a lounger and lifted her face to the late-afternoon sunshine. She was tired from the trauma of the day, but there was no way she could nap. Not with her mind racing. Maybe she could spend a few minutes writing.

Workmen were carrying drywall into Gram's house next door. Ryan saw her and waved, and she stiffened before waving back. She didn't know how to feel about what he'd told her.

The door slammed behind her, and Lucas strode toward her holding some papers. His mouth set in a grim line, he gave a short nod. "Mary said I'd find you out here."

She swung her legs to the deck and sat up. "Is Kelly dead?" Her voice quavered.

He pulled a chair closer to her. "She made it through surgery, but that's all I've heard."

There was a reserve in his voice she hadn't heard in a long time, but her tongue tripped over itself when she tried to form the question of what was wrong. Maybe she didn't want to know. The distance in his eyes felt like he had retreated clear to Alaska.

He held out the papers. "I made a list and realized we need to go back to the beginning. To Eric's murder and who he contacted after he found that egg. The danger now had to have begun then. I have his call log from his phone in the weeks leading up to his murder, and I'd like you to go over them with me. You'd know better than me if someone was a trusted friend or if a call was someone he might have confided in."

"Okay," she said.

His manner was still stiff, but he unbent enough to scoot his chair close enough for her to smell his cologne, a spicy masculine scent that made her want to move nearer. He'd tell her what was wrong when he was ready. Maybe he was tired of the chaos in his house and regretted opening his home to the horde. She wouldn't blame him if he felt like that.

He'd highlighted the different names on the list and she went down the first page line by line. She stopped at the last ten calls on that page—all to the same person. "I've heard him mention this woman, Lucille Godwin, but I can't think how she knew her."

Lucas took the paper back and studied it. "Ten calls, about a week before he died. Do you know exactly when he started going through your great-grandmother's belongings?"

"I'd thought it was that day he died, but the notes on his

computer showed he'd begun the process the week before. We'd both been busy and he hadn't mentioned it."

"He didn't mention a lot of things."

His curt voice made her shrink back on her chair again. What was eating him? If he wanted them to leave, where could they go? A hotel would be the only option, and it wouldn't be ideal with all of them plus two babies. They'd have to rent a house, and that wouldn't be easy with Beaufort's busy tourist season upon them. She needed to make this right somehow. Whatever *this* was.

She marshaled her courage, but before she could question him, he rose and pulled out his phone. She listened to him talk to Vince about Lucille Godwin, and when he hung up, her memory clicked into place.

"I know who she is. Eric mentioned she's an antique appraiser out of Savannah."

Lucas dropped back into his chair. "Ah, that explains it. And she might have been someone he confided in. He had to have shown the egg and provenance paper to someone to have figured out its value. We could stop to talk to her when we go to see Elizabeth on Monday."

"Good idea." She pursed her lips. "There are some nice furniture pieces, but we're talking a few thousand dollars per piece, not millions. I think it has to be the egg. But I saw the egg before I took the paint off of it. I don't think anyone would have known what it was in its gaudy red state."

"What if he brought the appraiser in to take a look at the furniture and she happened to see it? A trained appraiser might have suspected what it was. You did."

"I did see white porcelain under the chipped paint. It made

me curious, but I didn't suspect it was a Fabergé egg. I'll bet he talked to her about the provenance, and they realized it was a Fabergé egg despite the paint masking its beauty."

They went through the rest of the call list. Lucas tapped Gage Beaumont's number. "Chief Robinson had this name marked. It sound familiar to you?"

She studied it a moment, then nodded. "He was someone with a bike to sell—a collectible Harley Eric really wanted. He made an offer on it, but the guy sold it to someone else for more money."

"So that's a dead end." Lucas folded the papers and rose. "Thanks for your help."

He vanished inside the house before Carly got the courage to ask him what was wrong. Maybe it was for the best since she wasn't sure if she trusted men in general anymore.

———

Lucas tossed the papers onto his dresser and sank onto the edge of the bed. He wasn't proud of the way he'd treated Carly just now, and the hurt in her eyes reproached him. What was wrong with him? Was he running scared from his feelings, or was it something more?

The scent of gumbo wafted into his room, but he wasn't hungry. Not with his thoughts running around and around. Every time he was around Carly, he felt vital and alive. Alert and happy. He'd decided to keep his distance, but it would be hard to do when every cell in his body jumped to attention when he was near her.

Someone tapped on his door, and he looked up. "Come in."

Isabelle peeked inside his room. "Gram says dinner is ready." She held little Caroline in her arms, and the baby gave him a gummy smile when she saw him.

Lucas felt like the worst person in the world when he saw her happy little face. What kind of man begrudged safety to a tiny being like that, especially considering he was sworn to serve and protect? He should have felt privileged to be able to provide a safe haven for the infant. Instead all he could think about was how it affected him.

Isabelle's smile faded. "Are you okay, Lucas?"

"I'm fine, Isabelle. Just tired." He rose and went toward her. "You're doing a great job with Caroline. You must really like babies."

Her blue eyes lit up her face. "I love them. She's a really good baby. Not as good as Noah, of course, but I already love her. Here, want to hold her?" She thrust the baby into his arms without waiting for an answer.

Lucas juggled the infant into his other arm. "She's heavier than Noah."

"She's a little older." Isabelle's loving smile focused on Caroline.

The solid weight of the child in his arms roused a sensation of protection, and his arms tightened around Caroline. Noah was the first baby he could recall holding, and now here he was with another infant. The funny thing was he felt experienced and competent to do it. Crazy when he'd thought kids were little terrors.

He gave her back to Isabelle. "I'll join you in a few minutes. I want to wash up."

"Okay." She and the baby left the room, but she left the door open.

He stepped over to close it and heard voices from down the hall. Emily and Amelia.

"Dillard is suing me for divorce." Amelia's voice quivered, and she released a small sob. "I can't say it's a complete surprise, but I thought the money would make a difference."

"I'm sorry, sis. He's such a sleazebag. I don't know what you ever saw in him. What money are you talking about? It'll take ages for the bed-and-breakfast to pull in a profit."

"No, no, I mean the egg money."

"You told him about Carly's egg?"

"Well, sure. It's a fortune. Know what he said? He laughed and said even millions of dollars couldn't make him stay with me one more day." Amelia's soft sobs continued down the hall.

"I wouldn't put it past him to try to steal the egg. Carly asked us to keep it quiet."

"Not from my husband!"

A door shut, and he heard their footsteps coming closer. He left the door open a crack but ducked back. They said nothing more, though, as they went toward the kitchen.

Dillard knew about the egg. Lucas hadn't cared for the man from the first time he'd met him. He was all flash and no substance. Could any of these attempts to find the egg be fueled by Dillard's greed? Maybe not since he'd told Amelia he didn't care enough to hang around. But the divorce also meant Amelia would be in no hurry to leave here and go home. Lucas had wondered if living away from her grandmother's house would drive her home until it was ready for her to paint.

The original plan had been for them all to stay in the house while it was being updated, but the intensifying danger had worried him. And there was no turning back now. Once the die was cast, Ryan had jumped into the remodel with both feet. There were no working bathrooms now. And no kitchen. They couldn't move home until those rooms were ready for occupancy, and that would be weeks.

If he had it to do over again, would he still offer up their house? He thought about the quiet times he'd had with Carly, and a warmth spread through his chest. Those times had been special to him, but they also made it harder for him to step back.

He went to his bathroom and splashed water on his face, then stared at himself in the mirror. His eyes held more fear than he'd ever seen. Vince's words came back from earlier today. *"You ever think the good Lord brought Carly into your life on purpose? You're a stand-up guy, Lucas. She hadn't had the experience of meeting a man like you."*

What did that even mean—a man like him? He wasn't anything special—just a guy doing his job day after day. He'd faced death in his job plenty of times. Looking down the barrel of a gun tended to make a guy evaluate the worth of everything in his life. Relationships were every bit as hard as he'd always feared.

He wiped his face with the hand towel and hung it up. The thought of not seeing Carly every morning brought a hard lump to his stomach, but he'd done other difficult things before. This wasn't something he could decide overnight.

TWENTY-NINE

Carly rubbed her dry, tired eyes and turned off her com-
puter. The story was going well, and she was already up to ten
thousand words. Outside the sunroom's windows, the yard was
illuminated by security lights. Lucas had the place lit up like
a prison—but not to keep anyone from escaping. He wanted
plenty of notice if anyone was skulking around. He seemed
to think of everything.

Her mouth turned down at the memory of his distant
manner. What was going on with him? She hadn't had the
opportunity to ask him.

A shadow loomed in the doorway, and she jumped until
she realized it was Ryan. "You're home late."

"As always." He entered the room and dropped onto a
lounge chair where he propped his stockinged feet. "I could
just sleep here. And what are you doing up? It's after one."

"Couldn't sleep," she admitted.

"You seem to have that problem a lot."

"Comes with listening for a baby to cry." The scent of a
woman's flowery perfume drifted from his direction. "Big date
tonight?"

"Not so big. The average sort."

"Did you do anything fun?"

"Just went barhopping. How's the search going for your grandma's twin?"

"Slow. Lucas has a list of possible people after the egg. Roger Adams, the Russian mafia, and Ivan Bury. Lucas is trying to keep us all safe and the egg protected. It's been hard to find time to visit the woman he suspects might be Elizabeth, but we have a trip planned tomorrow."

He nodded. "I get it."

"Any idea when we can move back into the house?"

He hiked a brow. "You're eager to leave our humble abode?"

"I know it's a lot to have us here, and I just brought in another baby. The chaos can't be easy for either of you to take."

"We're both gone so much I don't consider it a problem. And I doubt Lucas does. He's always following his nose to uncover crime."

She had a quick flash of Lucas's face as a bloodhound and nearly laughed out loud. Something about Ryan's confession had brought down the wall that had been between them for so long. The admission of his weakness made her like him more somehow. Maybe because she no longer put him on a pedestal like she once had. It was hard to stand in the light of someone else's perfection.

"I think Lucas is tired of having us here. He's been distant," she blurted out.

Ryan shrugged. "Lucas is a hard guy to read. He's probably just immersed in work. I've seen the way he watches you. He's crazy about you."

Heat flooded Carly's cheeks, and she fiddled with the edges of her laptop. "I think you're exaggerating."

"I know my brother better than anyone. If he's acting strange, it might be because how he feels is freaking him out. He never thought he'd get married, you know. He was engaged once when he was in his midtwenties, and his fiancée couldn't stand worrying about him. He decided then and there never to let his heart get involved. And he hasn't. Until now."

Carly found it hard to breathe with Ryan's knowing gaze on her. She'd thought something was developing between her and Lucas, something more precious than the egg. But his recent behavior had made her doubt it. And since finding out the perfect Ryan had cheated, too, she wasn't so sure she wanted to get involved either. Lucas's change of direction had likely saved her from making a decision that would hurt them both.

If she ended up raising Eric's other child, any kind of relationship would move to the back burner. She'd have her hands full.

"I can see the wheels turning," Ryan said.

"Just thinking about Caroline. Kelly isn't doing well. She might not make it."

His eyes widened. "What would that mean for you?"

"I couldn't let Noah's sister vanish into the system. She might be adopted, and he'd never get a chance to know and love her."

"So you'd raise her?"

"Of course."

A slow grin spread across his face. "When did Lucas start acting weird? Yesterday when you brought the baby home?"

Ryan was right. She gave a jerky nod. "You think he doesn't want to get involved in case I'm stuck with Caroline?"

"I wouldn't want to put it quite that bluntly, but could you blame him? It's one thing to be prepared to raise one baby that's not your own, but *two*? And infants to boot? I mean, Lucas is a great guy, but he's not a saint. That's a whole other level of commitment, and it would be a lot to take that on."

He yawned and plopped his feet back to the floor. "I'm hitting the hay. Be patient with Lucas. None of this with Caroline may happen anyway. My motto is don't borrow trouble."

She told him good night and rose with her laptop in her hands. She'd told Lucas she would need to raise Caroline if Kelly died. No wonder he was running the other direction.

She'd nearly reached her bedroom when she heard the sound of sobbing coming from Amelia's room. In spite of her sister's standoffishness, Carly couldn't ignore her sister's pain. She rapped her knuckles softly on the door. "Amelia? It's me."

"You can come in," came the muffled reply.

Carly opened the door and crossed the dark room, illuminated only by the bit of moonlight streaming through the windows. She sat on the edge of the bed and touched her sister's shaking shoulders. Dillard's decision had swept through the family after dinner. "I'm so sorry, Amelia. I know you're hurting. Have you talked to him any more?"

Amelia shook her head. "I tried, but he isn't answering. What am I going to do, Carly? I didn't want to admit it to anyone, but my business isn't doing great. I can't keep the house without Dillard's income."

"You can always stay with Gram and me. The house will

be done soon, and you could base your business here. The exterior is going to look amazing, and it's bound to get you noticed in the area with so many historical homes. You're so talented, Amelia. You'll get through this."

"You got through Eric's death." Her sister paused and sniffled. "Divorce is like a death. There's rejection on top of it, but it's still loss. I guess you had a double whammy, too, when you found out about Eric and Kelly. I haven't been there for you like I should have, Carly. I'm sorry."

When Amelia took her hand, Carly returned the pressure. "You're going to be okay, Mel."

She hadn't called Amelia that in ages, ever since Dillard had sneered at her about it. Maybe some of Amelia's distance had to do with Dillard. Whatever had caused it, Carly felt the walls start to crumble.

———

Carly hadn't had much to say on the trip to Savannah to meet Elizabeth Durham. She and Lucas had brought Noah with them and had left Caroline with Carly's sisters. On the hour-long drive, Lucas had turned up the radio and she let her thoughts wander to the situation with the egg. They stopped at Lucille Godwin's antique shop, but it was closed for Memorial Day.

"Let's try calling her," she suggested. "There's an after-hours number. Let me try. Another woman might get her to open up." She didn't wait for him to nod before she pulled out her phone and placed the call. She turned on the speaker-phone.

It was answered on the third ring. "Lucille Godwin." The

woman sounded older, maybe sixty or so, but she had a lilt to her voice as if she didn't mind the call at all.

"I know this will sound crazy, Ms. Godwin, but my name is Carly Harris. My husband was Eric Harris, and I know he spoke with you several times by phone. He was murdered about ten months ago. Could you tell me about those conversations?"

There was a long pause before she answered. "I remember your husband. He claimed to have a line on a missing Fabergé egg. He brought a world of trouble down on me, though. I made some inquiries about its possible value and had a couple of Russian men approach me wanting information. I had to call the police to get them to back off. They actually threatened me if I sold it to anyone."

"I'm so sorry. Could you tell me anything about the men?"

"One was in his fifties with a bald head and hard blue eyes. He was bulky like he worked out. The other guy was younger and much skinnier, but he watched the door. I thought I heard him call the older man Dimitri, but I didn't hear clearly."

Carly exchanged a glance with Lucas. "Did they want to buy it?"

"That's what they said. Did your husband really find a Fabergé egg? Did the Russians kill him?"

"We aren't yet sure what happened. Is there anything else you can tell me?"

"Not really. The men scared me, though. You be careful, Mrs. Harris."

"I'll do my best." Carly thanked her again and ended the call. "Well, that explains a lot. Eric found the provenance papers right off and knew all along what we had. He probably used that paper to get the advance money from Ivan Bury."

"Makes sense." Lucas started the engine and pulled away from the antique shop to head to the Durham residence. "Another thing it might explain is why nothing happened until you found the egg. Maybe the Russians assumed Eric had sold it to someone else. They likely have been watching you and didn't see any evidence you knew anything."

Had Dimitri killed Eric? She turned her head and looked out at the historic homes as he drove to the Durhams' house and parked on the street.

Lucas turned off the engine. "Ready?"

She held out a shaking hand. "I'm nervous. What if it's not her?" Maybe she should have argued harder to bring Gram along. Her grandmother had a way of calmly facing every situation.

"But what if it is?" He glanced toward the house, a two-story brick Federal style with a black staircase leading to the entry. Black shutters framed the mullioned windows. "Let's find out."

She got out and lifted Noah from his seat in the back. He'd fussed a bit until he'd fallen asleep, and when the sun hit his face, he opened his blue eyes and started to squawk again.

"I'll take him. Those stairs are steep." He lifted the baby from her arms, and Noah snuggled against him, his fingers curling into Lucas's shirt.

The picture they made together seized her heart, and she pushed away the longing.

He led the way up the stairs. Elizabeth Durham was expecting them. Lucas had called and said he thought she might be able to help him with an investigation. He'd told Carly the woman sounded strong and alert on the phone. And very curious.

231

The door opened before they reached it, and a woman in the doorway looked so much like Carly that it took her breath away. The woman was clearly too young to be Elizabeth. Her scowl morphed into a dropped jaw the moment Carly stepped into view. The woman closed her mouth with a snap and took a step back. Carly's knees buckled, and she had to hang on to the railing to keep from falling.

"Detective Lucas Bennett." Lucas showed her his ID. "We're here to see your grandmother."

"Sh-she's expecting you." The woman backed away and didn't ask how they knew she was a granddaughter.

Lucas darted a glance at Carly and she saw the question in his eyes. She swallowed and managed a smile. "Thank you. I'm Carly Harris. What's your name?"

"Lainey. Lainey Durham Saunders." She shut the door behind them. "Nanna is looking forward to hearing what this is all about." She pressed her lips together. "So am I, and I'm not too happy you showed up here without explaining why you're here." Her eyes went to Carly and skittered away to land on Noah. Her dark eyes softened. "This way."

They followed her through a large entry with marble floors and a high ceiling with ornate crown molding into a parlor with walls covered in period wallpaper and furnished with historic velvet furniture. The wide painted trim was in perfect condition. The room looked too pristine to use, but the woman in the chair rose and smiled at them. Carly gasped, and it was all she could do not to gawk. Even Elizabeth's clothing, a flowing skirt and ruffled blouse, was similar to something Gram would wear.

They didn't need to ask if she might be Gram's sister. It was clear from the resemblances. And for the first time Carly realized if the surprise was in the custody of another person, the money would need to be split. If they were even willing to give up the surprise. For all she knew, it was a treasured memento.

Elizabeth glanced from Carly to Lainey, and she reached out to steady herself with a hand on the armchair. "I do believe I can see with my own eyes why you are here. Who are you?" The question was directed at Carly.

Carly sat on the sofa and held out her arms for Noah. The baby would steady her, and she snuggled the warmth of his small body for comfort. "I-I know this is going to be a shock."

"You're my granddaughter?" Elizabeth whispered.

Carly shook her head and wondered who Elizabeth thought had strayed into a secret relationship. "I believe you are my grandmother's twin sister."

Elizabeth settled back into her chair and held out her hand for Lainey, who rushed to her side. "I don't have a sister." She gave a shaky exhale. "That's a stupid remark, isn't it? When it's clear you are related. How do I have a sister?"

"Twin girls were delivered to an orphanage here in Savannah. They were each adopted by different families. My grandmother, Mary Tucker, didn't even know she was adopted, and I found the documents in the attic a few weeks ago. We've been looking for you ever since."

"Mary. Such a lovely name, and it goes well with mine." Elizabeth's hand shook as she brushed a stray lock of white hair out of her eyes. "I knew I was adopted, but I had no idea I had a sister. A *twin*, for heaven's sake! I want to meet her. Does she know you're here?"

Carly shook her head again. "I didn't want her to be

disappointed until we knew for sure. I don't think there's any doubt." She let her gaze linger on her cousin's face. "I'm thirty and widowed. This is my baby, Noah."

"He's darling," Lainey said, her voice trembling. "Can I hold him? I'm married, but my husband and I don't have children."

"Of course."

Carly let Lainey take Noah. She watched him stare at her, then nestle against her chest. What would a baby think? She and Lainey likely smelled different, so he could probably tell them apart.

She wanted to get up and hug the older woman. What a wonderful thing to have found her. "I'd love for you to meet Gram. We live in Beaufort. When would you like for me to arrange a meeting?"

Elizabeth stared at her granddaughter with a plea in her eyes. "Would it be too shocking for us to come now? Or could you fetch Mary and bring her here?"

"Gram is cooking dinner right now, and there is always enough food for an army. I'll give you the address and you can join us for dinner. She always wanted a sibling."

Elizabeth wiped tears from her cheeks. "So did I."

And just like that, the lost was found. Carly couldn't wait to see Gram's expression when Elizabeth walked in the door.

THIRTY

Lucas shot a glance at Carly as they pulled back into Beau-
fort. Flowers waved in a cheerful display of color along the
sidewalks, and everything seemed brighter and happier. Carly
had worn a smile all the way back from Savannah. "How are
you going to tell Mary?"

She turned bemused brown eyes his way. "I was just
thinking about that. I thought about letting it be a surprise,
but that might be too shocking with her age. If I'd had it to do
over again, I would have let Elizabeth know more information
before we just showed up. The resemblance between Lainey
and me was uncanny."

He wanted to say he could tell them apart easily because
of the gentle light in Carly's eyes and her caregiving manner,
but he kept that to himself. The distance between them needed
to remain.

Several police cars, lights flashing and sirens blaring,
zipped by going toward the river. "What's going on?" He
turned up his radio to see what had caused the commotion
and listened to the dispatcher. "There's a robbery attempt on-
going at the bank!"

"The egg! Go there now."

"I'll drop you off first. I don't want you and Noah in the line of fire. The robbers are armed."

Her eyes went wide, and she put her hand to her mouth. "Oh my goodness."

He turned on Boundary Street and zipped down to Bay Street. He pulled in the drive to his house and put the truck in Park. "I won't come in."

She leaped out of the truck and got Noah out of the back. "Let me know what's going on."

"I will." Once she was clear of the vehicle, he backed out of the drive and drove for the bank.

"Shots fired. Officer down, officer down," the radio squawked.

His veins turned to ice at hearing every cop's worst nightmare. He knew every one of the officers on the force, and they were all good people. Most of them had families. Praying it was only a minor wound, he got to the bank as quickly as he could. Police cars and vans surrounded the building, and an ambulance came screaming to a stop behind him. There was nowhere to park, so he pulled his truck as close to a police car as he could and left it in the street.

Paramedics got out of their vehicle, and Bernard hailed them from in front of the building. "He's over here." He spotted Lucas and waved him over.

Because of the crowd of people standing around, Lucas couldn't see which officer was down, and he stopped in front of Bernard. "Who was shot?"

Bernard's attention stayed on the paramedics blocking their view. "Brace yourself, Lucas. It's Vince."

Lucas froze, and his tongue didn't want to work. He licked his lips and managed to ask the question he feared most. "Is he dead?"

Bernard shook his head. "Chest wound. Don't know much more yet."

"Nellie. We need to get her."

"The perps got away."

"With the egg?"

"No. Response was too quick for them to get it, but they were yelling for the teller to get the box. They knew the number of the box, and they had a key as well."

Lucas rubbed his forehead. "Carly's key?"

"I don't know. Has she seen it lately?"

"I'll have to check. Last I knew it was in my safe." Lucas couldn't tear his gaze from the backs of the paramedics as they knelt over Vince. He wanted to be there encouraging his partner, but there was no room for superfluous bodies as they fought to save him.

"Go get Nellie," Bernard said. "She'll need you."

"I want to pray for Vince first." Barely aware of his surroundings, Lucas walked toward the huddled figures, and Bernard followed him.

He lifted his voice in a prayer for God to save his friend, for the paramedics and doctors to know what to do, and for Nellie and the twins.

"Amen," Bernard said, and several other officers echoed his word.

Lucas turned and ran toward his truck. Vince and his family lived in Port Royal, and Lucas drummed his fingers as he idled through slow traffic until he hit Ribaut Road. When he was able to drive faster, he pressed his foot to the accelerator and zoomed out to the ranch home.

Nellie met him at the door and didn't move to allow him inside. Her purse was on her arm, tangled in her long red hair, as if she'd been about to leave. "There's an officer down, and you're here. It's Vince, isn't it?" Her voice was strained, and her eyes were wet and full of fear. She grabbed his arm. "Is he alive?"

He embraced her and felt her trembling. "He's been shot, Nell. The paramedics are working on him now." He stepped back and let his arms fall to his sides. "Let's meet them at the hospital. Where are the twins?"

"At Vince's brother's for the weekend. I'll text him on the way and tell him to try to keep them from listening to any news until I can get to them." Her voice quavered. "Will he live?"

Lucas wanted to reassure her, but that wasn't fair either. "A gunshot to the chest, but he's still breathing, so we have to cling to hope."

She nearly fell as he escorted her to the truck, but he caught her before she could go down. Her face was set and strained, and she bit her trembling lip. He got her settled in his truck and got in to drive to the hospital.

"Vince is a strong man," he told her as he pulled out of the drive.

She gave a jerky nod. "I'm scared."

"So am I. We're all praying."

She fumbled in her purse and pulled out her phone, but her hands were shaking so much she had trouble typing. She finally managed to get the message sent and leaned forward as if to make his truck go faster.

The hospital wasn't far, but it felt like an eternity before he pulled into the lot. The ambulance came screaming past him into the ER bay. At least Vince hadn't been pronounced dead at the scene. It was all the hope Lucas could cling to.

———————

Carly had assembled the family in the living room, and Gram wore a mildly exasperated expression where she sat on the sofa. "Carly Ann, I have dinner to work on."

"It's only one, Gram. You have time, and this is something you need to hear. Something you will *want* to hear."

Carly glanced around the room and imprinted this moment in her memories. Isabelle held little Caroline on her lap in the chair, while Amelia and Emily were on the sofa with Gram between them. Noah sat in his bouncy seat and stared at sunbeams filtering through the glass.

She pulled out her phone and pulled up the picture of Elizabeth and Lainey before she knelt in front of her grandmother. "I want you to see something. Gather around, everyone."

Her sisters crowded closer to peer at the phone too. Emily gasped first. "Who are they?" Her voice was a whisper.

Gram stared at the picture for a long moment, then looked up. "Is that *Elizabeth*?"

"Yes. We found your twin. She lives in Savannah, and she's coming for dinner tonight. The other woman is her granddaughter, Lainey."

"You two look enough alike to be twins yourself," Amelia said. "I can't believe you found her! Do they have the surprise?"

"I didn't ask and I don't want anyone to bring it up tonight either. It's too soon. Let's get acquainted first, and we can worry about the surprise later. This is more important." She turned to their grandmother. "Gram has a twin sister and we have cousins!"

Her grandmother's fingers drifted to her neck. "I-I just can't believe it. I mean, of course I hoped we'd find her, but so many things could have happened. She could have died or moved so far away the chances of finding her were remote. And there she was, just an hour away. How many are coming tonight? I need to make sure I have enough food."

"You always have plenty. I think it's just Elizabeth, Lainey, and her husband. They don't have children."

"What about Lainey's mother or father? Are there any other relatives?" Gram asked.

The front door opened and shut with a slam, and Ryan, covered in drywall dust, rushed into the living room. "Where's Lucas?"

"At the bank. There was a robbery," Carly said. "What's wrong?"

"An officer was shot. It was Vince."

The words fell like an anvil on her heart. "No, not Vince."

"A gunshot to the chest. The ambulance just took him away."

"He's still alive?"

"Barely." He held her glance. "The robbers tried to get to the egg, but the police response was too fast. They got away. Vince was shot trying to stop them outside. They got away in a boat in the chaos. And they had a key from what I hear."

The key should have been in the safe. How had the robbers

gotten one? "I need to get to Lucas," she managed to say past the boulder in her throat. "He's probably devastated." Vince was a big teddy bear, and he'd been so good to her the night of the home invasion when Debby Drust had been shot.

"Bernard sent him to get Vince's wife, Nellie. They're probably at the hospital by now too." Ryan took her arm. "I'll drive you."

"I need to take Noah. He'll need to eat soon." She scooped up the baby and his diaper bag before following Ryan. "I'll drive myself. The car seat is in my vehicle."

He stopped on the porch. "You sure?"

"Yes. I'll drive, and you can ride with me." She got the baby situated in his car seat, then got behind the wheel and sped toward the hospital, praying as she drove.

She glanced at Ryan in the passenger seat. His face was pale and set. He'd known Vince a long time. "I can only imagine how Lucas feels right now. They've been partners a long time."

"This is why Lucas is scared of marriage. He doesn't want a wife to be on the other end of that phone call or visit."

What could she say to that? She'd experienced it herself, and it was horrible and terrifying. Nellie must be a mess right now. And didn't they have kids? She thought she'd heard Gram or someone say Vince had teenagers. But what was the answer? Every officer knew the risks when they pinned on the badge, and that decision affected every aspect of their life. Spouse, children, friends, parents. The effects from this shooting rippled through so many lives. She knew it firsthand after Eric's death. His parents still mourned deeply and always would.

She glanced in the mirror she'd put up to be able to see Noah's little face in the back seat. While her feelings for Lucas were real and growing—in spite of her efforts to stop them—what about her son? He'd already lost one father. Did she want to pursue a relationship with Lucas and have Noah and her face the possibility of another tremendous loss?

The thought made her gulp. It was just as well Lucas had been so strange lately. She needed to quit questioning his decision in her heart and move on herself.

She reached the hospital lot and parked as close to the ER as she could get. "He's probably in the ER waiting room with Nellie."

She hadn't been left in a waiting room by herself waiting to hear the news. The minute she'd seen Eric lying in the workshop, she'd known he was gone.

"I'll see you inside," Ryan said. "I want to get to my brother."

"I'm right behind you." She got Noah out and grabbed her purse and the diaper bag.

Finding the right things to say would be hard. Friends meant to help, but their platitudes didn't go very far into her grief. All she could do was sit with Lucas and Nellie and be there.

THIRTY-ONE

They'd been here only thirty minutes, but the wait already felt agonizing. Lucas paced the floor in front of Nellie, who huddled in a chair with her hands clasped in front of her. Her lips moved silently, and he knew she was praying even harder than he was. The hospital had rushed Vince into surgery, and they'd caught a glimpse of his white face on the gurney with tubes and machines attached.

He looked at the clock on the wall. Two o'clock. Bernard had called to check on Vince's condition, and he'd mentioned the team was reviewing video at the bank but had no leads to the robbers' identities. Not yet anyway.

Quick footsteps came his way, and he turned to see Ryan rushing toward him. His brother embraced him in a tight hug. "He's still alive?"

Lucas gave a jerky nod. "In surgery."

He released his brother and moved back as more steps came his way. Carly hurried toward him with Noah in her arms. A warm sensation gathered in his chest. She had so much on her plate today with having found Elizabeth, but she still came immediately. That was so like her.

She grabbed his arm with her free hand. "Any news?"

He shook his head. "The nurse said they'd try to let us know how things were progressing. It's all-hands-on-deck when an officer is injured, and I know they're doing their best for Vince."

He introduced Carly to Nellie, who made an obvious effort to gather herself and smile at Carly. "Vince has talked about you. Thank you for coming." Nellie reached up to take the baby's hand. "And this must be Noah. What a little doll."

"Thank you." Carly sat beside Nellie, and Noah reached for the other woman's long red hair. His waving hand managed to grab a few strands.

"Mind if I hold him?" Nellie asked in a low voice.

"Of course." Carly laid Noah in her lap. "Having children around during a trauma helps sometimes."

Nellie nodded. "My twins were a big comfort to my mother when my dad died." Her eyes filled with tears. "I don't want to bury my husband." She hugged Noah to her chest and rested her chin on his fuzzy hair.

"I know you're scared," Carly said. "Scared to lose him, scared of the future, afraid for your kids. Take one minute at a time. He's still breathing, and he's got good doctors working on him. They got him to surgery fast."

Nellie gulped. "You're right, I know you're right. I'm just so scared the doctor will walk in here and tell me he's gone. It's playing over and over in my head like a movie that's already happened."

"But it hasn't. We'll keep praying and trusting God in this. Vince is a big, strong guy. Hold on to your faith and on to hope."

Tears rolled down Nellie's cheeks. "I'm trying." With Noah in one arm, she reached out and grasped Carly's hand. "My kids want to be here, but I don't want them to hear bad news from the doctor."

"They're teenagers, right?"

Nellie's smile held pride. "Sixteen. Twins, Paisley and Paul."

"You need them here with you, and they need you."

"A-and if the worst happens, they should be allowed the chance to say goodbye to Vince." Nellie glanced at Ryan and Lucas, but before she could ask, Ryan turned toward the door.

"I'll get them. They're at Vince's brother's, right?"

"Yes. Thank you," she called after him as he hurried through the door. She slumped back and hugged Noah again.

The baby was beginning to fuss a bit, and Lucas thought he was probably hungry by the way he chewed on his fist. Carly took him and walked the floor a few minutes before she turned toward Lucas. "Is there a private room I could use?"

"This way." Lucas led her to a small consultation room. "This should work. I'll stand guard out here." He hesitated. "Thank you for coming. You're just what Nellie needed. You've been in her shoes."

He hadn't stopped to think much about what she'd endured when Eric died, but he was seeing it play out in front of him now. And she'd rushed to be here the minute she'd heard, even though it had to have been hard to step into a situation she'd already experienced. He suspected it was because of affection for him.

She tipped her head up. "I didn't have the hope she has. Eric was dead when I found him. But I know the fear she feels about her future and what will become of her and her children. I had my grandmother, and I know Nellie has you and her family too. She's blessed in that way."

"And the whole force will be there for them." He ran his hand through his hair. "Listen to me, talking like it's already happened. Vince isn't dead yet, and by God's grace, I pray he pulls through. But I'm scared."

She put her hand on his. "I wish I could help your fear and pain."

He set his other hand on top of hers and squeezed. "You already have by coming." Noah's complaints grew louder. "I think you'd better feed your son."

She nodded and slipped into the small room to find a comfortable chair. Lucas leaned his back against the door to protect her privacy and thought about all Carly had endured. Noah would never know his father, and Caroline wouldn't either. That realization stirred compassion for the baby girl being cared for at his house.

———

It was nearly four in the afternoon by the time the doctor dressed in blue scrubs entered the waiting room. Lucas shot to his feet with Noah in his arms. He took Nellie's hand, and she hung on to his fingers in a tight grip. Carly moved close on his other side as he examined the doctor's face for some kind of clue to the news he was about to deliver.

The doctor, a man in his fifties, glanced around until his gaze landed on the little group huddled together by the window. "Mrs. Steadman?"

Nellie nodded, and her grip on Lucas tightened. "I-is Vince going to live?"

The doctor's lips tipped up in what might have been a half

smile. "Well, he's not out of the woods yet, but we retrieved the bullet and stopped the bleeding. I'm cautiously optimistic he's going to make it, but his recovery will be a while. We're lucky the bullet missed his lungs." He reached out and touched her shoulder. "A nurse will let you know when he's in his room and you can see him."

"Thank the good Lord," Nellie whispered. "And thank you for all you did for him, Doctor."

"My pleasure." He released her shoulder and walked away at a fast clip.

Lucas embraced Nellie with his free arm, but she pulled away when a commotion at the door alerted her that Ryan had returned with the twins. The teenagers called out, "Mom!" and rushed toward her.

She hugged them. "The doctor was just here, and your dad is going to be okay."

It wasn't quite what the doctor said, but Lucas would have offered the same reassurance. He felt a little giddy himself at the news. He'd been dreading hearing that Vince had died. He watched Vince's little family celebrate, and it felt like watching a happy party through a window. On the outside looking in.

They'd want to include him if they knew he felt that way, but all he had was Ryan. It used to be enough, but now he wasn't so sure. He stared at Carly's beautiful face with her shining eyes and joyous smile. His arms tightened around the welcome weight of the baby in his arms.

Carly's smile widened when she saw him staring at her. "Wonderful news, just wonderful. I should probably go home and help Gram finish prepping for the most important dinner of her life." She wrinkled her nose. "Funny how easy it is to call your house 'home' when you probably can't wait to get the Tuckers out of there. We've taken over everything." Her smile wobbled and flattened. "Honestly, Lucas, I'm sorry for what we've done to your life. I think little Caroline might have been the final straw that added to the chaos."

"She hasn't been a problem."

"You sure? I could look for a house to rent."

"You know how impossible that would be with the busy season starting. Besides, I don't want you to leave."

He checked his impulse to say more when he couldn't commit to too much. His emotions and feelings were too chaotic and unfamiliar to be able to nail them down to talk about. Or even for him to understand them.

"I'll check on Kelly while you go on home. I'll be along as quickly as I can. I think Nellie will be all right now. She and the kids will be able to see Vince after a while, and they won't need me."

She lifted Noah out of his arms. "I'll relieve you of this guy. Don't leave the hospital if Vince and his family need you. We can handle things at dinner."

At her words he realized he didn't want to miss the happy drama that would be unfolding in his living room. He'd found himself an integral part of the Tuckers' lives, and he didn't want to be on the outside looking in. Not if he could help it.

"I'll be there." He watched her leave with the baby before telling Nellie to call him if she needed him.

He went up the elevator to the ICU and stopped at the nurses' station to ask about Kelly. He showed his ID. "Could you tell me how she's doing? We're taking care of her baby."

The reserve drained out of the nurse's brown eyes at the

realization he was more than a police officer. "No change. Still on a vent."

"Is she going to live?"

The nurse's gaze flickered. "We'll do the best we can."

His fingers curled into his palms. That didn't sound good. "Thank you. Is it possible to see her? I'd like to reassure her that her baby daughter is doing fine."

The nurse hesitated before pointing to the room. "Just a minute."

He thanked her and went to Kelly's room. Myriad beeping and suction noises filled the room. Tubes and contraptions were connected to her. Her eyes were closed, and she was so very pale that she hardly looked alive.

Though he wasn't sure she could hear him, he leaned down and spoke into her ear. "This is Detective Lucas Bennett. Carly Harris is taking good care of Caroline. She's eating and doing well. She and Noah enjoy being with each other too. But nothing can take the place of her mother. You need to fight hard to get well, Kelly. Come back to your baby girl."

There was no obvious response, but he put his hand on her shoulder and prayed for her before he left. He'd done all he could do for her, and she was in God's hands. It hurt to think her little girl might grow up without parents. With a heavy heart he made his way out of the hospital to his truck. The events of the past few days left him reeling, and he didn't know how to feel about much of anything. Especially Carly.

THIRTY-TWO

Gram put her hand on her stomach. "Heavens, I'm so nervous I have hummingbirds flying around in my stomach. What if she doesn't like me? Do I look all right?" She patted her white hair. Her updo was firmly in place with bejeweled combs and pins, and she wore a blue flowered dress with a flowing skirt.

Carly hugged her. "You look beautiful." She caught the aroma of Gram's Tabu cologne. Her grandmother had nursed the last bottle Grandpa had given her for as long as Carly had been alive, and it was nearly gone. The fragrance could still be purchased, but Gram saved the one Grandpa had bought her for special occasions. This meeting was so important to her grandmother, and she planned to do whatever she could to make it a wonderful evening.

The door in the entry opened, and Lucas's voice called out Carly's name. "In the kitchen!" she called back.

His footsteps came toward them, and he smiled when he caught sight of them. "Look at you, Mary. You're a vision. I need a kiss." He caught her in a hug and brushed his lips across her cheek.

She smacked him on the arm when he let go. "Don't be a

tease tonight, Lucas. I'm too scared to handle it." Her voice wobbled. "To think I have a sister is so amazing. I can't quite take it all in."

He grinned. "She'll love you. No one can help it. You're the Pied Piper and impossible to resist."

She smacked her lips. "I forgot lipstick. I'll be right back."

Carly smiled as Gram rushed from the room. "She's been like that ever since she heard. Thanks for trying to reassure her." She glanced at the clock on the wall above the sink. "Elizabeth and her family should be here any minute."

"Both of the babies asleep?"

"Down for a nap at the same time. In the same bed too. They like being next to each other, and it's adorable to see them all nestled together."

The smile faded from his hazel eyes. "I saw Kelly. She's still on a vent. No real improvement. The nurse wouldn't tell me much."

Carly winced. "I wish she had family here to look in on her, be with her."

"I talked to her a minute—told her Caroline was doing well and the children love each other already." He fell silent a moment. "I prayed for her, but I didn't have a good feeling when I left. I'll be surprised if she makes it."

He didn't seem as distant since Vince was shot. Maybe he needed her support regardless of how he felt about a relationship with her. She wanted to probe and ask what he was thinking, but now wasn't the time. Not when the big event was about to happen.

He turned toward the window. "I think I heard a car."

She followed him across the dining room to peer out the

front window. A white sedan was in the drive, and a man about Lucas's age got out of the driver's side. Carly's pulse sped up. They were here! Lainey exited the passenger side and opened the back door to let Elizabeth emerge. The older woman looked even more like Gram in the undiluted sunlight, especially with her hair up like Gram's.

Elizabeth had changed into something with more of a classic feel. Her black skirt and white blouse were tailored and refined. The black pumps gleamed, and she carried a tiny purse tucked under one arm. Her makeup was the perfect touch—not too much and in good taste. Maybe she was trying to impress her newly found sister.

Gram came down the stairs wearing a touch of pink lipstick. "Is she here?"

"They're climbing the steps to the porch right now," Lucas said.

"Oh my stars." Gram pressed her hand to her stomach. "Where are your sisters?"

"Getting ready. They should be down any minute. And the babies should be awake shortly as well. Go on into the living room, and I'll bring them in so we're not gaping at them in the foyer."

"You're right, I know you're right." Her flustered grandmother grabbed Lucas's arm. "Hold me up, Lucas. I just might faint."

"I've got you," he said, his voice soothing. He escorted her into the living room.

Footsteps clattered on the stairs, and her sisters came down. Isabelle held Caroline, and Amelia carried Noah. "Go on into the living room," Carly said. "They're coming to the door now, and I'll introduce everyone." Her sisters nodded and hurried for the living room.

The doorbell rang, and Carly rushed for the door and opened it. "Right on time. Come in. Gram is so excited to meet you."

Lainey was in the lead. "This is my husband, Holt." She gestured to the tall blond man at her side. "My grandmother is about to stroke out from excitement."

"So is mine. It's good to meet you, Holt. Come on in." Carly opened the door wide and stepped back to let them file in. "The rest of the family is in the living room."

Holt put Elizabeth's hand on his arm. "Steady as she goes, Grandma."

Elizabeth did appear a little wobbly, and Carly stepped past her to escort them. Was that a whiff of Tabu? Her grand-mother's signature scent couldn't be missed. How crazy that they wore the same cologne.

When she reached the living room, her grandmother sprang up and pressed trembling hands together. Her gaze went past Carly to the woman directly behind her, and her eyes widened. "Y-you look just like me. I mean, I look like you. I don't know what I mean."

Carly stepped aside to let the meeting evolve however it would, and Elizabeth took a step closer to Gram. "Mary. I've always loved that name." Her voice quivered. "I want to hear all about your life and everything."

"These are my sisters," Carly said after an awkward silence.

Elizabeth didn't take her eyes from Gram. "I'm so pleased to meet you." Her blue eyes filled with moisture.

Gram finally stepped away from the sofa. "Do you mind if

I hug you, Elizabeth? I've wanted a sister my whole life." Her voice trembled, and the tears gathering in her eyes rolled down her cheeks.

Mary opened her arms, and the two women fell into a tight embrace. Carly sniffled and realized she'd stepped into the circle of Lucas's arms. His grip steadied her, and regardless of what happened in the future, he was here for her now.

———

Lucas watched Carly scurry around the house all evening, making sure everyone was happy and had what they needed. It was so much in her nature, she couldn't sit on the sofa and let anyone else do the serving. She caught Lucas's eyes on her several times and exchanged smiles. One of the things about her that drew him was her giving nature.

He'd checked his safe and found the key. He reviewed his security videos and his gut tightened when he spotted a man wearing a ski mask sneaking in a week ago, before the family descended on his house. The man's back was to the camera at the safe, but Lucas could see enough to realize the guy had taken an impression of the key before he locked the safe back up. Maybe the headset he wore was one of those new safe-cracking tools that let him hear when the right combination was reached.

Mary and Elizabeth, though separated for almost seventy years, bonded immediately. Mary had begun calling her by the nickname Beth, and they seemed to have never been apart. Elizabeth told her about her only child, a son who had died in Afghanistan, and Lainey talked with all of the sisters as if they'd been friends forever. It was already eight, and no one showed any indication they were ready to leave.

Lainey sat on the floor with Carly and the babies, and they looked like twins themselves. Lainey's hair was straighter and a little longer, but they could easily be mistaken for one another. It was uncanny, though Lucas thought he'd be able to pick out Carly from her expression.

Elizabeth's phone rang, and she frowned. "It's the police. What on earth?"

Lucas stood from the side chair where he'd been watching the action. "You want me to take that?"

Elizabeth held out the phone. "If you wouldn't mind. I can't imagine why they would be calling me."

Lucas took the phone and answered the call. "Detective Lucas Bennett answering Elizabeth Durham's phone."

There was a pause before a female officer on the other end replied. "Is Ms. Durham all right?"

"Yes, she's fine. She asked me to answer her phone."

The officer identified herself. "There's been a break-in at her residence, and we were trying to see if anyone was injured. We found blood spatter in the living room and were concerned."

"She and her granddaughter are with us. The grand-daughter's husband too. I think those are the only residents of the house."

He glanced at Lainey's husband for confirmation since he had joined Lucas where he stood. Holt nodded. "Just the three of us."

Lucas switched on the speaker. "I have you on speaker-phone, Officer. Would you repeat what you told me?"

"Of course. A neighbor reported hearing gunshots from the residence at 7:25 p.m., and officers responded immediately. They found the back door breached. When they entered, they discovered the home had been ransacked. As they continued through the rooms, they found a large pool of blood in the living room. No body, though."

"Oh my stars," Elizabeth whispered. "I'm glad we were gone. I have security cameras."

Lainey rose and went to squeeze her grandmother's shoulder.

"I can tell you where to find the security cameras," Holt said.

"We'd appreciate that," the officer said. "The family won't be allowed back in to stay until we process the scene."

Lucas handed the phone to Holt, who gave the officer a list of four cameras and their locations.

Mary patted her sister's leg. "It will be okay, Beth."

It wasn't safe for them to go home, and Lucas had to be the one to tell them. He squatted in front of Elizabeth. "I'd prefer you to stay here until we're sure what's going on at your house."

He had no question what had happened—one of the parties after the egg had tracked her house. Had their visit today led them right to Elizabeth's door? And who had been shot? Could two of the factions have been there at the same time? Those were questions he couldn't answer, but Elizabeth and her family needed to know what they were all up against.

He glanced at Carly and her sisters. They stood in solidarity with their arms around each other. Carly's brown eyes were wide, but she gave him the nod he needed to start the story.

"There's something you need to know about your birth.

Your mother left each of you something of value when she couldn't keep you. Carly found a painted egg in an old trunk, and it opened the mystery of what had happened. She sells collectibles and decided to strip the old paint off the egg. Under it, she discovered a beautiful enameled egg that opened. The inside was pure gold."

"Like a Fabergé egg?" Lainey asked. "I love those."

Carly broke away from her sisters and came to join him. "It *is* a Fabergé egg—one of the missing ones. I believe it's the Hen with Sapphire Pendant. Ever since we found out about Gram's sister and began to try to find you, someone—or multiple someones—have been one step ahead of us."

Lucas told them about the break-in at Mary's house and the female burglar he shot. He moved on to Anna Martin's death and the break-in at Grace Adams Hill's house as well as the attack on Kelly.

"And someone tried to impersonate a Willard Auction House expert," Carly said. "I nearly gave him the egg but changed my mind."

"Someone tried to steal the egg from the bank today," Lucas said. "The danger around this is immense."

"Back up a second," Lainey said. "You said Grandma's birth mother gave each child something. You got the egg. What did Grandma receive?"

"It appears to be the surprise," Carly said. "That's probably what the burglars at your house were searching for."

Lainey perched on the arm of the sofa beside her grandmother. "This sounds terrifying. What would this surprise look like?"

"There are no pictures of it, but the descriptions say it's

a gold hen plucking a sapphire pendant out of a nest," Carly said. "The hen and nest are studded with tiny diamonds. It's thought the hen might have ruby eyes. That surprise might be inside a golden yolk, but no one is really sure. Have you seen anything like that?" She glanced from Lainey to Elizabeth.

Both women shook their heads. "It doesn't sound familiar."

"Do you have any old trunks or safes around that your mother left you?" Carly asked.

Elizabeth pursed her lips. "I have some antique furniture scattered throughout the house. I've never gone through looking for anything like this, though."

"I'd like to examine what you have once you're allowed back in the house," Carly said. "It's possible the burglars found it and made off with it, but I'd like to check."

Mary rose. "I'll sleep with Carly tonight, and you can have my room. Lainey and Holt, you can have the big bed, and there's enough room to put in a twin size bed as well. I'll freshen things up for you. Lucas, could you see to moving in a twin?"

He nodded. "There's an extra twin in Ryan's room. I'll move it over."

And just like that, the size of his newfound family grew.

THIRTY-THREE

This had gone far enough.

After a restless night of veering between praying for peace and trying to distract herself by writing a page or two of her novel, Carly grabbed her phone after breakfast and retreated to the sunroom while the rest of the family lingered over the pancakes Elizabeth had whipped up.

She motioned for Lucas to follow her. "I'm going to call the auction house and get that egg out of my possession. Maybe the danger will vanish when they know I don't have it any longer."

"I'm glad you thought of it on your own. I was going to suggest it."

She curled up on the lounge chair in a puddle of sunlight streaming through the windows. Her hand trembled as she called up Brian Schoenwald's number. As it rang through, she put it on speakerphone so Lucas could listen in.

"Schoenwald," the male voice said.

"Hello again, this is Carly Harris. I'm calling about the egg in my possession."

"Ms. Harris, I'm so glad you called. We're still on for Friday?"

"Could you come sooner?"

"I'm free today. If I can get a flight, I'll text you the number and you can have the police verify it's really me and I'm on that plane. I can be there by three this afternoon."

"I appreciate the extra care. There are a lot of security issues here around it. You're not wasting any time."

"We are prepared to deal with those security issues. It's what we do. And this is a find of utmost importance. I'll text you a picture of me boarding the plane also."

"I appreciate it," Lucas chimed in. "I'm an investigator with the police department, and I'll verify your identity."

"Of course, Detective." Mr. Schoenwald paused. "Are you prepared to relinquish custody of the egg to us immediately? If so, I'll prepare a security detail to pick it up. That will take a few days to arrange."

Carly's chest compressed in an almost painful rejection of doing just that. But she had to. The longer she insisted on hanging on to the egg, the more people would be in jeopardy. She had no idea who had been injured—or killed—last night, but the thought that she was responsible haunted her.

She locked gazes with Lucas and took strength from the strong conviction in his eyes and the slight nod he gave. "Yes. I think it's safest for everyone," she said. "Go ahead and arrange it. If it's what we all think it is, of course."

"Very good. I'll see you both this afternoon."

With the call ended, Carly dropped her phone and buried her face in her hands. "This is a nightmare, Lucas. If Elizabeth and her family had been home, they could be dead right now."

The cushion she was on sank with Lucas's weight, and his strong arm encircled her. "It's not your fault."

She leaned into the warmth of his bulk and felt the steady

beat of his heart against her side. The scent of his spicy cologne mingled with the soap he'd used in the shower this morning. It was a very appealing combination. Time seemed to stand still, and she didn't dare lift her chin to stare into his face. If she did that and he didn't kiss her, she didn't think she could stand the disappointment. Better not to go there when things had been so weird between them.

Struggling to find a somewhat normal tone, she clenched her hands together in her lap. "I know it's not my fault, but I feel like I should have stopped it somehow. Um, have you heard how Vince is this morning? And Kelly?"

He removed his arm from around her, and she felt bereft. A lump formed in her throat that he hadn't picked up on her vibes of how much she longed to be in his arms. She fumbled for her phone and swallowed past the lump.

"Vince is laughing and cutting up." He pulled out his phone and showed her a photo of Vince's family crowded around his bed. The big guy sported a huge smile.

"I'm so relieved."

"Me too."

"And Kelly?"

"No news about her. I did hear from the officer in Savannah, though. They've processed the house, and Elizabeth and her family can go in now. But I don't think they should stay until we know it's safe."

She finally thought she had her emotions reined in enough to meet his eyes. "I don't think Gram wants Elizabeth to leave. Like, not ever."

He smiled. "I picked up on that."

"Did Ryan come home last night? I never saw him."

Lucas rose and stepped away. "Yeah, about one. I don't know how he keeps those late hours."

"I was worried about him with everything going on."

"He knows how to take care of himself."

"I know he's trained with a gun, but anyone can be ambushed. Like Eric. And Vince."

Lucas winced. "True enough. I'll rouse the troops for a trip back to their house. They can get some belongings while you search the house for that egg surprise. It's only nine. We have time to get there, search, and return by three. It would be great if the surprise was found. Once the news is out that the egg's in the hands of the auction house, the danger all around should be over."

"Maybe this nightmare will be over soon and we'll be out of your hair. You've been a real trouper to deal with all of us. The crowd keeps expanding. The next thing you know, neighbors will think you're the one running the bed-and-breakfast."

His grin widened. "It hasn't been so bad."

Had his manner thawed a little? Carly thought so, but now that he'd moved away, she was glad he hadn't kissed her. It had been a moment of weakness and fear, and she needed to keep her guard up. While he seemed so different from other men she'd been around, there was no guarantee he wasn't just like Ryan. Or her dead husband, for that matter.

———

Carrying Noah, Carly walked behind Lucas through the trashed home. The doors to the entertainment center stood open, and wires and electronic parts had been pulled out. Several antique armoires lay tipped on their fronts. All the kitchen utensils lay scattered on the floor. Dressers with the drawers pulled and splintered were strewn around the bedrooms. All of Elizabeth's lovely things—destroyed.

The blood in the living room was a gruesome reminder of the violence done here last night. Still no word on who that might have been. Lucas tried to steer Elizabeth around it into another room, but the older woman stared at the stain and shuddered before moving to the kitchen at his guidance.

Lainey set a suitcase in the foyer as Carly exited the living room with Elizabeth. "Let me take the baby while you have a look around."

Noah's warm solid weight had been her comfort as she walked through the destruction, but Carly handed him over anyway. "Thank you. It's hard to know where to look. There's no safe anywhere? An attic or a basement that might hold old boxes from when your grandma was a child?"

Lainey adjusted the baby on her shoulder. "I hate the basement, so I never go there. Grandma doesn't either. She's afraid of all the 'haint' stories her mother used to tell her. I don't think either of us have gone down there. Let me show you the stairway." She led Carly to a utility room off the kitchen. "We had a furnace put in a few years ago, and Holt went down with the HVAC guy. He had to take a broom down to clear out the spiderwebs."

Carly shuddered. "I think I'd better at least give it a look, though."

Lucas grabbed a broom hanging on the wall. "I'll go with you."

He opened the door and flipped on the light. A weak yellow light illuminated old wooden steps that descended into a dark well below.

Holt stepped into the room behind them. "There's another switch at the bottom. I can show you. I didn't search much down there and spent as little time in it as possible. It's as old as the hills."

Lucas stepped away from the doorway to allow Holt to go first. "After you." Holt stepped down the stairs with Lucas on his heels.

"Call me when it's safe," Carly said from the second step down.

The place smelled dank and musty. It seemed like something out of *Poltergeist* or *The Amityville Horror*. She swallowed the sour taste in her mouth and moved toward the third step when Lucas called her name.

She could do this. She had to. Finding the surprise was the only way to keep everyone safe.

The odor of something dead grew as she descended into the dim light below. Though she knew it was a dead mouse most likely, the stench didn't help her nerves. It took all her courage to step onto the old stone floor and move toward Lucas, who was still sweeping out cobwebs overhead from the floor joists and hanging pipes.

Lucas had to stoop a bit, and Carly wanted to follow suit so she didn't slide her head into something icky, but it would be too hard to clearly see into every nook and cranny. She flipped on her phone flashlight and angled it around at the walls, hoping to find some kind of hiding space. It took fifteen minutes to examine the walls and find nothing.

The men waited for her at the bottom of the stairs, and she headed that way. She started to put her phone back in her pocket without remembering to turn off the light. The movement illuminated the ceiling. She hadn't thought of examining everything under the floorboards.

"Hang on, let me look around a bit more."

"Take your time," Lucas said. "If you see anything scary, just yell."

"Oh, I will." She shone the light under the floorboards and around the pipe all the way back toward where an ancient oil furnace sat.

Holt had told her they'd opted not to have the old relic cut up and hauled away because of the cost, and it loomed in her light like a scary torture device. What a scaredy-cat she was. She aimed the flashlight in that final space and squinted. Was that some kind of box clear in the back? She'd need someone taller to see better.

"Lucas, can you come here?"

"Coming."

The sound of his footsteps coming closer was a comfort. He reached her and took her elbow. "What is it?"

"See if you can reach whatever that is back there."

He added his light to hers. "I'll get it."

She squinted as it came into sharper focus. It was clearly an old chest. "Can you reach it?"

"I think I need a ladder. I saw one over at the foot of the stairs." He retreated into the dim light and returned with the ladder.

Carly's pulse pounded. The chest probably held tools or something else mundane. But she couldn't stop the hope that welled in her chest. Maybe this would all be over soon. She could leave Lucas and the police to figure out who had been behind it. All she cared about was that her family was safe.

Lucas propped the ladder against the old furnace. "This is an old octopus coal burner. It was gravity fed. They don't make them like this anymore."

"Thank goodness," Carly said.

He reached the top rung and leaned over the top to grab the chest perched atop a rough-hewn shelf. He grunted as he pulled it toward him. "Got it." It banged onto the top of the furnace, then scraped across the top until he could get it onto his shoulder.

She stood at the bottom of the ladder and reached toward him. "You can hand it down to me."

"I don't think you can lift it. It's pretty heavy. I've got it." He descended the ladder carefully, rung by rung. "Let's look at this upstairs."

She nodded and followed him to the stairs. They'd soon know what had been so carefully hidden all these years.

THIRTY-FOUR

Lucas set the chest on the floor of the kitchen and knelt beside it. The stench of the basement still filled his nose. "It's got a lock. I'll need something to break or pick it." He glanced up at Elizabeth and her family.

"There's an old ring of keys hanging on the wall to the basement." Lainey went to the utility room but came back almost immediately. "It's gone. Maybe the burglars took it. It's a good thing they didn't find the chest."

"Probably. It won't do them any good without a lock to try, though." Lucas yanked on the lock, but it was built to keep intruders out. He'd need an axe or something.

His phone rang, and his brother's face lit up the screen. "Hey, Ryan."

"Lucas, do you guys have Caroline?"

"No, she was sleeping. Isabelle was taking care of her."

"They're both gone. Caroline's diapers, clothes, and formula are missing too. Isabelle wouldn't have just gone for a walk and taken all the baby's necessities, including Noah's bouncy seat."

Carly crowded closer, and he put his arm around her. "Check the security cameras."

"I did. They don't show a thing."

"How's that possible?"

"I haven't looked closely enough to tell, but everything has been wiped out. Isabelle didn't call you to say anything about taking the baby somewhere?"

"Nope. She didn't have access to a car, right?"

"Right, and she doesn't have a license. Both our vehicles were gone, and Carly's is here. I have no idea where they went or why. I had a phone call about a problem at the house, and when I was done, our house seemed quiet, so I started searching for her. That's when I discovered she and Caroline were missing."

"Be there as quickly as we can. Call the police." He hung up and told the family crowding around what had happened. "I'll take the chest with us, but we need to find Isabelle and Caroline."

Carly bit her lip. "C-could someone have taken them?"

"Maybe. We don't know a lot about Kelly. She claims the baby is Eric's, but we don't know if that's true or not. If a member of Kelly's family decided to take Caroline and Isabelle stood in their way, they could have taken her too."

Carly's brown eyes were huge in her white face. "What about my other sisters?"

"Ryan didn't mention them. They were going out to lunch, weren't they?"

Relief lit Carly's face. "That's right. At eleven. I'll text them and tell them what's happening."

Elizabeth wrung her hands. "This is awful. Who could have done such a terrible thing?"

No one answered, and Lainey steered her grandmother toward the door. "Let's get out of here."

Elizabeth allowed her granddaughter to lead her out to their car while Lucas and Carly headed to his truck. Holt lingered to lock up behind them. Lucas put the chest in the back while Carly secured Noah in his car seat.

"I need to find Isabelle and Caroline. I'm scared, Lucas." Her voice wobbled, and her eyes filled with tears.

Though it was stupid and playing with his own emotions, he pulled her against his chest. "We'll find them. Ryan's already called the police by now, and they'll be all over this. Have faith."

He liked the feel of her in his arms. She fit perfectly. But he didn't want her to pick up the wrong vibe, so he released her. "Let's get going."

He waited until Holt was safely behind the wheel and pulling out with the women, then he flipped on his lights and siren to go around him and speed toward Beaufort. Carly looked straight ahead with her hands clasped in her lap. Her lips moved, and he thought she was probably praying like he was inside.

This wasn't good. In fact, it was terrifying. There was no reason for Isabelle to have taken all of Caroline's things. She wouldn't be trying to run off with the baby. He wished Kelly had a family member close by he could call. That was a black hole in the investigation. She had a few friends but her only family were her parents in Florida, and they were too ill to travel. If another family member wanted Caroline, they would have let Isabelle go.

Carly's phone dinged in her lap, and she lifted it to read. She gasped.

Lucas slowed his speed for safety. "What's happened?"

"I-it's from someone demanding the egg in return for

269

Isabelle and Caroline." Carly held up the phone. "He says no police or we'll never see them again."

His thoughts raced on proper protocol in a kidnapping. "What are the details of their demands?"

"I'm to retrieve the egg and wait for further instructions for delivering it. Once they get it, they'll let me know the exchange site in an hour. We can barely make it to the bank by then."

"Most of the time, giving kidnappers what they want doesn't work. They aren't even doing an exchange at the same time. You hand over the egg, and they'll vanish. You'll never know what happened to Caroline and Isabelle. I need to call in the FBI so we can find them before this goes down. We'll see how they say to handle this."

He didn't wait for her to agree but called Bernard directly. His boss promised to get the FBI there right away. They had a field office in Columbia.

"That's over two hours away!" he told his boss. "I'll try to stall them." He ended the call and increased his speed. "Text the guy back and tell him we're out of town and can't do the drop that quickly. Tell them you need overnight."

"Overnight! We can't leave my sister and Caroline in their hands that long."

"The FBI can be here in a couple of hours. Maybe sooner if they happen to have someone on a case nearby. Hold on, Carly. We'll find them."

His words sounded hollow, even to him.

Carly's hands trembled as she texted back the phone number and told him she was out of town and would need more time. She was a ball of nerves and struggled to keep from sobbing. Even trying to marshal her thoughts enough to make a coherent sentence was hard, and she fell silent as she waited for the kidnapper to return her text.

Lucas was on the phone to Bernard again, asking him to track her phone and see if they could discover the location of the man on the other end. What if her sister and little Caroline were in the hands of the Russian mafia? Would they really turn them back over?

Lucas ended his call. "We're in luck. There's an expert on child abduction in Savannah on vacation. They've called her in, and she'll be here within the hour. The FBI has more resources than local departments."

She wanted to feel relieved and optimistic, but her heart was a stone in her chest. Why had she ever found the egg? The hole they were in got deeper and deeper. No material item was worth what her family had endured. She wished she'd never opened that chest in the attic. Well, except for finding Gram's sister. That had been wonderful and necessary, even with the trauma of the burglary at their house.

Her phone dinged with a message, and her gut clenched. *You have until nine tonight.*

She moistened her lips. "They want it by nine."

Lucas nodded. He shot a glance at her, then reached over and took her hand. "Hang in there, Carly. At least now we know it's all about the egg. Caroline's family didn't take her or anything like that. Narrowing down our possible suspects helps immensely."

"How can that help? We have several possible groups after the egg—we have no idea who is running things in the shadows or how to find him."

"We have a few clues yet that might lead us to the right culprit. I still think Eric was the first casualty of someone's interest in the egg."

She gave a jerky nod. "I believe that, too, but there's no guarantee the person who took Caroline and Isabelle is the first one who learned of the egg."

He left his hand on hers. "Bernard has a lead on Dimitri, who seems to be in the area. He sent a couple of officers over to see if he could grab him. If we can find Dimitri to talk to him, we might learn something about the Russians."

Hope was elusive, and even that news didn't lift the terrible fear pressing down on her. "That's good. But it could be someone hired by Ivan Bury. And I didn't really believe Roger Adams had no knowledge of the egg. It's such an endless circle of possibilities."

"We'll lay all this out to the FBI and see what they can find."

"Do you really have any hope we'll get Isabelle and Caroline back safely?"

He squeezed her hand more tightly. "Hope is all we ever have, Carly."

She ducked her head. "Yes. If I hadn't had hope when Eric was murdered, I don't know how I would have gone on. Hope that God had a plan for my future, hope for building a life with my son, hope for finding my way."

"Our lives are so fragile. Maybe it's by design so we look to God."

His words brought some comfort but not enough. "They are both *children*. What kind of monster terrorizes children? Isabelle must be so afraid."

Her phone rang before Lucas could reply, and she snatched it up. "It's Dad." She swiped it on. "Dad, someone kidnapped Isabelle and a baby we've been taking care of. They're demanding a ransom."

"Ransom? We don't have enough money to attract a kidnapper."

"Where are you? It's a long story."

"I just landed at the airport. I was going to surprise all of you for Mom's birthday."

"I'm on my way back to town. I'll see you at the house. I should be there in half an hour."

"I should arrive at the same time. Where's my mother?"

"At the house. There's a lot to tell you." She closed her eyes in a brief moment of despair. "I heard from the kidnapper a few minutes ago."

"Don't call the FBI. That's dangerous to Isabelle."

She started to tell him that was out of her hands, but she bit back the words. It was a terrible thing when she couldn't trust her own father. His views and opinions were usually wrong. "I'll see you at home."

She ended the call and exhaled. "Dad is at the airport and on his way to the house. He said not to call the FBI."

"Trust me, Carly. We need to do this right if we want them back."

She caught his gaze and held it. "I do trust you. I hope you're right."

She broke eye contact and glanced at the clock on the

dash. Nearly one. They had eight hours to figure this out. And Mr. Schoenwald would be here in two hours and had already texted her a picture of him on the plane. It was too late to cancel the appointment with him. Maybe that was for the best. Once the FBI rescued Isabelle and Caroline, she wanted that egg in someone else's hands.

THIRTY-FIVE

The house was as chaotic as Lucas expected when he carried Noah inside with Carly beside him. Her dad was pacing in the living room while Mary, Elizabeth, and Carly's sisters wept on the sofa. Holt and Lainey sat quietly with Ryan in the living room. Lucas noticed the holstered gun on Ryan's belt. He'd been prepared.

Noah fussed on Lucas's shoulder, and he bounced him soothingly. He waited to tell Carly about Noah's hungry noises until she embraced her family and tried to calm them. Reassuring them seemed to have a positive effect on her, because the color came back to her cheeks and she seemed less despondent.

"Your little guy is hungry," Lucas finally said when the noise decibel lowered a bit.

She sniffled and came to retrieve Noah. "I'll feed him." She settled in an armchair and threw a light blanket over herself.

Kyle crossed his arms over his chest and glared at Lucas. "Why are you here and not out finding my daughter?"

"I'm waiting on a call that the FBI is here."

The older man paled and scowled. "You've signed their death warrant. When the kidnapper hears the FBI is involved, they'll kill the kids and disappear."

"We're going to find them first. The first few hours are critical, and we're lucky enough to have someone knowledgeable about child abductions in the area. We'll locate them."

Lucas wished he was as confident as he sounded. It would be tough to track down the kidnapper. Carly had nailed it when she went through the list of possible suspects. They still were uncertain which direction to go. But his words seemed to have calmed Kyle, who dropped his arms and slumped.

The older man settled into a chair. "What's the next step?"

Lucas couldn't explain his antipathy to Kyle Tucker other than he'd abandoned his kids, both the first group and Isabelle, and Lucas picked his words carefully. He didn't want to expose more than he should to this mercurial man. "We'll look at neighborhood videos to see who was in and out of the house as well as talk to neighbors. We'll check cams around town to see if we can spot Isabelle in a vehicle too. There's likely to be a clue to the person who took her. These days it's impossible to pull off something like this in broad daylight without someone noticing."

Lucas's phone rang, and he walked out into the foyer to take the call from Bernard. "What you got, Lieutenant?"

"Siela Chen from the FBI is here. And we just missed catching Dimitri. A neighborhood video showed he was in your house but went out the back door before we could grab him."

There was something Bernard wasn't telling him. "Carly and I will be right there. You have a car watching the house, right?"

"With two officers," his boss said.

"I'll have Ryan on alert inside. We'll be right there." Lucas ended the call and knelt in front of Carly. "We need to get to the station as soon as possible."

"I'm ready." She handed him the baby and tossed aside the blanket.

"I'll keep Noah," Amelia said. "No reason to take him with you."

Lucas handed over the baby before retreating to the foyer, where he found Ryan waiting for him. His brother wore a worried frown. "You think you'll find them?"

"FBI is here. We'll do our best. You see anything on our cameras at all?"

"Not a thing. I reset them this morning, but they'd been wiped."

Lucas gaped at his brother. "That would indicate whoever it was knew where they were. Or else it was a top hacker who knew how to turn them off remotely."

"My thoughts exactly."

Could this be someone they knew? Lucas couldn't wrap his head around that thought, but now it was lodged in his brain. It would explain how the perp had been a few steps ahead of them all along. He'd assumed it had been someone who had started searching for the egg before them, but that might not be true.

Carly joined them. Her face was pale and set, and her eyes were red. Realizing she'd been crying made him want to take her in his arms, and his fingers curled into his palms as he resisted the impulse. Her pain made his own heart hurt.

"I'm ready. Noah should be good for three or four hours. Long enough to meet Mr. Schoenwald and figure out what we're going to do about the ransom." Her eyes glinted with determination. Though she'd spent some time crying, she was clearly ready to enter the battle again and find her little sister and Caroline.

They left Ryan to oversee protecting the rest of the family and went out to Lucas's truck. As they started for the precinct, he told her about the cameras. "So I think someone we know is behind it all. And here's the key to the safety-deposit box." He handed it to her and she put it in her purse. "It's been copied, though. I saw it on the video after the breach at the bank."

She shook her head. "That's terrible, Lucas. Who would do such a thing?"

"I don't know yet. I hope neighbors saw something or a cam picked up the vehicle with your family in it. I'm guessing two people are involved. An acquaintance who is privy to the egg information and someone he's hired to carry out directives."

She chewed on her lip. "Maybe I should have taken Noah with me."

"Ryan is armed. He'll protect him and the rest of your family. Two officers are watching the house as well." He should have asked for a guard when they went to Elizabeth's, but he'd thought Ryan could handle it by himself. But there'd been no actual attack. Isabelle and Caroline's disappearance was peculiar.

The grateful smile she turned on him warmed his cheeks. "You're the best."

If he truly was the best, this wouldn't be happening to her and her family. He had to fix it somehow.

The whiteboard at the front of the room held pictures and dates. Carly spotted a picture of herself with the words *Intruder killed*. Eric's death was also on the whiteboard. The officers in the chairs wore identical expressions of grave determination. Beside Anna Martin's name were the words *Dimitri Smirnov ballistics matched to Kelly Cicero.*

She stopped and pointed at the board. "Smirnov shot Kelly and Anna?"

Lucas nodded. "Ballistics matched with a gun he used in another murder, but no one has been able to find him."

She sat at the end of the front row while Lucas went to stand by a dark-haired woman in her early thirties. She wore a gray suit, and Carly assumed it was Siela Chen from the FBI. The woman's calm, competent manner bolstered Carly's hope. Maybe she'd know what to do right away.

The woman came to stand in front of Carly, and while she didn't touch her, the compassion in her gaze warmed Carly. "I'm so sorry, Ms. Harris. May I call you Carly?"

"Yes, please."

"I'm Siela Chen. I know how hard this is for you. I'll likely ask you questions during the task force meeting. Time is of utmost importance. May I see the text message you received?"

Carly retrieved her phone and called up the message. "You'll see where I asked for more time. We have until nine tonight. We should comply with the ransom, right?"

Ms. Chen studied the phone's messages, then handed it back. "Lieutenant Clark printed out the messages Detective Bennett sent, but I wanted to verify every word." She shifted her weight on her black pumps. "Every case is different, and in this situation, I'm going to recommend you comply with the ransom demand. We'll have the drop site surrounded, and hopefully we can apprehend the kidnapper at the pickup." She turned when Bernard called her name. "We'll talk more later," she told Carly.

She went back to the front with Lucas and Bernard. "We'll have drones deployed that can follow the car after it leaves the pickup." She focused her attention on Carly. "You'll likely get instructions an hour or so before the drop on where to take the item. We'll have time to get our forces in place."

It sounded so easy, but Carly didn't feel good about it. The kidnapper had already told her not to call the police or the FBI. What if he got word she'd done just that and disappeared with Isabelle and Caroline?

She had her phone on silent, but it vibrated in her lap, and she glanced down at it as Bernard went over the deployment of teams to interview possible suspects while they waited for the drop to be set up.

You lied. And you didn't listen. Bring the egg to Hunting Island in one hour. I'm attaching a map of where to go. Leave the egg in the Y of the big tree and leave. Your sister will be released. If you bring the police, you'll never see her again. Go right now or there won't be time. Obey or else.

What did it mean that there was no mention of Caroline? Was it possible the kidnapper was related to her? Carly had a choice to make—do exactly as the kidnapper asked or tell Lucas and Chen about the text. Carly desperately wanted Lucas with her, but what if her actions resulted in the death of her sister? How could she take that chance? What was a priceless Fabergé egg worth when compared to Isabelle's life? Kelly's baby mattered just as much.

It would be easy enough to get the egg and drive out to Hunting Island, but she had to decide now—right now. She glanced around the room at the assembled team. Good officers, all of them. But with that many people involved, it became more likely she'd be seen. The problem was she was stuck without her vehicle. She'd come in Lucas's truck, and it would eat up some of her time to walk back to the house.

She had to at least tell Lucas and ask him to help her. But would he insist on notifying everyone else? It wasn't in his nature to go rogue, but she had to risk it.

The meeting was coming to a close, and she rose and went to the door, hoping Lucas would follow. And he did.

He caught up with her in the hall. "You okay? Chen will want to talk to you."

She took his hand and stared into his eyes. "Lucas, you have to help me. I have to take the egg out to Hunting Island, and it has to be right now. I have only one hour or Isabelle will die. I know you're going to tell me you have to let the team know, but you can't. I-I care about you even though I don't want to. And I think you care about me. If that's true, I need you to take me to the bank now without saying anything to Bernard or Chen."

His pupils expanded in his hazel eyes. She revealed how she really felt in her eyes and prayed he could read her expression. And that he cared enough to trust her intuition. Sometimes that was all a person had—their perceptions that couldn't be explained or analyzed.

He clasped her hand and squeezed it. "Okay, Carly, okay. Let's go now before anyone else gets here. Do you have your purse with the key to the box?"

The tender expression on his face told her more than mere words ever would. "Yes."

She let him lead her out the door to where he'd parked his truck. She climbed in and prayed she was right.

THIRTY-SIX

Taking Carly into the jaws of danger went against all of Lucas's knowledge and instincts. Yet here he was, doing just that.

He parked in the lot at Hunting Island State Park. "Ready?"

She nodded. "I'm not sure how we're going to make sure the kidnapper doesn't see you."

They'd gotten the egg out faster than expected. "I'm heading to the location first. We're half an hour early, which should give me enough time to get hidden where I can watch what's happening."

"I suspect he might already be there." Her phone dinged with a picture, and she lifted it to read the message. The picture was of Mr. Schoenwald in front of the bank. "Mr. Schoenwald is at the bank. I forgot to let him know what was happening."

"Send me his number, and I'll call him."

She tapped on her phone. "I sent it. Ask him to get a room and stay put until we resolve this. I want that egg gone."

He didn't blame her. It had brought massive trouble into her life. He placed the call while she got out. He told the auctioneer about the situation, and the man agreed to get a hotel room and wait. The concern in Schoenwald's voice amped up Lucas's own unease about what they were doing.

He'd ignored several texts from Bernard, which was bound to raise concern back at the station, but he'd been helpless to resist the depth of trust and emotion in Carly's brown eyes. He'd seen love there, and he couldn't lie to himself any longer.

He loved her and little Noah.

Her phone dinged again, and she paled. "Another text." She showed it to him.

I see you brought the police. Game's over. Goodbye to your sister and the baby.

Tears sprang to her eyes, and she stared around the area. "He's somewhere close. Watching us. I should have done what he said."

Lucas studied every person he could see: a young couple throwing discs, an older couple walking hand in hand toward the beach, a young mother with a toddler moseying toward the sand. No one stood out as a likely suspect, yet the kidnapper was out there.

He took her hand and moved her toward the truck door. "We need to get out of here. It could be an ambush."

Tears rolled down her cheeks as he opened the door and she slid in. He took another glance around and spotted a black cap that disappeared into the brush. "Stay put and lock the door."

He shut the door and raced in the direction of the movement he'd seen. Branches slapped his face as he plunged through the shrubs and bushes. He caught another glimpse of a male figure, dressed in a long-sleeved camouflage tee and dark jeans, running off through the trees. Lucas picked up his speed and tried to catch up, but the guy was fast.

He reached a clearing and didn't see where the guy had gone. Listening for any sounds didn't give him any direction. Had he lost him? The ground didn't yield any clues either, and Lucas paused to see if the man would make another move. He couldn't have gotten away so quickly.

The seconds stretched into several minutes, and he barely moved as he waited. An engine to his right caught his attention. It sounded like a small motorbike. He ran toward the sound, and a bike burst from the bushes and raced away from him. Breathing hard, he stopped and ran back toward the truck to let Carly know he'd lost the man. If he was fast, maybe he could still catch him. It would be slow going along the rough track out of here.

But when he reached the spot where he'd parked the truck, it was gone. He ran toward the road and saw it vanishing around a curve. He sprinted after it, but he soon realized he'd never catch her on foot. He reversed course and stopped to think. He knew this park well. Could he take a shortcut and cut her off? What was Carly doing?

Carly had a boulder in her throat as she saw Lucas trying to catch up to the truck, but she'd had no choice. The kidnapper had sent her a picture of Isabelle and Caroline sitting on a dock at Harbor Island. All she had to do was bring the egg and make an exchange right then and there. This was her only chance to retrieve them safe and sound.

She concentrated on her instructions. Harbor Island was just north of Hunting Island State Park. All she had to do was look for the right house and park. She was to leave the egg in the truck and walk back to get her sister and Caroline. The kidnapper would retrieve the egg, and she'd return with Isabelle and the baby.

It sounded almost too easy, but she had to cling to the hope of this working out or she'd go crazy. Her phone rang, and Lucas's picture filled the screen. Her impulse was not to answer, but the least she could do was let him know she was all right. She didn't have to tell him where she was going.

She swiped on the call. "I'll be back to get you in just a bit, Lucas. I'm sorry, but I have to do this. I have one last chance to get them."

"Carly, the kidnappers are lying to you." His voice was hoarse with emotion. "You can't trust them without any kind of assurance."

"Isabelle and the baby are just down the road. Not far. I have a picture. I can exchange the egg and get them to safety. I'll have them with me when I come back to get you."

"Honey, don't do this. You're operating on fear and desperation. That never leads to clear thinking. At least tell me where you're going. I can call for backup and we can make sure they don't escape the island with Isabelle and Caroline."

His plea caught at her heart. Was she not thinking this through? Maybe backup wasn't such a bad idea. "Harbor Island."

"I'll have the road blocked in each direction. It should be easy to catch them. You don't have to go. We've got them trapped in there. Don't go without help, Carly. Please."

She wavered in her conviction she was doing the right

285

thing. It had seemed an easy decision at the time. "I don't know, Lucas. What if they have a foolproof escape plan? They could hole up there and escape later after the police leave."

"A guy on a small motorbike got away from me. Do you see him anywhere?" Lucas sounded out of breath as if he was continuing to chase the truck.

"I haven't so far." She strained to peer ahead along the lane, but there was nothing but an old white pickup immediately ahead.

The highway was just ahead, and she slowed to turn north out of the park. Having Lucas on speakerphone was almost like having his presence with her. "You still there?"

"I'm here." He sounded even more winded.

She turned onto the highway and accelerated out of the park. A mile out of the park, she passed the white pickup she'd seen, but it held an older man and woman. Once she got around them, she tried to keep an eye on movement to the left and right of the road. "I still don't see the motorbike."

"Keep looking." His voice sounded strained.

He had to be trying to walk out of the park, and she felt terrible that she'd stranded him. "I'm sorry, Lucas."

"I understand."

A figure stepped from the tree line ahead of her and stood in the middle of the road waving his hands. She slammed on the brake, and the truck fishtailed, nearly clipping the man. The vehicle veered to the right of him onto the shoulder of the road. She squinted. Was that *Lucas*?

She sat with her hands gripping the wheel. This was stupid. Either she trusted Lucas or she did not. And she did.

Carly still had the connection to his phone, and his

strained voice came through the speaker. "Thanks for stopping. I'm going to hide under a tarp back here, Carly. Go ahead and drive to Harbor Island."

Lowering her forehead to the steering wheel, she took several deep breaths. "I'm sending you the text." She picked up the phone to talk into the speaker. "What do you think we should do?" She turned around and watched him through the back window.

He studied his phone for a long moment and frowned. "This isn't on Harbor Island. He's trying to lure you somewhere else. I recognize this place with the rocks. It's on Saint Helena Island. I've been there fishing with my dad. They were going to take the egg and you wouldn't have gotten Isabelle and the baby."

His head disappeared below the bottom of the window. "I'll direct you and you drive."

She hesitated, then put the truck in Drive and pulled out onto the highway. They'd know the truth in a few more minutes.

THIRTY-SEVEN

It was hot under the tarp, and Lucas wiped sweat from his brow. The dot on the map was nearly to Saint Helena Island. "The turnoff is ahead," he said into the speakerphone. "Make a right onto Cee Cee Road."

He winced at the realization of her next turn. It felt like a bad omen. She made the turn, and he stayed hunkered down past the few signs of civilization. "Right ahead onto Coffin Point Road."

Expecting her to freak out a little, he tensed, but she made the turn without comment. He directed her to the next two turns. "You'll see a white shed soon without a house. Turn left into the drive and park. Try to hide in the trees or behind the building as much as you can."

He held on as she made the turn, and the truck jerked and bumped over the rough driveway. The shade from the trees was welcome, and he poked his head out from the tarp as the truck stopped behind the building.

He jumped out and went to open her door. "I texted Bernard to have backup at Saint Helena Island in case they can snag him. And Chen is heading this way with Bernard. The Coast Guard is coming too. Let's get out to the boathouse."

The enclosed boathouse in the picture appeared dilapidated and unused, and he suspected the kids might be locked inside with a second kidnapper. A boat was docked there as well, and they could be inside it, so Lucas and Carly had to be careful not to allow the kidnapper to sail off with them. He eyed the shed as they passed, but it was open to the elements and wouldn't be a suitable place to keep anyone prisoner. As far as he knew, there was no other building nearby that was empty.

Now wasn't the time to tell her that he was proud of her courage. In fact, it wasn't the time for any type of emotion that might cloud their thinking, so he took her hand and squeezed it instead. "This way."

With her slumped shoulders and downturned face, he knew she felt like she'd messed up. "Good job, Carly. If you hadn't agreed to his demands, he wouldn't have sent you the picture of the location. We still wouldn't know where they are. At least this way we have a shot at freeing them."

Her head rose and a slight smile lifted her face. "Really?"

He squeezed her fingers again. "Really." He released her hand and stepped in front of her with his gun drawn. "Stay behind me. Watch for any movement."

His every sense hyperalert, he watched for anything in his peripheral vision and studied the terrain ahead as well. They crossed the road to the sand, and the Saint Helena Sound stretched in front of them with the rocks he recognized poking above the water. Gulls perched on the rocks, and he spotted a couple of dolphin fins cutting through the waves. The boathouse was boarded up and had a weary, abandoned appearance.

If only they could have approached in the dark. He didn't

like the exposed sand and bright sunlight, but this was the hand they'd been dealt. He was determined to rescue those kids. The wood on the pier bowed under his weight, and he paused to check the safety of walking out on such a rickety structure. "Go back to the truck. I don't think the pier will take the weight of both of us."

She shook her head. "I'll wait here and watch for any movement."

He didn't like her exposed position, but with her chin up and her gaze firm and determined, there would be no persuading her to retreat. He chose each footfall carefully along the rotted boards until he stood at the boathouse door. The boat he'd seen in the picture still rocked in the waves, and it didn't appear to be seaworthy. The starboard side listed like it was taking on water. That left the boathouse as his main area of interest.

A sound from the boat caught his attention. Maybe he was wrong. Would the kidnapper have stashed the kids in a sinking boat? He approached carefully and studied the craft. It bounced in the water more than it should, considering the slight waves in the sound today.

Someone is inside.

Could be the kids, but it could be someone guarding the boathouse. He wavered and glanced from the boat to the structure. His sixth sense told him to focus on the boat, so he moved closer and tried to peer into the wheelhouse. No movement. Would someone be below deck? It didn't seem safe or pleasant with the craft taking on water.

Holding his gun ready, he stepped aboard the boat and felt it sink a bit under his feet. Another noise came, this time clearly from the wheelhouse. It might have been the noise a baby would make, and he wished Carly could have heard it. She would know.

He eased along the deck toward the wheelhouse, and something zinged by his head. A bullet. He ducked down.

The gun's report seemed to have come from the bow, so he moved that way. If the kidnapper was aboard, did that mean the kids were here too?

"Leave the boat or I'll shoot the kids!" a muffled male voice yelled. "And throw down your gun."

Lucas crawled on his hands and knees toward the voice. Leaving the kids on a sinking boat wasn't an option. The baby would drown before he could get to her, and he had no idea if Isabelle could swim. "Give yourself up!" He spotted a boat speeding toward them. "The Coast Guard is coming. It's all over."

Another bullet plowed into the boat's soft wood near his head. Something about the man's voice seemed familiar, but he couldn't quite place him.

Carly's distant voice carried to his ears. "If you hurt those kids, you'll be facing the death penalty. Let them go. It's all over."

She was going to get shot. Lucas motioned for her to get down, but she continued to approach. He would have to take the shooter out before he could shoot Carly. Lucas leaped to his feet and charged the bow of the boat.

The shooter stood to aim, and Lucas didn't see either of the children around. Roger Adams was firing, and Lucas's finger jerked on the trigger as he dove toward the deck. An expression of surprise widened Roger's eyes and he tumbled to the deck.

Carly was the first one to the wheelhouse, which stank of old urine, seawater, and dirt. She found Isabelle holding Caroline under a counter with a tipped chair barricading the way to them. "Isabelle!" She scrambled over debris to reach her sister and tug the obstructions out of the way.

Isabelle began to cry when she saw Carly and scooted on her bottom toward her. With the chair out of the way, Carly stopped to gather them both in her arms. "It's okay." The soothing words were as much for herself as they were for her sister. She felt weak with relief. Gunshots, a sinking boat, and the near miss of even finding them had drained every bit of her adrenaline.

Limbs trembling, she helped her sister from the floor and took the baby. "Let's get out of here." Caroline snuggled her face into Carly's neck. They'd done it. Found them both safe and unharmed.

They exited the wheelhouse as Lucas was talking to the Coast Guard. She caught a few words. *Kidnapped, ransom, gunshots.* Would his weapon be taken from him again? A quick peek on her way to find the kids had shown Roger was dead.

But someone had been at the park watching her. Who had that been? This wasn't over until they uncovered all the shadowy figures who had stalked them. If that ever happened. No matter what, she planned to get that egg out of her possession.

She helped Isabelle onto the spongy dock. "Be careful, it's not very safe." Carrying Caroline, she stepped gingerly along the boards until they reached solid ground.

Isabelle's expression was set and scared. She kept glancing

from right to left as if she thought someone would jump out anytime. It made Carly jumpy too. What if the other person involved was lurking around? She hustled the kids to the truck and got them inside to wait for Lucas.

Heat shimmered in the air, and she reached over to start the engine and turn on the AC. They had no car seat for the baby, so she planned to sit in the back and hold her while Lucas got them home. A thought struck her, and she grabbed her purse to make sure the egg was still there. The weight reassured her, and she dug into the contents until her fingers brushed the enamel finish.

It was safe.

And in a few hours, it would be someone else's problem. She couldn't wait to get it out of town and into a collection where it could be admired by everyone. She let out a sigh of relief when she saw Lucas jogging toward the vehicle. All she wanted was to get everyone home so she could hold Noah and assure herself everyone she loved was safe.

Lucas slid into the driver's seat. "Bernard is *not* happy with me, but he'll get over it. Teamwork—we did it." He glanced in the rearview mirror and smiled when his gaze caught Carly's. "Good idea to keep the baby back there. Isabelle, you okay?"

"I'm fine," she said in a tired voice. "Can we just go home?"

The ordeal had been grueling, but something about her sister's manner alarmed her. "Maybe we should have a doctor look at both of them and make sure they're okay."

Isabelle whipped her head back and forth. "No! I want to go to bed. Take me home." Fresh tears ran in dirty tracks down her face. "I just want to forget what happened."

"The police and FBI need to talk to you," Lucas said. "I'll

have them come to the house instead of going to the station, though."

Isabelle's eyes widened. "I don't have anything to say."

"We have to figure out who did this."

"You shot him!"

"There is someone else," Lucas said. "And he might come back."

"He won't! He said . . ." Isabelle shut her mouth and turned her face to the window.

And she said nothing more all the way to town. They made a brief stop for Carly to return the egg to the bank's safe-keeping before going home. When Lucas pulled into the drive and turned off the engine, Isabelle ran for the door.

THIRTY-EIGHT

Lucas tried Isabelle's door again with Noah in one arm. Locked. Lifting a brow, he glanced at Carly. "Now what? Bernard and Chen are downstairs waiting to talk to her."

The minute they'd reached the house, Isabelle said she was sick and raced to the bathroom. They heard her retching inside and had given her space. Since then, she'd locked herself in her bedroom and refused to come out.

Carly wore a worried frown as she bounced Caroline up and down in her arms. "Is it trauma or something more?"

"You know her better than me. Could she have been more involved than we know?"

"I can't believe she'd put the baby in danger."

He knocked on the door. "Isabelle, you need to face this. We just have a few questions."

Carly touched his arm. "Let's leave her alone for a while. It's been a traumatic day, and she's probably overwhelmed. If she sleeps awhile, she might be in better shape to answer questions."

He allowed Carly to pull him from the door, though he didn't like it. There were too many questions to be answered, like who was the other person working with Roger? There had to be at least one, and that man was still on the loose.

They went down the stairs and into the living room, where Bernard and Agent Chen waited on the sofa. They showed obvious disappointment when only he and Carly joined them.

"She won't come out, so I decided to let her rest for a while. We'll try later," Carly said.

Bernard rose from the sofa. "We've got your statements. Call us when she's out of her room, and we'll come back. I'm going home to have dinner with my wife for the first time this week."

Chen's smile landed on Caroline. "I'm so relieved this ended happily. You have my number."

Lucas and Carly walked them out. Fatigue pressed down on Lucas's shoulders. It had been quite the day, and it wasn't over yet. He smelled the aroma of fried chicken wafting from the kitchen and heard the soft voices of Mary and Elizabeth talking. Amelia and Emily had taken Lainey and Holt out for dinner, and Carly's dad had left without telling anyone where he was going. He'd been gone when they got home.

Lucas carried Noah back into the living room and laid him on a blanket on the area rug. Carly put Caroline beside her baby and handed toys to both of them. She gestured to the old chest in the corner of the room. "We've got a little time before dinner. We could go through that while we wait. Elizabeth told us to take a look whenever we wanted."

Though all he really wanted to do was fall into bed and nap awhile, he lugged the chest over to the sofa in front of her. "Have at it. I think I smell coffee. Want some?"

"Sure." She yanked on the chest. "I forgot it was locked."

Coffee forgotten, he went to the basement and retrieved some tools. A few minutes later, the lock released and he lifted the lid. The odor of mildew and must rushed out, and he wrinkled his nose as he stared down into the pictures and papers inside.

Carly let out a mewl of dismay. "I was sure we would find the surprise inside."

He plunged his hands into the contents, lifted them out, and laid them on the floor. "Looks like old pictures."

She picked up a handful of pictures and shuffled through them. "Aunt Elizabeth will probably treasure these. They're probably of her grandparents and their parents. Some are really old."

He took a stack of pictures, too, even though he had no idea what they were looking for in them. Many were of Elizabeth's house while it was being remodeled. "Seems like these were taken in the 1930s and 1940s. They did a big remodel on the house and added on the new kitchen."

They plodded through the photos, and he was sure there was nothing of interest until Carly gasped and showed him a picture. "Look at this."

He took the photo and stared at it. Two babies on an old bedstead. Beside one was an egg and beside the other was another object more round than oblong. In the black-and-white picture, they were both dark. Painted?

He lifted a brow and stared at Carly. He touched the round object. "The surprise?"

"I think it has to be!"

He flipped the picture over and found spidery handwriting

on the back that he read aloud. "Elizabeth and Mary, age two weeks. Always remember Mama loves you."

Carly took it from him and stared at the front again. "I have to show Gram and Aunt Elizabeth."

───

Gram and Aunt Elizabeth both cried when they saw the picture of themselves as babies. Carly left it in their possession and went back to the living room, where she found Lucas perusing his phone. The babies had fallen asleep entwined around each other, and she smiled to see Major curled up beside them too.

Carly settled on the sofa beside Lucas. "If you could find Dimitri, maybe he'd talk."

"I doubt it. The Russian mafia is loyal to a fault."

"It might only be Dimitri and the mafia doesn't know about it."

"Then how did Ivan Bury come to know about it? And how does Roger fit in?"

She blew out a frustrated breath. There were still big voids in their knowledge. "Will you be getting a copy of Roger's phone calls? Maybe we can figure out who his contact was."

"Already got it. It's on the printer. Hang on." He went out of the room to his office and returned with a sheaf of papers.

She took half of the papers and pored through them while Lucas studied the other ones. Only unfamiliar names were on the list, and she laid the papers aside. "Nothing."

"I might have something."

Lucas's voice held a strange note—trepidation maybe—and she moved closer to him to see. She recognized the number instantly. "Dad? Dad talked to Roger?" It wasn't possible for her dad to be mixed up in this, was it? "D-do you still have Eric's phone call list handy?"

"Yeah, it's in my office."

While he retrieved it, she ran through the rest of the calls. Her dad's number appeared eleven times. Eleven! That wasn't a random call about selling things at an auction. How had her dad gotten to know Roger?

"Eric talked to my dad too. Why would he do that? They were never really close."

"Your dad just traveled out of the country," Lucas said. "I'm not sure why he would do that if he was involved in this."

Her gaze met his. "Was he really out of the country, though? Can we find out?"

"I can check his passport. But, Carly, this might explain why Isabelle doesn't want to talk. She's fifteen. Could your dad have been manipulating her? She's crazy about Caroline. What if he promised she could keep the baby if she helped him? Kids that age are easily swayed. They don't have clear thought processes in place yet. And she longed for his approval and felt abandoned when he left her. He might have just asked her to keep him informed of what we're discovering."

Why did it hurt so much to know her dad might be involved in this? He'd left her and her sisters long ago. She'd always known they meant little to him in the grand scheme of things. But could he have had anything to do with Eric's murder?

"What about Eric?" She navigated through her thoughts like a minefield, not sure she wanted to disturb a possible bomb of information that might blow up her life even more.

COLLEEN COBLE

"Let's go back to your original list." He picked up a pen. "Eric found the provenance. Your dad would be the logical person to call, right? He lived in the house all his life until he married. Kyle was often at his grandmother's house where that chest had been until she died. Maybe Eric thought your dad knew exactly where the egg was and whether it was of any value. For all he knew, Eric might have thought it had been found and sold long ago."

"But Dad knew nothing about it." She spoke slowly, feeling her way through the possibilities. "When Dad heard there might be a priceless artifact, he was intrigued. Why would he contact Roger Adams?"

"Maybe Eric didn't tell him everything. So your dad took it from there and called Roger to see if he had anything that might help him find the egg. Roger might have gone to see Eric on his own to see what else he could find out. Maybe he and Eric struggled and Roger shot him."

Carly frowned. "Why didn't Eric take the egg and sell it?"

"Maybe he realized it was wrong. He backed out of letting anyone go through the chest. Or maybe he only found the provenance and hadn't found the egg before he was killed."

She nodded. "The items were all still in the chest, so nothing was gone but the provenance. The provenance could have been right on top and Eric missed the egg wrapped in the shawl. I didn't find it until I shook out the shawl."

A movement came from the doorway, and a very pale Isabelle moved into sight. Her tearstained face was set and determined. "I can answer most of those questions."

THIRTY-NINE

Carly shot to her feet and went to embrace her sister. Isabelle trembled like a frightened puppy in her arms, and Carly led her to the sofa. "You feel hot. Are you still sick?"

She smoothed Isabelle's blonde hair, which was a rat's nest of tangles that included dirt from the ordeal this afternoon, and she caught a whiff of vomit. The poor thing. "Are you sure you want to talk about it now?"

Isabelle rubbed her eyes. "I have to. I can't sleep until I tell you. I'm so ashamed. I knew better, but I thought if I did what he wanted, he'd love me. He's never loved me, not really. Neither has Mom."

Carly held her while she sobbed on her shoulder. "I love you, Isabelle. So do Gram and our sisters. I know it hurts."

Isabelle lifted her head when Caroline began to fuss. "I'll get her." She rose as if her bones hurt and stooped down to gather the baby in her arms. Caroline settled as soon as Isabelle snuggled her against her chest, and her eyes closed.

"She loves you too. So does Noah."

Isabelle shook her head. "I can't believe I let him talk me into this."

Lucas exchanged a glance with Carly. "Start at the beginning."

"Okay." Isabelle released a shaky exhale. "Dad left me here without a word. You saw all that. But the day after we got Caroline, I saw him drive by. And he'd said he was going to Italy! I texted him and asked what was going on. He swore me to secrecy and told me we would be rich, really rich. That he would buy me whatever house I liked, and we'd have a happy life. We'd buy an island if I wanted."

Carly could hear his persuasive voice in her head. Their dad had always been a big dreamer. He'd invested a lot of his salary in schemes he'd heard about. The next big one would get them out of debt and make her mother happy. It never happened. She'd hoped a new family had helped him break into a new life with new habits, and it pained her to hear that her sister had endured so much disillusionment too.

"Go on," Lucas said.

"I heard you talking when I came downstairs. You guessed most of it. Eric called Dad to ask if he knew about some fancy jeweled egg. Dad didn't and Eric only told him about Gram being adopted and who the nurse was. Dad did some research on his own and found that Roger guy." She shivered. "He was scary. Roger was supposed to go through the shed and see if he could find the egg, but Eric came in. Roger panicked and killed him. Dad was so mad." She fell silent and sniffled.

Carly closed her eyes as a mental picture of that horrific moment came. If she'd been there, Roger would have shot her too. When she opened her eyes, Lucas's hazel eyes were fixed on her, and she sank into the sympathy she found there. Or was it more than sympathy? Did she dare hope it was—*love*?

She dragged her focus from Lucas and prodded her sister to continue.

"Then Dad found out a guy named Smirnov had found out—probably from Roger. Dad called him a loose lip. This Smirnov and his men had broken into Aunt Elizabeth's house and were there at the same time as Roger. Roger killed one of them and got away, but Dad was afraid the Russians would be out for revenge and coming after him. He'd wanted to find the surprise, too, but he decided he'd settle for just the egg. It would be worth a lot by itself."

"Do you know how Ivan Bury plays into this? He gave money to Eric and Kelly," Carly said.

Isabelle shook her head. "I never heard anything about him."

Lucas picked up Noah, who had begun to squawk. "So your dad concocted the scheme to ask for the egg as a ransom for you and Caroline."

Isabelle looked down at the baby. "He wanted me to take Noah, but I wouldn't do it. I knew Noah would need to nurse. Most nursing babies don't take well to being switched to a bottle all at once. I didn't want to traumatize him. I knew Caroline would be just fine either way as long as she had me."

Carly's eyes burned at her little sister's words. She'd done the best she could with the father they had. "You're a wonderful sister, Isabelle. And aunt. We're lucky to have you."

Isabelle shook her head and sobs erupted from her throat. "I shouldn't have gone along with it, Carly. I knew he was wrong."

Carly struggled to hold back the hot words about their father that wanted to pour from her mouth. "But you wanted him to love you. He's very good at manipulating his girls."

She rose to get Noah, whose fussing had become a hungry wail. "What's our next move, Lucas?" Settling back on the sofa, she grabbed her cover-up and began to feed the baby.

"I'll need to let Bernard know about this. We'll pick up your dad."

Isabelle's lips trembled. "Will he be sent to jail? Charged with kidnapping?"

Lucas shrugged. "Well, he has custody of you so it's not against the law for him to take you somewhere. We'll figure out the charges. People have died because of his actions. While he didn't murder anyone directly, he covered up the murders, both of Eric and of whoever died in Elizabeth's house. Did Roger kill Anna Martin? Did he break into the Hill home? And what about Kelly? Who attacked her?"

Isabelle put her head down to rest on Caroline's. "I don't know."

It was such a tangled web that Carly wasn't sure they'd unravel it without talking to the Russians. She glanced at the clock. "I'm going to set up a meeting with Mr. Schoenwald tomorrow morning and get that egg out of here."

"Oh no you're not."

She turned at the sound of her father's voice. He stood in the doorway aiming a gun at Lucas. "Toss your gun down, Lucas." Sweat dripped from his red, sweating face, and his eyes were wild. "There's been a change of plans."

Another man stepped into view from behind her father. He prodded Ryan and the older women forward with a gun that was much bigger than her father's.

The man with the M16 had hard green eyes that looked them over like a slab of beef. He was bald, and he looked like he worked out. He'd ushered Ryan and the older women into the room with them and had made them all throw down any weapons. Lucas recognized him from the files. Dimitri Smirnov. Lucas judged the guy to be in his fifties, and his craggy face was a road map of scars illustrating his violent life.

Kyle held up his hands. "Look, let's work together on this. I've got information you don't have."

Smirnov sneered. "I'm going to have the egg, which is all that matters. It belongs to me. I've been searching for it all my life, as my father did before me. My great-great-grandfather was one of the Bolsheviks who stormed the palace. It was in our family until Sofia Balandin's grandfather took it and disappeared. After all these years, it will finally be back where it belongs."

"How did you hear about the egg?" Lucas asked. "Did Roger Adams contact you?"

"Adams put out some feelers to sell it. I wasn't about to buy what belonged to me already. I started following him and it led right to all of you. I had the advantage with my tech people and plenty of men to watch the lot of you."

Carly put her hands on her hips. "Why did you shoot Kelly? You left her baby crying from hunger in the bedroom."

Smirnov shrugged. "I didn't kill it, did I? The Cicero woman had her chance to tell me what she knew and help me get my egg, but she refused."

His twisted logic left Lucas speechless. Did he really think the egg belonged to his family? They'd stolen it from the Romanovs.

"Your family stole it," Kyle said.

Smirnov's attention swung back to Kyle. "You've gotten in my way for the last time." He pointed the assault rifle at him, and Carly screamed, "No!"

Smirnov glared at her. "Here's what's going to happen. You're going to go get the egg and bring it back while everyone stays put right here. Do what you're told, and you all might walk away." His gaze swung back to Lucas. "Except for this guy. You're the one who killed my Debby, and there has to be retribution for that."

"It was self-defense," Ryan said, but his comment didn't elicit a response from Smirnov, who continued to glare at Lucas.

Lucas glared back. "You ever think her death was your fault? You sent her in there." He felt naked and helpless without his SIG Sauer, but it was on the floor four feet away.

Smirnov stepped forward and drove the butt of his M16 into Lucas's stomach. The air left his lungs in a painful whoosh. He buckled and fell to his knees. Mary screamed and stood from her seat on the sofa, but she sank back when Smirnov turned the rifle her way.

Noah still in her arms, Carly rushed to his side, and he leaned against her, gasping for breath. She stared up at Smirnov with angry eyes. "I'm not going anywhere unless you assure me you won't touch him. None of this is his fault."

"If you want that baby of yours to grow up, you'll do exactly what I say." Smirnov glanced at his watch. "You have twenty minutes before the bank closes, so you'd better get going." He held out one arm. "Give me the kid."

She rose to her feet and shook her head. "I'm taking him with me. He'll need to eat, and you don't want him screaming."

"That will make you get back here sooner then, won't it? There and back should be all of fifteen minutes."

She stared back without moving.

"Fine, take the kid with you. You have half an hour, or people start dying."

Lucas regained his feet, but his legs felt weak and unsteady. At least Carly would be out of here. If he could talk to her, he'd tell her to go straight to the police station and not to the bank, but he knew her. She'd never run the risk of Smirnov following through on his threat. Knowing the man's criminal background didn't reassure Lucas either. The man had murdered before, and he'd do it again. He had no compunction about taking human life.

Carly snatched up her purse and rushed from the room and out of the house with Noah in her arms. A minute later, the engine of his truck started. Would she warn the police or fully obey Smirnov? Lucas wasn't sure of the best course of action himself. One thing for sure, the killer wasn't leaving with the egg unless he had a hostage. He'd know they'd call for help the second he was out the door.

Four family members were still out to dinner, and they could come back anytime. They needed to be warned to stay away, but Carly might think of that. Bringing in more people would muddy the situation even more. This was far from over.

Caroline began to cry, and Isabelle jiggled her on her lap. "I need to get her a bottle."

Smirnov jerked his head toward the next room. "Don't try anything funny or I might have to blast your grandmother." His M16 veered from Mary to Elizabeth and back again.

"Though since I don't know which one is which, I could take out both of them."

"Don't be so dramatic," Isabelle said. "I'll be right back with the baby bottle. Two minutes tops." She handed the baby to her father and hurried from the room.

"What would your grandmother say about the way you're acting?" Mary asked in a soft voice. "And don't tell me she's dead and it doesn't matter. It does matter."

Smirnov blinked and looked away without an answer.

Just Lucas, Kyle and Caroline, Ryan, and the older women were left with the glowering killer. He was as unstable a person as Lucas had ever seen in his days as an officer. Extricating them all alive from this was going to be tricky. Smirnov might just blast them all as he left. Lucas needed a strategy.

He glanced longingly at his SIG in the pile of pistols and phones before glancing around the room. The lamp or a side table might work, but Smirnov was likely to shoot him before he got hold of them. He would need a distraction, and once Carly returned, she might provide that as Smirnov examined the egg to make sure it was real.

It was the only hope they had.

FORTY

Carly had never felt such searing terror. Her family was in the crosshairs of a maniac, and she wasn't sure any of them would escape alive. She prayed for their safety all the way to the bank, where she parked and got Noah out of the back seat. He was happy, kicking his legs and smiling, without any hint of the trauma unfolding.

She pasted a placid expression on her face as she went inside and spoke to the teller about accessing her box for the third time today. In minutes she had the egg in her purse and was back out in the beautiful late-afternoon sunshine. Her phone dinged several times, but she ignored it until she was back in the truck with Noah in his car seat.

She glanced at her phone. She had a message from Amelia that Dillard had arrived in town and wanted to reconcile. They were on their way home. Carly quickly texted her back.

Hostage situation at the house. Do not attempt to come in! I will keep you posted. Pray!

A flurry of more texts came, and she dropped the phone back into her purse. It would take all of her thought processes to figure out how they were going to stay alive. She didn't trust

Smirnov, not for a second. She had to cling to her faith to even be able to put one step in front of the other.

Smirnov had disarmed them, but there was a chance he wouldn't examine her purse when she came in. He'd want her to hand over the egg so he could gloat over it. At least that's how her imagination saw it playing out. She had no gun in the car, but could she get one? Her thoughts tumbled with the options of who might give her a gun without too much argument.

Dillard!

Amelia's husband had a concealed-carry permit, and they were still at Breakwater Restaurant. She grabbed her phone and shot off a text.

Can I borrow Dillard's gun?

Her sister agreed quickly, and Carly turned the truck toward the restaurant. She glanced at the clock on the dash. She had fifteen minutes to get back. Her family clustered together at the curb and waved when she saw them.

Amelia and Dillard ran forward, and she rolled her window down. "I have to go now or he'll start shooting. I need your gun now, right now."

Dillard nodded and pulled it from the holster. "Do you know how to shoot?"

"I'll figure it out."

He kept hold of the gun and leaned in the window. "Thirty seconds to show you how to switch off the safety." He demonstrated how to do it. "Take off the safety, aim, and shoot. Try for the largest target—his chest. In fact, let's leave off the safety. Just be careful when you grab it. It would be best if you could get it to Lucas somehow."

She put it into her purse gingerly. "Thank you. I have to go *now*." She had a quick impulse to leave Noah with them, but Smirnov would know she'd talked to someone and he might shoot everyone.

"Pray, just pray. When I'm gone, wait fifteen minutes, then go to the police and tell them what's happened."

"We don't even know what's happened," Emily said, her voice choked with emotion. "Who's in there?"

"Tell them Dimitri Smirnov has everyone hostage. Extreme precautions, please." She ran up the window and started forward with a jerky pump of the accelerator.

The delay had cost her three minutes. She sped toward the house and pulled into the driveway with eight minutes to spare. Her pulse pounded in her throat, and she felt nauseated at the thought of taking Noah into the cesspool of danger. Out of the corner of her eye, she spotted one of Ryan's workers on the porch at Gram's house. If Smirnov saw her hand Noah over without saying much, maybe he wouldn't overreact.

She had to try it.

She got the baby out of the truck and ran to the worker. "Here, hold the baby a minute. I'll be back." She thrust Noah into his arms. "Don't come to the house. Danger!"

His jaw dropped. "Hey, come back!" he called as she ran toward Lucas's house.

He made no move to follow her, so he must have heard the panic in her voice. Glancing back, she saw him carry Noah into Gram's house.

She raced up the porch steps and ran inside. "I have the egg."

Smirnov appeared in the doorway to the living room. "What you don't have is the kid. Why'd you do that?"

"Why do you think? I can't trust you not to hurt him. I didn't tell the guy what was going on or to call the police. He's just babysitting until this is over."

"You'd better pray the police don't show up. Let me see the egg."

She went into the living room and exhaled with relief when she saw Lucas and her family still alive. She set her purse on the table and reached in to lift out the egg. It would be the last time she touched its smooth porcelain surface, and she nearly threw it into his hands. It had brought her nothing but heartache.

"Did you ever find the surprise?" she asked him.

He shook his head. "But this will do. There's time to find the rest later." His hands smoothed the white surface and greed filled his face.

Her gut clenched, and she exchanged a fearful glance with Lucas. This wouldn't be over if Smirnov got away. They had to end this now.

———

Smirnov's smile as he ran his hands over the egg made Lucas shudder. The man had plans for them all, and they weren't good ones.

Carly glared at the killer. "Now let them go. You have what you came for."

The man's green eyes lasered in on Lucas. "Not quite all. I need a hostage, and the killer over there will do just fine. Remember, if you call the police, I'll put a bullet in his brain."

The man had already said he wanted retribution, so Lucas

had no high hopes of escaping this alive, but at least Smirnov wasn't trying to take Carly. That had been his biggest fear. His gaze locked with Carly's, and she looked from him to her purse and back again. She mouthed something while Smirnov gloated over the egg again.

Gun?

He thought that's what she meant. Had she managed to get hold of a weapon somewhere? He gave a slight nod. "Let's get out of here if we're going."

Smirnov tucked the egg under his arm. "The rest of you go to the basement. I'm going to lock the door to give us some time to get away." He gestured with the rifle to Lucas. "You lock them up."

Carly began to cry. Tears poured down her face, and her nose ran with the fury of her sobbing. "I need a t-tissue," she hiccupped. She grabbed her purse and dug in it.

Smirnov took a step toward her and raised the M16. "Put that down."

"I just need a tissue," she wailed. "The least you can do is let me wipe my nose."

He spat out a foul word. "Get your tissue and get in the basement."

Her eyes widened, and she looked out the window. Smirnov made a half turn to see what had startled her, but Lucas kept his gaze on her, looking for his cue. Her hand came out of her bag with a Smith & Wesson. There would never be time for him to get it and shoot before Smirnov turned and shot her.

Before he could fully form the thought, Carly pulled the trigger, and the shot went through the picture window. The killer half turned toward her, and she shot again. Red bloomed on the back of his left shoulder, but he was still moving and the gun was heading toward her. Lucas threw himself forward and tackled Smirnov before he could pull the trigger. They grappled together for the rifle, rolling over and over.

Smirnov got in top position over Lucas, squeezing Lucas's neck.

Lucas flailed at the grip but couldn't break it. Spots danced in his vision, and he fought back, getting his knee up to push the other man off.

He nearly managed to throw him off, but Smirnov slumped against him as pieces of what looked like pottery rained down.

Lucas rolled the limp body off and sat up. The remnants of the ceramic lamp lay around them, and Ryan held the base of it in his right hand. Lucas jumped up and rushed to Carly. She was so pale that Lucas thought she might faint, and he got up to steer her to a chair.

"Easy." He pushed her head between her legs. "Deep breaths."

Ryan was prodding the downed man with his foot. "He's out."

"Tie him up. There's rope in the basement."

Ryan nodded, and Lucas went back to tending to Carly, while Mary and Elizabeth rushed to help him. Mary put her hands on Carly's shoulders. "My poor girl, are you all right?"

"I'm fine." Carly got up in a jerky motion. "I have to get Noah." The faint strains of hungry wails came from somewhere outside.

"I'll get him," Ryan said.

Mary pressed her granddaughter back in the chair. "You were so brave! How did you manage to shoot him like that?"

When Carly's laugh came, it was shaky. "Eric had me hold his firearm a time or two, but the real advice came from Dillard. He told me to shoot for the largest target, which would be the chest. I missed the first time."

"You did great." Lucas didn't want to think about how his heart froze when Smirnov swung his rifle her way. He pulled out his phone and called 911 to request assistance.

He watched Carly, who was beginning to regain her color. He couldn't have lived if Smirnov killed her. That knowledge changed everything.

FORTY-ONE

Brian Schoenwald put down the loupe. "It's a genuine Fabergé egg."

The small room at the bank felt claustrophobic to Carly as the confirmation sank in. She imprinted this moment in her memory—the hum of the fluorescent lights overhead, the distant murmur of bank customers and employees, the warmth of Lucas's hand as he took hers and squeezed it, and the awe in Schoenwald's dark eyes all coalesced in a moment of history.

He handed the provenance papers back to her. "It's a shame the surprise couldn't be found. I'm going to have you put the egg back in the safe for now. My security team will be here tomorrow, and we'll take custody of it until the auction. I want time to circulate pictures and publicize it before the sale, so let's plan a date out about three months. And we will, of course, keep your identity secret."

Carly nodded. "I appreciate that."

No one had ever discovered the identity of the man who'd found the last lost egg, but this situation was different. She held no illusions the news would stay secret—not when her father would go on trial. All the news about the egg would have to be revealed, but at least the egg would be out of her control.

Brian rose. "The last missing egg sold for thirty-three million dollars, but it had the surprise in it. Still, it was in 2014, so this egg without the surprise may still bring close to that sum. We will see, but I'm appraising the egg at twenty million. If you find the surprise, that estimate would bump to forty million. Thank you for trusting us with your exceptional piece." He glanced at his watch. "I have an online meeting and must run back to my hotel. I'll see you tomorrow. Call if you need anything."

While Brian made his way out of the bank, Carly and Lucas put the egg back in the safety-deposit box. The surprise had to be at Elizabeth's house somewhere. "Could we take another look at the pictures in the chest we found at Aunt Elizabeth's house?"

Lucas shrugged. "Sure. It's still in the living room. I think Elizabeth and her family are going back home today. I'm sure you're as exhausted as I am after the debriefing with the police last night."

She nodded and they went to his truck. The interrogation had gone on until after nine. No one was certain that all the guilty parties were accounted for. Smirnov likely wouldn't talk, and unless Kostin regained his memory and spilled what he knew, they might never know for sure. Kelly's condition had worsened, and Carly had a rock in her stomach at the thought of Caroline losing her mother.

They found the family gathered around Amelia, who was sobbing on the sofa in the music room with a sister on each side of her. The older women hovered close, and so did Lainey and her husband. Carly dropped her purse on the table in the entry and rushed to join the group. She knelt by Amelia. "What's happened?"

"I-I overheard Dillard talking to his *girlfriend*! He was trying to placate her about being gone and said it was only until he got his share of the egg auction money."

"Oh, honey, I'm so sorry." Carly leaned into an embrace with her. "What are you going to do?"

Mascara had left streaks of black around Amelia's eyes when she pulled away and lifted her chin. "I kicked him out, and I never want to see him again."

After consoling her sister a few more moments, Carly stood. "The egg will be auctioned in a few months—probably the end of the summer. I want to take another look around for the surprise."

Lucas went to grab the chest and lugged it over to the chair where she settled. "I think you should search everything yourself. You're the only one who knows what it should look like."

Lainey dropped onto the floor by Carly's feet. "Describe it to us."

"It's gold and round, not egg shaped. It's supposed to be the egg's yolk. Probably about two to three inches, though no one has seen it. And if the items inside happened to have been taken out, it would be a very small bejeweled hen with a sapphire pendant in its beak. There would be some kind of nest as well."

"I've seen nothing like that," Lainey said.

An image of the egg painted red flashed through Carly's head. "It's possible the yolk was painted."

"What color?" her aunt asked.

"Could be any color. The egg was painted red. In its natural state it could be darkened with age and use and look more like brass."

The frown on Aunt Elizabeth's face cleared, and she smiled. "Like brass?"

"You have something in mind?"

She nodded. "Maybe. I think I have a picture." She scrolled through the pictures on her phone. "My mother loved painting furniture. She would strip pieces she liked and refinish them and then paint birds or other wildlife on them. I love hummingbirds, and before she died, she renovated a bedside table for me. It's got a round brass pull on the drawer. Maybe it really is brass, but it's the only thing I can think of that's round like you describe. Ah, here it is."

Carly took the phone and studied the photo of a Bombay chest with beautifully painted hummingbirds and flowers on the front of it. The top drawer pull was the only round one, and the ones on the other drawers were more ornate. The size looked right. She zoomed the picture bigger on the phone and studied it more closely. "It looks like there might be a crack around the middle."

Her aunt nodded. "I always assumed it was from the mold when the brass was poured."

Carly tried to tamp down her excitement in case she was wrong. "I need to take a look."

"Of course. We're heading home now anyway. You can follow us there now."

"Let's all go," Gram said. "Just in case."

The air of suppressed hope in the air was enough to get all of them moving quickly for the door.

———

Noah was beginning to fuss, and Lucas jiggled him while Carly squatted in front of the dresser. The painting was stunning, and she touched the very realistic hummingbird with awe. "Your mother was an amazing painter."

Aunt Elizabeth spoke from her right side. "If you look through the house, you'll see her paintings in nearly every room. She never sold them, but she could have made a lot of money if she did. They are exquisite."

Carly stared at the drawer pull. She dug the screwdriver she'd brought out of her bag and detached the round ball from the drawer. "It appears to have been glued to the bracket. On the back side it's still perfectly round and fits into an indentation on the bracket." She brought out another tool and carefully pried it loose. "I hope you don't mind that I'm disassembling it."

"Of course. Do whatever you want. If we find out it's just a drawer pull, I'll buy another or repair that one."

But Carly's heart was trying to pound out of her chest the more she handled it. It was too heavy to be a normal drawer pull, and it didn't have the same appearance of brass. She was a pro at identifying metals and historical items. This was gold.

The ball warmed in her palm, and she stood with it in the sunlight streaming through the window. Her pulse thudded in her throat as she prepared to twist the ball, but her fingers didn't want to work right as she struggled to open it. She wiped damp palms on her khaki shorts and gave it another try. It moved a smidge, just enough to make her redouble her efforts.

"It's loose!" She gently lifted the top off.

In her palm lay the missing surprise: the exquisite hen taking a sapphire egg pendant out of a gold wicker basket. The hen and basket were on a gold stand. The brilliance and detail of the rose-cut diamonds were unmatched.

Lucas put his hand on her shoulder. "Breathe."

"I-I can't." Her voice came out in a squeak. "I've never seen anything so beautiful." She knew her aunt was dying to touch it, too, so she handed it to her.

Aunt Elizabeth took it reverently in her palms. "Oh, Carly. How wonderful."

Everyone gathered around to stare at the treasure in her hands. Carly couldn't wait to see it in the original egg, complete and whole. "I assume you want it reunited with the egg and sold together? We'll split the money between you and Gram."

"Between you and Elizabeth," her grandmother said. "That chest was left to you."

Carly shook her head. "It belongs to you, Gram. You and your sister. But the biggest treasure of all is that we've found each other. Nothing compares to that."

"Amen," her aunt said. "And yes, of course. The egg needs to be complete." She let Gram hold the surprise next.

Carly had a sharp pang at the thought of the egg going into someone else's collection. What if it was a private collector and he hoarded it so no one else got to enjoy it? "What if we specify it has to go to a museum? It might mean a little less money, but all the world could see and enjoy it."

"I like that idea," Lainey said. "It's not all about the money."

Her grandmother smiled at her. "I think you're right, sugar." She handed it back to Carly. "It's in your hands." A bell rang from somewhere. "Is that the doorbell?"

"I'll get it." Holt went past them out the door and down the stairs. A few seconds later he yelled up the steps for them to come down.

Carly tucked the treasure into a soft cloth she'd brought just in case and put it in her purse. They all trooped downstairs to see Holt standing in the entry with a man in a gray suit. He was in his fifties with wings of gray at the temples of his dark hair. He carried himself with an erect, almost military bearing.

His dark blue eyes scanned through the people and landed on her. "Ms. Harris? Allow me to introduce myself. I'm Ivan Bury."

Lucas's free hand dropped to the butt of the gun at his waist, and he stepped in front of her. Ivan held up his hand. "I am unarmed, and I mean none of you any harm. I wish to talk, that is all."

His Russian accent was faint, and Carly didn't get a sense of danger from him. "Let's go into the parlor." She glanced around. "All of us. Anything you have to say you can tell everyone."

"Of course."

"This way." Holt led the way to the parlor.

Carly perched on the sofa with the older women on either side of her. Her sisters and Lainey found seats on sofas and chairs scattered around the room while Lucas and Holt stood. Even with the baby in his arms, Lucas looked ready to take on a challenge, and Holt was tense as well.

Bury smiled. "I can see you equate me with the men who have tried to harm you. That is the furthest thing from my mind. I've been on a quest to return as many of the lost art treasures to Russia as possible. I wish to buy the egg, not steal it. It will be on display for all people to see and enjoy in the Fabergé Museum in St. Petersburg. We have nine of the eggs so far, and yours would be a most welcome addition. I will pay you the appraised value and will add a bonus of ten million dollars."

Carly's heart leaped at the thought of her egg being with others where they originated, but she had questions first. "You gave a hundred thousand dollars to Kelly two different times. What is your role in all of this?"

"Kelly heard I was searching for the imperial eggs and contacted me. She sent me a picture of the provenance papers and said she and her fiancé needed funds to finish the search. It seemed to be enough proof that the investment would be worth the risk. When your husband was murdered, I knew others were after the egg, and I thought the extra funds would ensure I got the egg first. That did not turn out well, of course."

Carly winced at the word *fiancé* as it seemed to indicate Eric had made the decision to leave her. But then, it shouldn't have come as a surprise. She glanced first at her grandmother and then her aunt. They both nodded, so she turned her gaze back to Bury. "We accept. On one condition." At his questioning expression, she smiled. "You seem to have a lot of resources. Could you find Sofia Balandin?"

He smiled. "I'll see what I can do."

FORTY-TWO

Fifty million dollars, twenty-five million for each of the twins. The amount left Lucas speechless. Even split between Carly and her sisters, it would be over six million for each of Mary's granddaughters. He glanced at Carly riding silently beside him in the truck. It was just like her to share it even though it belonged to her.

He was nearly home after depositing the surprise at the bank, and there was so much he wanted to say. He cleared his throat. "How's that novel coming?"

"Slower than I'd like. But I've figured out where to introduce the love interest."

"It's a romance?"

"Of course. What's life without love of some kind?" She glanced back at her sleeping baby. "Family, friends, it's all intertwined."

"I suppose it is. I've been afraid to get close to someone special for fear of loss. People leave or die or fail you in some way. It's always been safer to keep my distance."

He pulled into the park at the marina instead of going home. The feelings bubbling in his chest were overwhelming, and he was going to burst if he held them back any longer. He'd rather not have an audience either. Her dark eyes were questioning, but she said nothing as he stopped the car.

"Take a walk with me?"

Still silent, she nodded and he retrieved Noah from his car seat in the back. The baby's grin made him smile in spite of being as nervous as someone on his first date. "Don't tell your mom," he whispered in Noah's ear. "But I love her and I love you too."

He carried the baby around to join her where she stood under a palm tree. Her uncertain expression tugged at his heart. This was uncharted water for her, too, even though she'd been married. The things she'd been through this past year were enough to shake anyone.

They walked to a vacant bench. A Marine band played in the distance, and recruits laughed and hooted along the green space and the water. Graduation week kicked off today, and families there to see their kids graduate had swelled the population.

"You okay, Lucas?" Noah's hand waved in her direction, and she kissed it.

"Better than I've been in a long time." Where was his courage? He had faced down a gun barrel pointed at him this week better than he was faring right now. "I'm glad it's over."

"Me too. The egg and the surprise will be safely home in Russia, and I can concentrate on getting Gram's house finished. And I'm hoping Ivan Bury finds Sofia—her grave or whatever happened to her."

"Now that your grandmother doesn't have to worry about how you'll earn a living, do you think she'll still want to mess with a bed-and-breakfast?"

Carly hiked a brow. "Maybe not. I always knew it was her way of taking care of me and Noah."

How did he even begin to say all the words clogging his throat? "I know I've been weird lately. I was afraid, Carly." His gaze locked with hers. "Afraid of letting down my guard and allowing the feelings I have for you to run wild. But it's too late. I can't stop them now even if I wanted to. And I don't want to."

"Y-you have feelings?"

"I love you." He ran his hand through his hair. "I can't believe I'm saying that, but it's true. It wasn't supposed to happen. The last thing I wanted to do was fall in love with someone with a baby. Now it looks like there will be two babies, but you know what? I like kids, which was a big surprise to me. And I already love Noah. Little Caroline too."

He took her hand and she clung to it in a tight grip. "I've seen how strong your love is, how you put other people ahead of yourself, and how brave you are. I want to be like you when I grow up."

"You're way braver than me. I'm a wimp."

He slipped his arm around her and drew her closer to him and Noah. "You're the bravest person I know. You put it all on the line without holding anything back. Do I have a chance? We can take our time. You're still dealing with a lot."

When she shook her head, his stomach bottomed out until she said, "It's too late for me too. I tried to change how I feel about you. I tried but I couldn't." Her eyes turned tender. "You realize you've never even kissed me, and here you are telling me you love me."

"I think we should remedy that." He leaned closer, savoring

the moment. Rushing in would spoil future memories, and he always wanted to remember the light in her eyes and the way her lips curved into a beguiling smile before parting a bit in anticipation.

"Kiss her already, you sap!" a Marine called from a laughing group of graduates.

So he did just that. And it was every bit as wonderful as he'd dreamed.

———

Balloons bounced gaily in the palm trees and peeked out from the Spanish moss draping the live oak trees in Gram's backyard. Blue tablecloths on the long serving tables fluttered in the breeze off the water. That same breeze tried to tug free the "Happy Birthday" signs taped to the gutters over the back deck.

Carly carried the large birthday cake to the table. The happy colors of the Polish pottery cake plates made an inviting display for the many guests roaming Gram's gardens, though the cleanup would be a bear. The number of guests had ballooned since it was now a party for two. Carly's attention went to her grandmother standing close to her sister. The Marine band playing in the distance added even more of a festive touch to the day.

She stared around the yard until she spotted Lucas showing Noah the hummingbirds flitting around the red rose garden at the side of the house. She smiled to see the palindrome *Sagas* on the shirt he wore. The last few months had seemed like a saga or two. Lainey held Caroline on her lap on the deck. The process had been started for Lainey and Holt to adopt the baby since

Kelly had succumbed to her injuries a month before. Caroline's grandmother had Parkinson's, so her grandparents were unable to care for her. Eric's mother had made noises about wanting her but had finally admitted she couldn't handle caring for a baby. It was the perfect solution and would ensure Noah got to see his sister often.

Carly motioned for Gram and Aunt Elizabeth to join her at the serving table, and the guests stopped talking and crowded around the sisters. Lucas and Noah came to stand beside Carly. "Let's sing 'Happy Birthday.'" She began the song and the guests chimed in. Everyone clapped when the song was over.

She had cut the cake, and Lainey handed Caroline to Holt so she could help Carly serve it. Carly heard her gasp, and Lainey grabbed her arm in a tight grip as she stared toward the side yard. Carly turned and spotted Ivan Bury and an elderly woman making their way slowly across the grass. The woman's white hair curled around her smiling face, and she wore a touch of pink lipstick. Her sleeveless pink-and-white dress was enhanced by a strand of pearls. She was tiny and frail, barely five-two. She clung to Bury's arm, and her bright blue eyes behind her glasses stayed fixed on Gram and Aunt Elizabeth.

Could it be?

A lump formed in Carly's throat, and she couldn't have spoken even if she'd tried. Guests began to notice her fixed gaze on Bury and the woman, and Gram finally noticed too.

Her grandmother turned toward the couple, and she reached out and grabbed Aunt Elizabeth's hand. "Beth," she said in a hushed whisper. Aunt Elizabeth turned and put her hand up to clutch her pearl necklace.

Bury reached them and smiled. "Another guest would like to add her birthday wishes to both of you. I'd like you to meet your birth mother, Sofia Balandin Kostin."

Kostin?

No charges had been filed against Charlie Kostin, and they'd heard he'd returned to New York. He hadn't been involved with the mob at all. Now it was clear why he'd come to town.

"My girls," Sofia said with a slight accent. Her voice was strong and assured. "Both so beautiful. Never did I think to see you again this side of heaven. May I hug you?"

She opened her arms, and Bury kept his arm on her waist to steady her as her two daughters approached and nearly fell into her arms. The three of them were crying, and so were Carly, her sisters, and Lainey. Carly smiled so hard through her tears that she thought her face would crack.

She looked up at Lucas and found a shimmer of moisture in his eyes too. None of them had thought Ivan Bury would find Sofia alive. They'd assumed he'd take them to a graveyard somewhere.

Gram led Sofia to a nearby chair and both sisters sat close to her. Carly caught only bits and pieces of their conversation and knew they were telling each other about the past seventy years. So much to catch up on, and it was for their ears only. She moved away with Lucas and found a lawn chair where she could recover her composure.

Bury followed them. "I believe I have fulfilled my promise."

"I can't thank you enough," Carly said, her eyes brimming again. "Look at them."

He turned and his smile broadened. "I wish you had seen

Sofia when I told her I'd found her daughters and they wanted to see her."

"Where was she?" Lucas snatched his cake away before Noah could plunge his chubby hands into it.

"In New York. She is Charles Kostin's grandmother. She told him a few months ago about the egg and the surprise she'd split between her daughters, and he'd promised to try to find them."

"So he wasn't trying to find the egg—only the twins?"

"I cannot say he wasn't interested in locating the treasure. He was most disappointed to hear I'd purchased it. He wished to know how much I'd paid, but I did not reveal that, of course.

"Sofia didn't think the egg and surprise were worth all that much back when the twins were born. The market was glutted with Romanov art at the time, and Sofia thought it was merely a trinket she passed along to her daughters. She married a few years after your grandmother and aunt were born and had one more child. When the junk dealer found the egg in 2014, Sofia realized the value of what she'd given them and remarked to her family that she hoped it had given them a good start in life. That set Kostin on a search, though he didn't mention the hunt to Sofia."

"What a fascinating story. Thank you." Carly's mind spun. Shouldn't some of that side of the family share in the wealth? "How many of my cousins are still alive?"

"Kostin is the last."

It would be easy enough to talk her family into sharing with one more person. Bury had been more than generous. After the surprise was reunited with the egg, the new appraisal was forty million, and he'd given them fifty million. Life-changing wealth for the entire family had shifted a few things. Gram no longer wanted a bed-and-breakfast, so Ryan was simply updating the home per Emily's specifications. Amelia had painted it a pale tan with the traditional "haint" blue on the porch ceiling. Black shutters added the final touch. Another month and they'd be able to move back in.

"Thank you for that," Carly said. "And for everything."

"My pleasure." He smiled again and wandered back to stand near Sofia.

Carly watched him go. "What a crazy two months it's been."

"The best months of my life." Lucas handed her the baby. "Can you hold him a minute? I have something I need to do."

She settled Noah on her lap and immediately had to rescue her necklace from his grasp. Her fingers clutched her necklace when she realized Lucas had slipped to his knees and was pulling a velvet box from his pocket.

His hazel eyes were smiling yet quietly confident. "I was going to wait until we were alone, but I think your family would like to share this moment with us. After all, they've shared everything else we've gone through together. Is that okay with you?"

She couldn't talk so she nodded.

He opened the box to reveal a large ruby ring studded with diamonds around the band. "Have we taken enough time for you to know you want to marry me? I know without a doubt I don't ever want to lose you. Will you marry me, Carly?" He pointed to his shirt. "The sagas of our lives are about to converge if you're willing."

Her throat was still as full as her eyes, and she nodded

before managing to squeak out, "Yes." She took the ring from the velvet and gasped, her voice finally coming back. "It's by Fabergé!"

"It seemed meant to be," he said in a husky voice. His hand trembled as he took it from her and slipped it onto her left ring finger. His warm lips brushed her hand as he sealed the ring in place.

At the sound of clapping, she tore her gaze from his smiling face and saw her family clustered around. Gram was crying, and Carly realized she was too.

Lucas leaned closer and brushed a tear from her cheek with his thumb. She sank into the love in his gaze and knew this was where the hard road of the past year had led her. Right into Lucas Bennett's arms.

EPILOGUE

Friends, family, and strangers crowded Litchfield Books in Pawleys Island. Authors clamored for a book signing at the famous bookstore, and Carly was honored to have a spot. The beautiful blonde owners stood by her side, handing opened books to her as she needed them.

Carly sat at the table with a dwindling stack of her books. The line was moving slowly because so many remarked on the palindrome on her shirt that read *Must sell at tallest sum*. She couldn't believe so many of her friends had made the trip from Beaufort for her first book signing. Even her great-grandmother, Sofia, had made the trip from New York.

Three-year-old Noah had escaped Lucas's hand, and Carly caught him as he tried to knock over a stack of her books. Lucas—with their new son, Joe, in his arms—came to retrieve him. "Sorry. He's fast." He tried to take Noah's hand, but her big guy resisted.

"Noah can stay with me. You want to help Mama?" she asked. He nodded and climbed into her lap, then reached for a book. She looked up to see who was in line, and Emily smiled proudly down at her. Ryan was beside her. "You don't need to buy a book," Carly told them.

"Every sale counts for the bestseller list." Emily pushed ten books her way. "Just sign your name. I'm giving them as gifts."

Ryan pushed another ten at her. "Same for me."

She shook her head. "You guys."

The bestseller list sounded like a dream that could never happen, but she'd thought that plenty of times over the past three years. She had recommendations from agents to change the time setting from 1955 to something more historic, and she'd listened. *Beneath the Palmettos* was now set in early 1900 on a defunct plantation, and her agent had sold it to Harper-Collins in a bidding war. While the time period changed, the basics of the story hadn't. Love lost and found. Life broken and restored. And she hoped it resonated with readers the way it did in her own life.

She gave the books to her sister and Ryan. Something had changed for Ryan. He and Emily had been dating for a month now, too many dates to count. Maybe it had been seeing how fragile life really was when they'd all thought they were going to die. Maybe it was the happiness Ryan saw radiating from his brother's face. Whatever had happened, Carly hoped things progressed well for him.

She signed so many books that her hands cramped. Even Ivan Bury came and bought twenty copies for gifts. The bookstore ran out just before closing, and owners Wendy and Olivia turned off the lights with happy smiles as she and Lucas walked to their truck with their kids.

"Ice cream?" Lucas asked. "Gilbert's is still open. This is where our journey kind of started. We could go past your old house if you like and see if the new owners are in the yard."

Her life with Eric seemed so long ago. With his death she'd thought her life was over, but she'd been so wrong. With Joe in her arms and Noah in Lucas's, she stood on tiptoe for a kiss. "I have all I need right here."

A NOTE FROM
THE AUTHOR

Dear Readers,

I've been obsessed with Fabergé eggs for many years and am so thrilled I've finally been able to write about that obsession and bring it to you! I have noodled on an idea for the eggs for at least twenty-five years, so creating this story has been a true labor of love. I hope you enjoyed reading it as much as I enjoyed writing it.

I love hearing from readers, so let me know what you think!

Much love,

Colleen

colleen@colleencoble.com

colleencoble.com

ACKNOWLEDGMENTS

Thank you, Team HarperCollins Christian Publishing, for all you have done for me through the past two decades! Dear editor Amanda Bostic has been with me through thick and thin and has set my suspense free to fly. My marketing/publicity team is the best out there, and no one has better covers than me. ☺ The love and support I've felt travel all through every department all the way up to Mark Schoenwald himself. I couldn't resist using his name in this book. He's been an awesome leader and is such an encourager.

Julee Schwarzburg is my freelance editor, and she has such fabulous expertise with suspense and story. She smooths out all my rough spots and makes me look better than I am. I couldn't write without her.

My agent, Karen Solem, and I have been together for twenty-four years now. She has helped shape my career in many ways, and that includes kicking an idea to the curb when necessary. She loved the idea of the Fabergé eggs right from the start and encouraged me to jump in.

My critique partner and dear friend of twenty-five years, Denise Hunter, is the best sounding board ever. Together we've created so many works of fiction. She reads every line of my work, and I read every one of hers. It's truly been a blessed partnership.

I'm so grateful for my husband, Dave, who carts me around from city to city, washes towels, and chases down dinner without complaint. But my Dave's even temper and good nature haven't budged in spite of the trials of the past year.

My family is everything to me, and my three grandchildren make life wonderful. We try to split our time between Indiana and Arizona to be with them, but I'm constantly missing someone. ☹

And I'm grateful for you, dear readers! Your letters and emails make this journey worthwhile! God knew I needed you to be whole.

And this was all God's doing. He knew the plans he had for me from the beginning, and I'm thankful for every day he gives me.

DISCUSSION QUESTIONS

1. Carly was fortunate to have a supportive grandmother. Grandmas are the unsung heroes of many of our lives. What do you think would have happened if Carly didn't have Gram to turn to during her trials?

2. It's easy to make snap judgments about other people like Lucas did about Carly. Have you ever been wrong about someone? If so, how did you handle it?

3. Carly tended to mother everyone. Have you ever known someone like that—or is it you yourself? What do you think makes someone have that type of nature?

4. Have you ever had the desire to write? What did you do about it?

5. Being on the police force can be challenging. What other jobs put pressure on home life?

6. How does trust in another person grow? Is it hard for you to lower your guard to trust?

7. At the end of the novel, Mary is reunited with her twin, Elizabeth. Have you ever witnessed or experienced a touching reunion of some kind?

8. Carly was quick to share the proceeds from the sale of the egg. Would you have done the same or kept the proceeds all to yourself since the item was left to you?

ABOUT THE AUTHOR

Colleen Coble is the *USA TODAY* bestselling author of more than seventy-five books and is best known for her coastal romantic suspense novels.

———

Connect with her online at colleencoble.com
Instagram: @colleencoble
Facebook: colleencoblebooks
Twitter: @colleencoble